PRAISE FOR

"Grace Hawthorne captures the spirit and tobacco-stained flavor of the 20's with a sharp eye and acerbic keyboard. Any student of old-time politics in general and Southern politics in particular should put this book on their must-read list."
— *Rob Levin, president, Bookhouse Group*

"*Shorter's Way* is a delightful journey through the researched and remembered landmarks of Atlanta's rich history."
— *Martha Tate, psychotherapist and workshop leader*

"The women in *Shorter's Way* are terrific. Who wouldn't want Laine's courage or Miss Amanda's guidance? Grace Hawthorne captures Southern women, politics, and race in the 1920s.
— *Lyn May, creator and editor of* Wise Women... Now, *a website for older women who write.*

"'Those years taught Willie the value of a good story.' So remembers Willie Shorter in *Shorter's Way*, and it's clear from the very first page that Grace Hawthorne knows the value of a good story too."
— *John Gentile, professor, Kennesaw State University*

"The whole book is... a clear new chapter in the eternal struggle between 'what is right' and 'the way things are.'"
— *Donald Davis, storyteller and author*

"I am familiar with Grace Hawthorne's ability to make her characters come alive."
— *Lisa Wiley, Carter Presidential Center*

SHORTER'S WAY

SHORTER'S WAY

a political love story about
rambunctious Georgia politics
in the 1920s

GRACE HAWTHORNE

DeedsPublishing

Published by Deeds Publishing
Marietta, GA
www.deedspublishing.com

This is a work of fiction. Names, characters, places, and incidents either are products
of the author's imagination or are used fictitiously. Any resemblance to actual events,
locales, or persons is purely coincidental.

Library of Congress Cataloging-in-Publications Data is available on request.

ISBN 978-1-937565-55-8

Books are available in quantity for promotional or premium use. For information write
Deeds Publishing
PO Box 682212
Marietta, GA 30068

info@deedspublishing.com.

First edition 2013

10 9 8 7 6 5 4 3 2 1

ACKNOWLEDGMENTS

I am putting this list in alphabetical order simply because I cannot thank everyone at the same time. Each of you has had a part in making this book possible. My heartfelt thanks to each and every one of you.

The Atlanta Cluster Group of the Southern Order of Storytellers which is my creative family.

Martha Church whose legal skills and sharp eye for logic and grammar kept me honest.

Feriel Feldman who introduced me to Bob Babcock, my editor and publisher.

Lyn May whose encouragement and non-Southern viewpoint were invaluable.

Diane and Wilton Rooks, whose knowledge of Atlanta history kept me on target.

Martha Tate, my storytelling buddy, who was my constant and trusted sounding board.

And finally to Jim Freeman, my husband, who read *every single version* of the manuscript and always had something valuable to add. He stands alone in his belief in this story, his encouragement and his infinite patience.

To Freeman

CHAPTER ONE

WILLIE SHORTER'S OFFICE SMELLED LIKE shit. Manure to be polite, horse manure to be specific. The odor drifted up from the deserted Morganton Livery Stable downstairs but Willie hardly noticed any more. The afternoon heat however, was inescapable. The black oscillating fan simply moved the heavy air around the room and Willie found it hard to stay awake. He pushed himself out of his rump-sprung chair, headed out the door and down the back stairs in search of a breeze.

"Villie! Come, come!" Sol Goldman urgently summoned him.

Willie walked across the street to Gold's Mercantile where Sol stood beside a colored man wearing faded overalls.

"This is Mr. Cunningham. He's a good customer, but he's got himself some big trouble." Sol looked at Cunningham and jerked his thumb toward Willie. "Tell him."

Experience had taught Nelse Cunningham to avoid dealing with white men whenever he could, but Mr. Goldman had always treated him with respect, so he couldn't very well refuse.

"Well Sir, Mr. Bull Rutledge, he hired me...."

"Harman Rutledge's son?"

"Yes, Sir. You know him?"

"I know *of* him," Willie said.

Sol looked disgusted. "Bad man, he would kick a dog just to hear him yowl. Go on, tell Villie vat he done."

"Well Sir, he said he'd pay me $5 to clean out a couple'a acres back'a his house and I done it. Then he said I'd busted up part of his fence. Now he's not gonna pay me. 'Sides that, he's gonna take my mule to pay for the fence. How I'm gonna farm without that mule?"

"You are lawyer, Protector of Poor, Villie, so you help him, yeah?"

"Sure, I'll help."

Nelse shook his head. "I 'ppreciate your help Mr. Goldman, but I ain't got no money to buy a lawyer."

Willie smiled. "Don't worry about that, I'll think of something."

From the time he first opened his law office, Willie's main thought was his political future. In gold letters he introduced himself to the world, "Willie Shorter, Attorney at Law. Protector of the Poor."

How could he possibly say no? Willie had known men like Bull Rutledge and Nelse Cunningham all his life. And God knows he knew about being poor. He'd been born out of wedlock and by the time he was three, his 18-year-old mother, gave him to a widowed neighbor, climbed aboard a Greyhound bus and disappeared.

Aubrey Shorter was left with a skinny, silent child. Aubrey had a knack for saving lost, injured animals and Willie certainly looked the part. He carried the boy into the kitchen and pulled a chair up to the big wooden table. He padded the seat with a couple of Sears Roebuck catalogues and sat Willie on top. The boy watched as Aubrey mashed up some cornbread in pot likker and offered it to him. "Go ahead try it, Boy," Aubrey said gently. "You'll like it."

That was the beginning. Aubrey not only gave Willie his first taste of real food, he also gave him comfort, a home and a last name.

Willie had come a long way in the intervening years. Although there wasn't much legal business in a town like Morganton, he was slowly building a reputation by taking cases like Nelse's, cases no one else wanted. Willie had big dreams. In his secret heart, he planned to be governor of the state someday and maybe even president. He hadn't decided yet. He was only 29, so there was plenty of time.

Willie brought his attention back to Nelse's predicament. Everybody in the area knew the Rutledges. The old man was mean as a snake and Bull was trying to live up to his father's dubious expectations.

"Mr. Cunningham, you come by my office about 3:00 next Monday. I ought to be able to sort this out by then."

Willie didn't need a week to deal with the likes of Bull Rutledge, but it never hurt to let the client think you had expended a lot of time and effort on his part.

Right on the stroke of 3:00 Willie saw Nelse's form through the frosted glass of his office door. The old man hesitated and Willie got up to open the door for him.

Nelse walked in slowly, took off his hat and looked around. There was no place to sit. Books, newspapers and boxes of legal papers covered every table, chair and desk in the room and a good portion of the floor as well. Willie transferred papers from two chairs to the top of his desk. Then he sat down and motioned for Nelse to sit opposite him.

"Make yourself comfortable. Hot enough for you?"

Nelse was not accustomed to making small talk with white folks, so he just nodded and waited for the younger man to continue.

Willie took a deep breath and smiled. This was the best part of his job…well the second best part. Matching wits with wise-asses who thought they could push people around was fun, but elaborating on the story afterward ran a close second.

"Mr. Cunningham, I reckon you'd like to know what happened." Nelse nodded. "The first thing I did was to call Bull and tell him I wanted to talk to him *here* in my office. Well, of course he balked at that idea until I threatened to talk to him at his *daddy's* office. He sure didn't want that. When he showed up, I asked him if he had a contract for the work he hired you to do, something that laid out the terms of the agreement in writing.

"I was pretty sure he didn't and when he admitted that, I started reeling him in. I carefully explained that since I had taken your case, he'd have to hire a lawyer too and that was going to cost a lot of money. Then I explained that when I got him on the stand… under oath …before a judge… at the courthouse… in front of *all* his friends… I was gonna ask for that contract. When he testified he didn't have one, the judge would probably throw the whole thing out of court and he'd be stuck paying court costs.

"He was sweating bullets by that time. I let him suffer a minute, then I pointed out that ole mule was gonna cost him a whole lot more than it was worth. I also suggested that his daddy wasn't gonna be impressed when he realized he'd be the one footing the bill for Bull's foolishness. On top of all that, his friends were gonna have a good laugh at his expense."

Nelse knew better than to interrupt a man in the middle of a yarn, so he waited.

"By then Bull was up pacing the floor, begging me to help him out. I took my time, but finally I admitted there might be a way to make the whole thing disappear. In order to keep it strictly legal, he'd need to pay me a consulting fee and then I would do my best to talk you out of taking him to court.

"I quoted him $25 and he started pulling money out of his pocket as fast as he could. He finally came up with $24.95 and I told him that would do."

Nelse appreciated a good story as much as the next man, but he still hadn't heard anything that would solve his problem.

Then Willie carefully laid three five-dollar bills on the desk. "I took the rest of the money as my fee, and this is your share."

Nelse just stared at the money.

"Go on, take it. It's yours."

Carefully Nelse reached out his hand, took the bills, folded them one by one and pushed them deep into his overall pocket. "Mr. Shorter, I'm much obliged to you for gettin' me all this money. I think I knows where I can get me another mule…"

"No, no, no!" Willie grinned from ear to ear. "You get to *keep the mule* free and clear."

"I gets to keep the mule *and* the money?"

"Yes Sir."

"Praise the Lord! My Misses been prayin' for a miracle and it looks like you done made one sure enough."

Nelse stood and Willie knew he was anxious to leave. At the door the old man turned, "Mr. Shorter, if there's ever anything me or my family can do for you, you just let me know."

Willie smiled. "You never know, Mr. Cunningham, you just never know."

After Nelse left, Willie walked home to Miss Dorothy's boardinghouse. An afternoon thunder storm had settled the dust and lowered the temperature slightly. All in all it had been a good day, but instead of feeling satisfied, Willie was restless.

After supper, he decided to get the car and go for a drive to cool off and clear his head. He left the boardinghouse through the back screen porch and walked to the end of the block where he parked his Model T Ford. That 13-year old car was his pride and joy. It was a two-door touring car, with a tan body, black fenders and a black canvas roof.

Under normal circumstances, Willie could never have afforded such a car, but he had won the Ford in a poker game. As a rule he wasn't much good at poker, he could never keep a straight face. That night however, Lady Luck smiled on him and the fact that his opponent cheated, made the win that much sweeter.

As he drove along the gravel road leading out of Morganton, Willie thought about Nelse. Then he let his mind wander back to his days selling Peruna and Bibles on the back roads of Georgia with Uncle Aubrey. Between the 20 percent grain alcohol in Peruna and the solace offered by the Good Book, they brought a lot of comfort to their rural customers. Those years also taught Willie the value of a good story.

When Willie was 17, Uncle Aubrey passed away. The boy felt like a part of his body had been amputated; he was wounded and unbalanced. Gradually he healed, but even after all this time, the smell of collard greens and cornbread still hit an empty spot in Willie's soul.

Don't worry, Boy, I won't ever be far away. Just keep listening, I'll be here.

Initially Willie sold the remaining stock of Bibles and Peruna to another salesman and bummed around for a couple of years. He did odd jobs, lived in boardinghouses. He played cards and shot pool with men twice his age and learned about the ways of the world. The men he met bragged about their conquests and Willie also got a varied—if somewhat lopsided—education about women.

Until he met Hannah. She was a particularly helpful young widow who owned a boardinghouse where Willie lived for a summer. She took a special interest in his sexual education; smoothed out the rough edges and taught him the finer points of dealing with women. Willie smiled at the memory.

"I haven't done so bad, Unk," Willie said out loud, "Managed to get in and out of law school, mostly because of all the books you made me read and the savings you left. You told me to do some good, and I'm trying, but damn it, Unk, I'm just not moving fast enough."

But he *was* making progress. One of the habits Willie picked up from Uncle Aubrey was reading as many daily newspapers as he could get his hands on. At the time, the south had very little industry and south Georgia had even less, but according to the *New York Times*, that was changing. The big cotton mill owners from New England knew high-grade cotton grew well in Georgia red clay and as unions took over up North, the mill owners turned to the ready, eager supply of cheap labor in the south. By 1920, much of the cotton mill industry had moved south, and with it came cotton mill injuries. That's where Willie fit in. For several years he had taken workers' cases no one else wanted.

Normally, when a serious injury occurred at a saw mill, paper mill, or textile mill, the company doctor took care of it and then the injured party was fired. Willie had been building his law practice winning small settlements and doing a little good for his fellow man in the process.

He took the mill owners to court. The judgments weren't large and Willie took half of the settlement. Even so, his clients might end up with as much as $100. That was almost six month's pay for most of them and a hell of a lot better than nothing. Because he didn't ask for too much, the big employers weren't too concerned and his clients were grateful. Willie made enough to pay the rent on his office and his room at Miss Dorothy's boardinghouse.

What he needed now was something a little bit different, a little bit bigger; a case that would get him noticed throughout the state. Something to catch the attention of the big boys in high political places like Atlanta.

CHAPTER TWO

THERE WERE NO CHILDREN IN Ford Crossing. From the time they were born, they were destined for life in Claxton Mill. The town just accepted the fact that on their tenth birthday, kids quit school and started working 12-hour shifts, six days a week. Since this was south Georgia and the Bible Belt, God still insisted on Sunday as a day of rest.

Laine Becker was no exception. For all her 18 years, dull cotton fields with white cotton bolls growing on black stalks defined the boundaries of her life. Gravel-road dust painted everything tan. The hot Georgia sun sucked the color out of clothes hung out to dry, while it burned people brown. By the end of summer even the grass and trees looked faded. The only color—if it could be called that—was red Georgia clay. Just a little bright color was all she wanted. Was that too much to ask?

"Elaine Becker, don't make me come in there. We gotta get the weedin' done. Now get up!" Louise Becker yelled to her daughter from the back porch.

Slowly Laine swung her long legs over the side of the bed. Still wearing the old dress she slept in, she shuffled outside where Louise handed her a hoe and headed across the hard-packed dirt of the back yard to the garden. It was late April in south Georgia and the pre-dawn air was still cool, but as soon as the sun came up, the temperature would rise quickly. Laine started chopping weeds as she moved along the rows of tomatoes, squash, cucumber and pepper plants that were just coming up. Nearby, Louise looked for grub worms and crushed them underfoot. "Sonofabitch," she hissed under her breath.

Laine smiled. If confronted, she knew her mother would deny ever saying such a thing. As much as she hated weeding, Laine knew how much her mother loved that garden and the small patch of zinnias, which were the only flowers hardy enough to survive in the heat and fight it out with the weeds without much help. The flowers in the garden were the only thing that set their house apart from every other house in town.

Like match boxes laid out in neat rows, mill houses for workers all looked alike. White washed, two rooms wide, a tin roof, a front screened porch supported by four-by-four posts, a small fenced in front yard. The front door opened directly into the living room, a narrow hallway gave access to the front bedroom where Jeb and Louise slept. The girls' bedroom was in the back separated by the bathroom; the boys slept in the living room.

About 5:00 the two women stacked their hoes against the back porch. Louise went in to fix breakfast. "Better get in the bathroom while you got the chance." Laine nodded.

"Mornin' Lainie," her dad said as he walked out of the bathroom and headed into the living room to wake up JW, his oldest son whose lanky body was sprawled on a roll-a-way bed. His younger boy, Bo, slept on the couch.

Although Jeb loved all his children, he had a soft spot for his first-born son. JW had been working in the mill nine years and was the hope of the family. He had a knack for mechanics; could just listen to a machine and know what was wrong with it. He was next in line to be a fulltime fixer, the best job in the mill. Fixers kept the machines running and without them the whole operation shut down. Even now while he was learning the job, JW made 10 cents an hour more than Jeb, who'd been working in the mill for 20 years. "Get up boys, time's a wastin'."

In the bathroom, Laine splashed water on her face, brushed her teeth, pulled on cotton underwear, a loose, faded dress and tied a kerchief over her hair. She stuffed her feet into a pair of shoes run down at the heels and went into the kitchen.

By the time she got there, Jeb and the boys were seated in mismatched chairs crowded around the kitchen table with its faded oilcloth covering. The room was so small the icebox was kept on the back porch. Louise wouldn't allow curtains because they blocked the air. Her one indulgence however, was to always have fresh flowers on the table. Zinnias when they were in bloom, wild flowers when nothing else was available.

The family gobbled down cold biscuits, coffee or milk. The shift started at 6:00 and anybody who was late stood a good chance of being fired. More workers than jobs meant the bosses had a never-ending supply ready to step in at a moment's notice.

Jeb knew he was lucky to have his whole family working for Claxton. So far, they had avoided getting the common mill diseases and with all of them staying healthy, the Beckers just managed to get by.

Louise insisted her family eat a balanced diet and sent them to be examined every time the mobile clinic bus rolled into town. Standing up during 12-hour shifts, six days a week took its toll on even the young, strong ones. Laine knew people thought her mama was crazy cramming vegetables down her family and cleaning everything with lye soap or alcohol, but she understood. She'd seen too many of her friends and neighbors get pellagra or typhoid or TB. If somebody working for the mill got sick, they went to work anyway or got fired.

Breathing lint was an unavoidable part of millwork, but Louise did her best to protect her family from everything else. Everybody's worst fear was getting injured at the mill. Humans were no match for fast-moving, spinning machines and limbs didn't grow back.

The Beckers worked hard and were proud to be one of the few mill families who didn't owe their souls to the company store. They tried to pay their bills on time and once in a while have a little left over.

Jeb and JW finished breakfast, grabbed their lunch pails and left for the mill. With practiced skill mother and daughter gave the dishes "a lick now and promise to do better later" as Louise always said. That done, they ran to catch up with their men. Bo left with them but headed in the other direction to Claxton Mill School. The school provided lunch for five cents a week. The big red brick building housed grades one through five. Since kids went into the mill at ten, there was no use for the higher grades.

At eight, Bo was too young for mill work, but he helped out earning a little extra money "haulin' dinners." He left school at 3:00 p.m., picked up lard cans full of food from Ole Miss Hattie and delivered them to the workers. He did the same thing at 6:00 p.m. and again at 9:00 p.m. While the workers ate, Bo watched over their machines. He couldn't wait to go to work at Claxton Mill full time with the rest of the family.

Bo knew Laine would be upset when he quit school, because that would be the end of the free library books he brought home by the bagful for her to read. He made fun of her because she always had her nose in a book, but she just swatted him. "You may be plannin' to spend all your life workin' in the mill, but not me. Just because I had to quit school after fifth grade, don't mean I'm not gonna get educated one way or another. I'm leavin' this place just as soon as I can."

Laine dreamed about leaving every morning as she made the short walk from her house to Claxton. It lay like a big brown lizard along the banks of the Senoia River. Inside, the machines and the people were covered with gray fuzz. The dark wooden floors were seasoned with an oily compound that was supposed to keep the dust down. It didn't.

Everybody worked standing up. Constant attention was required to spot broken threads quickly and tie them off immediately. The work was repetitive, boring and nerve racking. The huge room was always hot, the humidity kept high with mists of water sprayed from the ceiling to keep the static electricity down. It didn't help much either.

On her first day at the mill, Laine was terrified by the ear-shattering noise, the whirling machines and the concentration it took to do her job and not lose a hand or an arm. For the first week, she went home every day with a splitting headache. Louise went out on the back porch, took the ice pick and chipped off a handful of shards from the block in the bottom of the icebox. She put them in a rag and held it to Laine's head. "Hang in there, Baby, it'll get better."

It didn't get better and Laine never accepted the fact that the mill was all life had in store for her. JW, however, genuinely enjoyed going to work. He finally showed his sister how to live with the noise. He taught her to listen to the rhythm of the room. She gradually came to see the whole thing as a huge dance floor where people and machines moved in and out together with prescribed steps and motions as elaborate as any cotillion.

Point, touch, turn, change, watch your partner, mind the rhythm, point, touch, turn, change. She listened and dreamed of real cotillions, with beautiful people in rainbow-colored gowns, who lived exciting lives far away from the dusty cotton mills of Georgia.

The six o'clock whistle signaled the shift change and Laine caught a glimpse of her twin sisters Callie and Bessie as they headed home from working all night. The girls made as much as grown women by working the night shift. They would soon be sound asleep in the bed Laine had just vacated.

Bessie had hated to quit school, but she had no choice. The family needed the extra income to keep going. Callie, on the other hand, couldn't wait to get out of school and start work. She knew the town kids called her a lint-head but she didn't care. Her life centered on Claxton Mill, the mill town and the mill families. She took things one day at a time and squeezed as much fun out of life as she could.

Once inside the mill, the Becker family split up to go to their assigned jobs. As she walked down the line of machines, Laine felt the heat closing in and knew that by the time her shift was up, she'd be covered in lint and sweat that flowed from the kerchief covering her hair into her eyes and ran from her arm pits down her sides.

The supervisor told JW to start filling batteries, the wheel-like contraptions that held a number of spindles of thread that fed the looms. It wasn't his normal job, usually beginners did that. However, he did what he was told.

The deafening clatter of the machines pressed down on Laine's shoulders, but she hardly noticed any more. The lint particles, which everyone breathed, swayed and danced in the rays of sun that came in through the high windows. The rhythm and the noise stayed at a steady roar. The heartbeat of the mill was as constant as the air in Ford Crossing.

High above the floor, a tiny sparrow sailed in through one of the open windows. It disturbed the dust and the light and distracted one of the dancers. JW glanced up for just an instant as he leaned over one of the whirring machines. As if irritated by his lack of attention, his spinning partner grabbed his right hand and pulled him into her metal embrace. He screamed in pain.

Although the clanking noise in the cavernous room became second nature to the workers, a human scream cut through all the mechanical clatter and buried itself in the heart of every person on the floor.

Louise heard it first. She'd heard it before. So had most of the old-timers and they knew what it meant. It took Laine a split second longer to realize what had happened. Instinctively she looked to where her mother and father worked and saw each of them looking back at her. She breathed a sigh of relief.

Then she heard a second scream and realized it was her mother. But Louise wasn't hurt; Laine could see both her arms and she was running, running toward the far side of the building. Then she saw her father run in the same direction.

Instantly she thought, *JW! It must be JW, but he doesn't work in one place; he goes wherever he's needed. But it can't be him. He can't be hurt. He's too quick, too strong, too steady.*

Only family members left their machines to investigate when somebody got injured. Everybody else kept working. Veterans had seen enough in their time. They had no curiosity left.

As Laine ran down the center aisle, she saw people's eyes. Sorrowful, staring, resigned. Just as she saw her mother's back and her father kneeling over a body on the floor, the shift supervisor caught her. Although he did his best to hold her, she wrestled loose and caught a glimpse of JW as her father and three other men lifted him onto a stretcher. Her brother's arm was bloody up to his shoulder, his face pale, his teeth clinched against the pain.

She tried to follow him through the aisles, but hands kept holding her back. In the background she could hear the supervisor yelling for everyone to mind their business and keep working.

"I have to get to him…"

"Leave him alone, Child."

"Let the men handle it."

"There's nothing you can do."

"It's in God's hands now."

She pulled away from the workers holding her. "That's my brother. I've got to get to him…." Things started to close in and Laine saw her mother's stricken face just before the world went black.

CHAPTER THREE

LIKE HE DID EVERY DAY, Willie read the papers, not just the local news in the *Atlanta Journal* and the national news in the *Atlanta Constitution,* but out-of-town papers and the small town weeklies. When he could find them, he even read the papers published by the mills.

On this particular morning, Willie had his feet propped up on the desk with the holes in his shoes offering a little ventilation. Willie always wore those shoes when he met working folks for the first time. He made sure he crossed his legs so the holes were clearly visible. Poor folks tended to trust a man with worn out shoes.

On a more practical note, the shoes were soft and comfortable and Willie had no intention of replacing them. On the rare occasions when he met with someone more prosperous, or someone he wanted to impress, he hauled out his one pair of Florsheims and gave them a good polish.

Willie reached for his cup of day-old coffee and picked up the *Claxton Mill News* from Ford Crossing. Nothing of interest on page one or two, but then a small article on page three caught his eye.

"Louise and Jeb Becker, their daughter Elaine, twins Callie and Bessie, and youngest son Bo, wish to thank their friends and neighbors for their prayers and good wishes following the unfortunate accident to their oldest son, JW. A bright boy, 19 year-old JW was in line to be a fixer, a dream he will now have to abandon. However, in the spirit of taking care of its own, Claxton Mill has already found a place for JW. He will be coming back to work after a short period of recovery. Young and strong, he has a job waiting for him as a doffer."

Willie sat back and thought about the article for a long time. It was a pretty common story, one he had heard many times in his days on the road. Rather than being angry, families were usually grateful for whatever small compensation the companies gave them. Willie bristled at the unfairness of the Becker's situation, but he had to admit his reaction was not entirely altruistic. He saw his efforts to get fair compensation for the families in a Biblical light, like throwing bread upon the waters. You give a little, you get a little back. Glancing back at the article, he wondered what a fixer did.

Wanta know something, Boy? Get a book. Look it up.

How many times had he heard that before? He wandered around the office until he found a couple of books and some old dusty pamphlets about mills. He sat back down and started making notes. It didn't take him long to discover that a fixer was well respected, well paid and essential to a successful textile mill. That was good. He made a note of it.

A doffer, on the other hand, was women's work. When each heavy roll of cloth was finished, it was removed from the machine or "doffed." Sometimes the company assigned the work to old men. Willie made a note of that, too.

The article did not mention paying the family any compensation. He also wrote that down. Then he hunched over the desk and read the article through several more times. The oldest son, bright, strong, on his way to a good future. Injured through no fault of his own. Family probably counting on him to take over as the main breadwinner in a couple of years when his dad was too old to work. The article gave the names of the other kids, probably younger, and a good bet they were all employed by Claxton Mills which was a big northern-owned company… the biggest employer in the state.

Willie smiled slightly. He reviewed his notes, tapping his fingers on the desk while he considered the possibilities. This just might be it. It might work. Not one to leap before he looked, Willie started searching the book shelves again, mumbling to himself. "Somewhere, somewhere, somewhere…" finally he pulled out a heavy volume covered in dust. He brushed off the cobwebs and carried the book to his desk. *A History of Workmen's Compensation Cases in Georgia.* "All right, let's see what we can find."

Hidden in the midst of all the dry reading, Willie found some interesting facts. He turned to a clean page in his tablet and started a new category.

An hour later, he decided to check out Claxton Mills. More digging through books, pamphlets and newspapers turned up more interesting facts. As it happened, Claxton was not only the biggest employer in Georgia; it was an industrial giant throughout the south. Claxton Textile Mills, Inc. employed lots of people which probably meant that no one had ever dared to speak out against them, no matter what they did.

That was exactly the kind of fight he was looking for. Willie's mind raced. If he took on Claxton Mills, he'd get lots of publicity. He'd be known as the one lawyer who wasn't afraid to challenge the big boys on behalf of the little people. If he won and got a nice settlement for the family, he'd be a hero. Of course, there was a chance he would lose, but even if he did, he'd still be a hero for trying.

As for Claxton Mills, well, if he ever came face to face with the bigwigs there, he could make them understand it was nothing personal, just business. It was never wise to burn bridges you might need to cross later on.

Willie had one more resource to check out, the Over-the-Hill Boys Club. He had stumbled onto this fount of knowledge by accident when he was looking for office space. Their headquarters sat a block off South Main on an unnamed side street and looked like a cross between a run-down store and a warehouse. A large hand-lettered sign over the door announced, "Morganton

Memorial Museum, Home of the Over-the-Hill Boys Club." Willie was intrigued.

On his first visit, he met Pappy Hinshaw, a retired newspaperman, who was happy to have company. He poured Willie a glass of ice tea from a gallon jug kept cold on a block of ice in a number 10 galvanized wash tub. "Didn't start out to be a museum. Pretty much everybody around here knows I'm a notorious pack rat. One day my wife, Eleanor, laid down the law. Said either the junk went or she did. Well, I had to think about that for a while, but truth is, I couldn't live without either one. So I moved the junk out of the house into this vacant storehouse. My stuff was safe and Eleanor stopped talking about leaving. I just put up the sign for a joke."

However, little by little the Museum's collection grew as other men—and some women too—discovered a place in Morganton for their accumulated leftovers. Some of the men who dropped things off lingered to talk and smoke and the Over-the-Hill Boys Club was founded.

"You're supposed to be over 60 and retired to join, but as long as you've got time on your hands and a good story to tell, you're in. Speakin' of stories, there was this one time some poor lost Yankee actually paid hard cash to come in and look at our 'exhibits.' The Boys sure got a kick outta that."

Willie recognized a treasure when he saw one. He made it his business to meet the rest of The Boys. He found out Chauncey Kennon, his landlord, was a member. Before he retired, Chauncey was a jackleg attorney who knew both the law and the loopholes. He had practiced in Atlanta for years where he made some friends and an equal number of enemies.

Philemon Van Norman Ledbetter—known to all as PV— was president of the local bank. He viewed himself as Southern aristocracy because his family went back six generations. PV and Mother Ledbetter knew everyone worth knowing and all the juicy stories the other old families didn't want anyone to know.

Willie first met Sol Goldman at the Museum. As in many small towns, Gold's Mercantile was a general store that offered groceries, guns, plows, piece goods, notions, work clothes, boots, shoes, ribbons, ladies' hats, cosmetics, medicines, fishing poles, and cleaning supplies. If it wasn't on the shelves, Sol would gladly order it. He had strong ties to the Jewish community in Atlanta and throughout the state.

Joe Laundry owned farmland all over south Georgia, which was worked by Joe's sons, daughters, and large extended family of brothers, sisters, aunts, uncles, nieces, and nephews. To Joe's way of thinking, it made no difference if you were male or female, as long as you were kin and made enough to buy seed, pay the taxes and keep the land in the family.

Sol and Joe could only claim to be associate members of the Boys Club, because both of them were still gainfully employed.

This rather unusual collection of men became Willie's mentors and, in many ways, his family. Whenever he needed advice or council or something more than just facts and figures, he headed over to the Museum.

Following his research on Claxton Mills he walked over to consult The Boys. Pappy, PV, and Chauncey were sitting on the bench outside smoking, trying to outdo each other with tall tales and watching the unfortunates who still had to go to work.

"What'chall know about cotton mills?" Willie asked as he inserted a nickel and took a Co' Cola from the rusty red cooler just inside the door.

"Well," Pappy said as he shifted positions to get more comfortable, "most folks in south Georgia started out raising cotton. Being tenant farmers meant they had to turn over half the crop to the land owner. That didn't leave enough to buy starts for the next planting, put food on the table for their families and feed the chickens or cow if they had 'em. So they were always in debt. When the mills came, farmers flocked to town to get jobs. If they were lucky, they moved into one of the company-owned houses."

Before Pappy could take a breath, Chauncey chimed in. "I got a friend lived in one of those mill houses. Not such a bad deal. House had five-rooms, a porch on the front and back. Mill charged him 50 cents a week rent and he had to send one person for every room to work at the mill. If he'd been living in town, it would'a cost him at least twice that much. On top of that, the company provided a school for his kids, at least until they were old enough to go to work in the mill."

PV's social circle did not include mill families, but he wasn't about to be left out of any discussion. "Actually, from what I hear, Claxton's one of the better mills around. Mother's maid told her that in Ford Crossing, Claxton built the playground, the recreation hall, and the ball park. They sponsor a baseball team, community dances and deliver fruit baskets at Christmas. Oh, and here's the best part, Claxton supplies *burial plots* for the workers. 'Cradle-to-grave,' that's Claxton's slogan… at least that's what I've heard."

Willie stayed around swapping stories for a while. Then he finished off his Co' Cola, put the empty bottle in the wooden case that served as a doorstop, and headed back to his office. There was a bounce in his step and a smile on his lips. Willie was on his way to save the Becker family, whether they needed saving or not.

CHAPTER FOUR

WILLIE SPENT THE REST OF the week getting things in order for his visit to Ford Crossing. First he got a haircut with the idea that it would grow out a little before he actually met the Beckers. He didn't want to look too "done up." Then he stopped by the Esso gas station on the corner to ask Leon for directions. Strange that in all his travels with Uncle Aubrey he couldn't remember ever going to Ford Crossing. Next he hung his one suit out on the clothes line in the back yard to give it a good airing.

Saturday morning he got up early and was the first of Miss Dorothy's boarders to sit down at the long oilcloth-covered table in her kitchen. He could smell biscuits and the scent made his mouth water. Slowly the other boarders shuffled in. The crowd was usually sparse on Saturday.

"You get your days mixed up?" Miss Dorothy asked with a smile as she took a big pan of biscuits out of the oven and brought them to the table. She couldn't remember the last time she had seen Willie show up for Saturday breakfast.

Willie grinned. "No, Ma'am, I gotta go check out a mill down in Ford Crossing."

Before anyone reached for the biscuits, Miss Dorothy bowed her head and indicated the men at her table should do the same. "Mickey, it's your turn."

Mickey was 45 and a little on the slow side. He worked as a stock boy at both Gold's and the Red and White Grocery. He also did odd jobs around the boardinghouse. "God is great. God is good. Let us thank him for this food. Amen."

The split second he finished, a blur of hands snatched up the biscuits. Miss Dorothy went back to the kitchen for more. For someone who had grown up without a woman's cooking, Willie thanked his lucky stars every time he sat down to eat at Miss Dorothy's table. He and Uncle Aubrey had done all right, but greens, cornbread and fried meat were about all they ever ate.

Following the unspoken rule at all Southern tables to "take two and butter 'em while they're hot," Willie broke open one of his crusty, hot biscuits, held it to his nose and inhaled. By the time Willie buttered his biscuits, Miss Dorothy was back with scrambled eggs, grits, sausage, and coffee. Jars of homemade peach preserves, fig preserves, and crabapple jelly and a jar of honey were lined up down the middle of the table.

The six men who lived at Miss Dorothy's knew each other and were friendly enough, but food always trumped conversation, especially on Saturday. Not everyone showed up for breakfast, which meant extra servings for those who did. Willie gave his undivided attention to the mound of food on his plate.

When he sopped up the last drop of honey with the last piece of biscuit, Willie finally pushed back his chair, loosened his belt, patted his stomach and sighed with contentment. He was the last one to leave the table, and before he went back upstairs, Miss Dorothy handed him a paper bag. "Thought you might need a sausage biscuit or two. It's a long drive down to Ford Crossing."

Willie leaned down and kissed her on the cheek. "Dorothy, if I wouldn't have to fight it out with every other man in the county, I swear I'd run off with you."

"Get outta here," she said…but she was smiling.

Willie decided to wear his old shoes, an ordinary pair of pants and an old shirt, but at the last minute he reconsidered and put on his second best pair of pants, a better shirt and a tie. He didn't change his shoes. He didn't plan to actually talk to anyone on this trip, but then you never know. Prosperous, but not too successful, that was the ticket.

The sight of the Model T never failed to give Willie a rush of excitement. As he drove through Morganton headed south, he hardly noticed his surroundings. His mind was busy deciding what he was going to do with the settlement he planned to get from Claxton Mills.

Several miles before he got to Ford Crossing, the air inside the car began to throb with the bass notes of the huge machines that kept Claxton Mill running. Involuntarily his heart started beating to the same never-ending rhythm.

As he got closer to the mill, a high-pitched buzzing noise made his ear drums vibrate like some pesky insect aiming for the middle of his head. The sound made the hair on the back of his neck stand up and set his teeth on edge. "How in the world can people live with that 24 hours a day?" Willie asked out loud. He tried to concentrate on something else, but his brain refused to cooperate.

As he drove around town, Willie was surprised. He'd seen mill towns before, but he'd never really looked at one. Claxton Mill hunkered down along the banks of the Senoia River. Willie estimated the building at about two football fields long, much bigger than he had imagined. Claxton Commissary, the company store, occupied the corner across from the mill.

Up a slight incline not too far away, white, frame houses stood in neat rows. Upon closer inspection, he distinguished between the houses that belonged to the supervisors and those that belonged to the workers. The bigger houses farther from the street belonged to the bosses. A mill hand's house looked like a square box, with a tin roof that extended over small screened porches front and back.

Front yards were either close-cut weeds or hard-packed dirt. He noticed chickens in several back yards and small vegetable plots in others. He had expected the town to look run down, but everything was neat and clean. If it hadn't been for that infernal noise, Ford Crossing would have been a nice little town.

Next to the Baptist church was a school and a baseball diamond with wooden bleachers. Around the corner was a community center. Everything had the name Claxton on it…including the graveyard. Obviously, The Boys had been right. Claxton Mills took care of everything.

Still, something about the town made Willie feel uneasy. It took him a minute to realize he didn't see any people. No one working in their yards, no one shopping, no kids playing. Curious. Then it dawned on him that everything and everybody in Ford Crossing ran on Claxton Mill time. The people were either working in the mill or sleeping after coming home from the night shift. Willie shook his head, *What a way to live!*

Ford Crossing had one main intersection, but no traffic light. Willie didn't see many stores, probably because Claxton Commissary sold everything mill families needed. The exception was Caruther's Furniture Store which was in between the post office and the Greyhound bus station. There was also a train station. Unusual for a town to have both.

Willie finally completed his inspection and headed back to Morganton. The flat land for miles around Ford Crossing was covered with low-growing, dark green cotton plants. Come late summer most of the leaves would turn brown, dry up and fall off, exposing the plant's black skeleton. The wealth of the south hung on these dead plants. Soft, white tufts of cotton bursting from tough, black cotton seeds.

When he got back to Morganton, Willie spent the afternoon in his office, doing research and making notes. After 6:00 he walked over to Charlie's bar for a beer or two.

The next morning he got up early again. "Lord have mercy, two days in a row? You must be preachin' somewhere to get up this early on a *Sunday*." Willie gave Miss Dorothy a peck on the cheek and sat down to breakfast.

As soon as he finished, he went back to his room, brushed his teeth, lathered his face with Burma Shave and made sure he got a nice, close shave. He added a little Old Spice for good measure. Then he took out a clean white shirt. He didn't put it on.

I'm glad to see you remember what I taught you, Boy. Wear a clean shirt driving with the windows down on gravel roads and you gonna be wet and soggy 'fore you get where you're going.

So true. Willie covered the shirt with an old piece of sheet. If he found a place to wash up and change, fine. If not, he'd pull over to the side of the road, stretch his legs and change into his clean shirt before he knocked on the Becker's door. He put a tie on the hanger with the shirt. No need for a jacket, it was too hot and besides, he didn't want to look like a mill owner. Although he wore his old shoes, he took the trouble to put a nice, high shine on them. A little Brillcream on his hair was the finishing touch. Then he picked up his tattered briefcase and headed for the door.

Most good folks were going to Sunday School as Willie left Morganton. The way he figured it, by the time he got to Ford Crossing, the Beckers would just be getting out of church and he'd catch the whole family at home. He wanted his first meeting to be all business, but if they invited him to stay for Sunday dinner, that would be fine, too.

When he got to Ford Crossing, he stopped at a Pure Oil filling station with a single gas pump out front. He bought a gallon of gas and found out from the attendant where the Beckers lived. Then he went into the restroom, washed his hands and face, slicked down his hair again and changed into his white shirt and tie. He knew his car had already attracted some curious glances.

It only took him a minute to find the Becker's house. He stopped and got out of the car. Before he went to the door, he leaned over to flick the dust off his shoes with a rag he kept for that purpose under the driver's seat. Finally he walked up to the front gate. Since no dog came to greet him, he let himself in, walked across the yard, up the steps and knocked on the door to the screened porch. He was not prepared for what happened next.

CHAPTER FIVE

THROUGH THE DOOR HE SAW a young woman walking toward him. The sunlight streaming in from the back of the house set the red in her hair on fire and outlined her long legs, slender waist and shapely hips through her thin cotton dress. Her face was beautiful, full lips, golden skin, but when she looked at him, it was her eyes that made him catch his breath. Her lashes were long and thick and her eyes were dark brown, almost black. They held him in a steady gaze.

"Is this the Becker residence?" he asked when he got his voice back.

Laine Becker looked at the man standing on the porch. He was about six feet tall, good-looking and since there wasn't any lint on him, she figured he was a city man. His dark curly hair was slicked back and his blue eyes lingered a little bit longer than necessary on her bosom before they got back up to her face. She hesitated. When he smiled, she felt a catch in her stomach. She'd had the feeling before, but never quite so strong. She smiled back.

"Dad," she called over her shoulder, her eyes still locked on Willie's, "there's somebody here wants to see you."

Jeb came to the door, surprised to see a man wearing a tie on his front porch. "Yes Sir, can I do somethin' for you?"

Willie became all business. "Mr. Becker? My name's Willie Shorter. I'm a lawyer. My office is up in Morganton. I heard about your son's accident and I'm right sorry such a terrible thing has happened to your family. I wonder if I could come in and talk to you for a minute or two."

Jeb studied the man in front of him. The only people he knew who wore white shirts and ties were mill owners or preachers. He didn't trust either one. In his experience, they came around looking prosperous, but in the end, they always wanted something. He'd never met a lawyer before, so he wasn't sure what to expect. Still, the young feller seemed polite and Jeb was slightly curious about what he might want. He pushed the screen door open slowly.

Willie walked in and found himself surrounded by the whole family. The older woman was a faded copy of the girl with the dark eyes. He easily identified JW because his right arm was bandaged from shoulder to fingertip. Twin girls just beginning to blossom and a small boy made up the group. They all stared at him without a word.

Jeb made introductions all around. "This is my wife, Louise, our oldest daughter, Laine, I reckon you can figure out which one is JW, that's the twins Callie and Bessie, and Bo's our youngest." Still nobody moved.

Finally Laine spoke, "Won't you sit?" she indicated the well worn, plaid couch. As soon as Willie sat down, everyone else found places to sit. It was clear this was going to be a family discussion.

Willie knew better than to get down to business too quickly. "I was down here yesterday drivin' around a little. Pretty town." Willie knew he was not telling them anything they didn't already know. In a town the size of Ford Crossing the sight of a strange man driving a car no one recognized would be more than enough to get folks wondering who he was and what he wanted.

"I couldn't help noticing your garden out back, Mr. Becker. Tomatoes are lookin' good."

"Credit for the garden all goes to Louise. That's her doin'."

Willie nodded toward the kitchen. "Then I'll bet those zinnias came out of the garden too. Nice to have a woman's touch." Louise gave Willie a shy smile, clearly pleased to be singled out for a compliment.

He tried to keep his eyes off Laine, and for the most part, he succeeded. When she leaned over to serve him a glass of ice tea, he didn't exactly look, but he couldn't help noticing she was not wearing much under the old housedress. With a supreme effort he finally got down to business.

"Mr. Becker, I reckon I better explain why I'm here. I read in the *Claxton Mill News* about JW's injury. Now I know the mill took care of fixing him up, and I'm not saying they didn't do a good job." Willie took a breath and slowed down. "Mr. Becker, I hate to say it, but, Sir, you know JW's never gonna be a fixer with his right hand the way it is. And being a doffer...well, that's no job for a young man with such promise."

Jeb waited. So far he hadn't heard anything he didn't already know. Laine watched Willie. He noticed that she seemed to hang on his every word, but he was careful to direct his comments to her father.

"The point is, Sir, with JW out of the picture, there's not gonna be anybody to take your place," he glanced at Bo, "for a long time and if you're like all the mill families I know, you need everybody working and making as much as they can just to stay afloat."

Jeb continued to wait. He still hadn't heard anything new. Laine met Willie's eyes with a steady stare when he glanced her way.

Willie was beginning to feel a little uncomfortable, so he kept talking. "The thing is, Sir, I have had some experience and more than a little success in...dealing with situations where somebody working for a big company has been hurt, through no fault of their own."

Willie waited for half a second to see if that was going to get a response, and when it didn't, he forged ahead. "For instance, there was this man over in Hardwood, that's a sawmill town up in the middle of the state. Anyway, he got his hand cut off by one of those big saws. Company doctor fixed him up and they were gonna give him $10 and call it even. But Sir, the man came to me and told me that he'd worked for that sawmill since he was a boy and that $10 wasn't gonna last him any time at all. He needed something to tide him over until he could find another job, but saw-milling was all he knew."

The family listened so Willie went on spinning a tale. "Well, the man's story touched my heart and I decided to see what I could do." Now he was really warming to his subject. "I took the sawmill to court and in the end they paid the man four times that much. And I'm glad to say that the money helped him get by until he could figure out something. What he did was make himself a kind of hook for that missing hand and he's now working on a logging crew and doing just fine."

Willie finally stopped. He was reasonably proud of the yarn he was spinning. The bones of the story were true, but like any good storyteller, he had added details to make it truer and more entertaining. Willie looked at Jeb who continued to sit silent as a post. Laine reached for a pencil and started writing notes on the back of a used envelope. Willie took a swallow of ice tea and started in again.

"The point I'm trying to make is this. That man was old and it doesn't take too much skill to run a board through a saw. But JW here, well, he's a young man with potential. Even the write-up in the mill paper said so. And as far as I know, Claxton hasn't offered y'all any money to compensate for his injury. I know they're gonna keep him on, but working as a doffer he's never gonna fulfill his potential as a major wage earner in this family."

Silence.

Willie was getting more than a little frustrated. By this time he had expected the Beckers to be clambering for money from Claxton Mills. Then all he would have to do was settle on a figure. For want of something better to do, he decided to just stop talking and see what Jeb would say. He looked around the room and waited.

Finally Jeb spoke. "Are you sayin' that you think we oughta let you make a legal fuss about this?"

Willie brightened. "Yes, Sir. Now the way I see it…"

"Mr. Shorter, you don't know how things work in a mill town. All of us, 'cept Bo, work at Claxton Mill. Bo goes to the Claxton School. We rent this house from Claxton. Even though we try not to, we still owe money at the Claxton Commissary. All our friends and neighbors work for Claxton.

"If we raise a ruckus, they might give us a little money, but as soon as it was over, they'd fire us all. We'd have to move outta here and it's a good bet no other mill would hire us. Now, we're all mighty upset about JW gettin' hurt, but we'll work this out on our own. We don't need no lawyer with good intentions makin' things worse."

Willie heaved an inner sigh of relief. He could almost hear Uncle Aubrey's voice.

Once you get 'em to object, Son, you're on your way to closin' the deal.

"Mr. Becker, you are one-hundred percent right and that's the beauty of this plan. We're not going to court. We're not going to get within a country mile of a court, no Sir, I can guarantee that. Normally the first thing I'd do is write up a petition and file it with the court. But I'm not even going to do that." He saw a glimmer of interest and began to reel in his line.

"Here's what I'm proposing. I'll draw up a petition, but instead of filing it, I'll *show* it to Claxton Mills and give them a chance to do the right thing so I won't *have* to file it. I'll be asking Claxton Textile Mills, Inc., for $30,000." The family gasped. Laine didn't look up. In fact, she didn't react at all; she was too busy scribbling.

"Thirty thousand dollars!" Louise said. "There ain't that much money in the whole entire state of Georgia…maybe not in the entire United States of America."

"Oh we're not gonna get that, nowhere close," Willie admitted. "See, for this to work, everybody's gotta think they won. So I'll list $30,000 in the petition that I show to Claxton Mills."

Jeb spoke up again. "The supervisor, Blix Reeve's, gonna laugh you out'a his office the minute you start talking about money like that."

Willie smiled. "Mr. Becker, I got no intention of talking to the local supervisor. I'm going to go right to the top and talk to the *owners* of Claxton Mills, even if I gotta go all the way up North to do it."

CHAPTER SIX

ACTUALLY WILLIE ALREADY KNEW THAT Claxton had their southern headquarters in Atlanta and he was reasonably certain that's where the negotiations would be conducted.

Atlanta was the magic word and Willie had already started thinking about the daily news reports he was going to send to the *Atlanta Journal* giving the details of his efforts to protect the poor from the big corporations that were "pulling the feathers out of the golden goose one at a time. The golden goose which is the hard working people who daily endanger their health, yea, their very lives to produce cotton goods that are so expensive they can never hope to enjoy the fruits of their labors." He could hardly wait to see that in print.

He might even get his picture in the paper if he played his cards right. And if he was lucky and stirred up enough dust, the story might get moved up from local coverage in the *Journal* to national coverage in the *Atlanta Constitution*. He had the whole thing worked out.

It's simple, Boy. Based on the time-honored tradition of horse trading. Know what you're willing to settle for before going in. Ask for a lot more than you expect to get. Keep the trading going back and forth. Give in on a major point. Hold a trump card. Make the other guy feel like he has taken you to the cleaners. Take his money and run.

With infinite patience, Willie explained what he had in mind. First there were the facts, which they had already discussed. Then there was the process. After he had presented his case, he would let Claxton Mills talk him into being reasonable. He would offer to settle for half the amount. They would put up a fight, of course, and offer a fourth. Willie would decline. They would insist. Take it or leave it. Then Willie would play his trump card. The twins.

"What's my girls got to do with all this?" Jeb asked, suddenly on his guard and protective.

"Bessie?" Willie said with his best smile, "how old are you girls?"

Before she answered, Bessie looked to her father. He nodded. "Thirteen."

"And you work at the mill, right? How long have you been working there?"

"Nearly three years," Callie answered.

"We make near 'bout as much as Laine cause we do night work," Bessie said proudly.

Willie sat back. "Well, there it is. We've got 'em."

He knew he had the Beckers as well. He explained there had been a law on the books in Georgia for just over three years that girls had to be 14 before they could be hired to work full shifts and even then they couldn't do night work.

"Now I'm gonna reluctantly agree that we'll settle for only a third of what we were originally asking, and in return, I won't file a complaint against Claxton Mills for violating the child labor laws. It'll be a gentlemen's agreement. They'll figure they saved themselves a lot of money and we'll walk away with a big cash settlement."

Laine got up and came to sit by her father. She handed him the envelope, which was covered with numbers. She cupped her hand over her father's ear and whispered to him for some time. Eventually he nodded his head. Laine looked directly at Willie. Although he wasn't exactly sure how, he knew the balance of power had shifted and he was entering a new phase of negotiation.

In a soft, polite voice, Laine began. "Mr. Shorter, we 'ppreciate what you're tryin' to do to help us. Now accordin' to what I think you've been sayin', you're gonna ask Claxton Mills for $30,000. They're gonna refuse and you're gonna say you'll settle for $15,000. They're gonna say no and offer $7,500. Then you're gonna threaten them with the twins and agree to take $10,000. Is that right?"

Willie was taken aback. He was used to talking to clients about generalities; he didn't usually have to get too specific. However, he recognized the figure of $10,000. That sounded right. He smiled and nodded his head.

"And how much are you gonna charge us for all this help?" Laine asked.

Willie was back on solid ground. "You don't have to worry about a thing. I'll take this case on a contingency fee."

"And how much does a *contingency* cost?" she insisted.

"It won't cost you a red cent. You don't have to worry about that."

Jeb spoke up, "Now Mr. Shorter, I may not know about the law, but I know we ain't gonna get somethin' for nothin'."

"Well, yes Sir, you're absolutely right again. What that means is that if we win, I take a percentage of the money we get for my fee."

"How much?" Laine asked keeping her voice low and her eyes steady.

"Half," Willie answered softly.

Laine started whispering to her father again. The conversation went back and forth for some minutes. Again Jeb nodded to his daughter and Laine continued.

"So, after all's said and done, we run the risk of making Claxton Mills mad and getting everybody fired for $5,000, is that right?"

Willie had never run into a woman like this before. He wasn't quite sure how to figure her out. "That's one way to look at it I guess, but they aren't gonna fire anybody. The twins are gonna insure that." Again he was met by a roomful of silent stares. "You see, if I report Claxton, they'll have to replace all the children under 14 who're working in all their mills and hire adults in their place. Now that's gonna cost them a lot more than $10,000 because they've got mills all over the south."

"Can you guarantee that my family'll be safe, Mr. Shorter?" Laine asked.

Willie looked at the people in the small room and realized the risk he was asking them to take. He had drawn up a number of petitions, three by actual count, and he had bluffed his way through each time. The odds were in his favor, especially with the twins as his trump card, but there was no guarantee.

"I'm 99 and 44/100 percent sure…but no, I can't absolutely guarantee that it'll turn out like we planned."

Laine grabbed another piece of scrap paper and covered all the available space with figures. Then finally she handed the sheet to her father.

Jeb took his time before he spoke to Willie. "Son, we understand that you're goin' to a lot of trouble for us. But there's got to be something more than money you're getting out of this. What is it?"

Willie thought for a long time. Finally he looked Jeb in the eye and said, "Publicity, Sir. I want to run for governor in the next race and I need something that will get me some statewide publicity. If I take on the biggest mill in the south, that's news."

"You get the publicity win or lose, that right?"

"It's a lot better if I win, but yes Sir, I get the publicity either way."

Laine leaned over and pointed to a figure on the bottom of the paper. "Well, Son, here's the way I see it. We'll go along with your idea, and if you settle without going to court—and we're countin' on you to do that—then we get two-thirds of the settlement and you get one third. That's $6,666 for us and $3334 for you. Laine decided you oughta get the extra dollar for all your hard work."

At first Willie didn't know what to say. He'd never had a client out trade him before. And he'd certainly never been out traded by a woman. It was clear this girl had a lot more going for her than a pretty face and a dynamite body. Clearly she knew how to make numbers talk. Willie was good with round figures and anything he could divide by two. It took him a long time to figure out higher math like fractions, something Laine seemed to be able to do in her head.

Still, this was a dream case. Hard-working family, lots of kids. He did his best to turn the facts and figures over in his mind and wisely consider his options. Finally he decided that he'd come out ahead either way and bowed to his betters.

"It's a deal," he said and shook hands with Jeb.

CHAPTER SEVEN

THAT NIGHT LAINE LAY AWAKE in the small bedroom pondering Willie Shorter for a long time. He was handsome in a rugged sort of way and she wondered what he saw when he looked at her. She got out of bed, stripped off her threadbare gown and stood before the full length mirror on the back of the door appraising herself with a critical eye.

When she was 13, her chest was still flat as a pancake. Every night she had prayed for boobs, although she didn't say "boobs" to God for fear of offending him just when she needed a favor. "Please don't let me stay flat-chested all my life." Apparently God had listened and approved of her choice of words, because the next year He had answered her prayers abundantly.

Now whenever the preacher quoted his favorite scripture, "My cup runneth over, surely goodness and mercy shall follow me all the days of my life," Laine smiled to herself and wondered if, despite what she had been taught in Baptist Sunday School, maybe God did have a sense of humor after all.

The same summer she got boobs, she had also grown to her present height of five foot six inches. Even being critical, Laine had to admit that adding three inches and a few extra pounds had done wonders to transform her from a skinny kid into a very pretty girl. She turned from side to side looking at herself from all angles. "Not bad," she decided. "I bet I'm as sexy as any of those big-city girls he's used to seein'." She slipped her gown back on and got back in bed with a satisfied smile.

The change in Laine's body wasn't lost on the boys in town and it surely didn't go unnoticed by her mother. Louise wasted no time in sitting down with her oldest daughter to have a long serious talk. Years before she had explained where babies come from, but this new development required a different kind of mother-daughter discussion.

"Honey, it's clear your body's changing and you're gonna be what my mama woulda called 'voluptuous.' I know you're only 14, but what that means is all the boys are gonna look at you and think you're one kinda girl and it's your job not to be that kind." Laine looked blank so Louise tried another approach.

"What I'm saying is, they're gonna think you're easy. Most men are just after one thing and when they get it, they don't have no respect for you anymore. And worse than that, once they get what they want, they're gonna brag to all their friends and before you know it, you're gonna have a reputation."

Laine was genuinely puzzled. "Sounds like you're mad at all the men in the world, Mama. I thought you liked Dad. I hear you and him laughin' in bed sometimes and…"

"That's a whole different thing," Louise said and smiled in spite of herself. "The thing is, Lainie, all women have got something men want. It's a contest, Honey, you got it and they want it and they're gonna tell you every kind of thing to try to get you to give it away, 'specially the first time. But Laine, once you've gone all the way with a boy, things is different. A pretty woman like you is gonna have men hangin' around all the time, like flies to honey. The trick is to find the right man to fall in love with and get married. Then makin' love is not only alright, it's wonderful."

"What's it like, Mama?"

Louise hesitated. She'd always made it a point to be honest with her girls—and the boys, too. She didn't like the way some women pussy-footed around the truth and then acted all surprised when one of their kids got themselves—or someone else—in trouble.

"Well, Sugar," she said finally, "it's like all the energy in the world is concentrated in one place and it feels so good you can't stand it. When that happens, Lord," she took a quick breath, "it's like coming down the first big hill on the roller coaster sittin' in the front car with your hands in the air. Nothin' in the world's better or more fun, if.... and that's a big if... if you do it with the right man. So just hold out until you find the right one."

"When were you on a roller coaster?"

"What? Lainie, are you payin' attention?"

"Yes, Ma'am. I understand about being careful and all...it's just...when were you ever on a roller coaster?"

"Oh, I'll never forget it. For some reason, the mill took a bunch of us to the State Fair once when I was a girl. We went to the Southeastern Fairgrounds at Lakewood up near Atlanta and there was this huge wooden roller coaster called the Greyhound. It was the tallest thing I'd ever seen. The cars made this clackety-clack noise going up the incline—way up above everything—and then just dropped down the other side. It looked really scary and I didn't want to ride it. But somehow your dad convinced me to go and to sit in the front seat with him. I don't know what made me do it. Anyway, he put his arms around me and held me real tight the whole time. When I got off that thing, my heart was poundin' and my legs were so weak I could hardly stand up. The rest of the kids went off to ride other stuff, but your dad stayed with me all afternoon. I think that's when I knew he was the one."

"How'll *I* know?"

"Oh you'll know," she said with a far-away look in her eyes and a smile on her lips, "you'll know."

"Is makin' love ever sweet and romantic like at the picture show?"

"I don't think I'd call it sweet, at least not on the way up. It's frantic and kinda wild, I guess you'd say, but afterwards... well, yeah, then it can be kinda sweet. Least..." she glanced at her daughter's face, "...least that's the way it is with your dad and me. I know some women don't like it, but I think that's just 'cause they was never with the right man. You just look for somebody like your dad and you'll be OK."

Laine often remembered her mama's words. Louise had been right about everything. The boys had come around, and the men too, and Laine discovered she could get them to do almost anything she wanted for a kiss or a real close dance or a grope in somebody's pickup, but she always stopped before things went too far.

As to finding somebody like her dad, Laine had a list of exactly what her perfect man should be. First, he had to be good looking with a strong, wiry body and dark curly hair like her dad and JW. And he had to have blue eyes. She liked blue eyes. Then he had to be quiet once in a while. She didn't like boys who talked all the time. He had to listen sometime. And laugh, that was important too. And he had to be able to dance, not just crush the breath out of a person pretending to know what he was doing. He had to be a really, really good dancer.

As to his personality, well, he could be gruff sometime. Her dad was, but he loved her mama and his kids and they all knew it. He held the babies on his lap when they were little, made toys and played with them when they were older, taught them how to do things. He wasn't afraid to love his kids. Even now, sometimes her dad would give her or the twins an unexpected hug or bend down and kiss the top of the boys' heads when they were sitting at the kitchen table.

So far, nobody she'd met had fit the bill. She'd known most of the boys in Ford Crossing all her life, and none of them came anywhere close to living up to her standards. They were either too shy or too silly or too pushy. And if you added all of them together, they wouldn't be anywhere near as smart as she was. How could she fall in love with somebody who was dumb as a post?

She realized that at 18 lots of people considered her an old maid. Most of her friends got married when they were 15 or 16 and started having babies right away. It was just what everybody did. She sorta liked the idea of having a big family, but she also knew once that happened, she would be stuck in some mill town for the rest of her life.

That led her thoughts back to Willie Shorter. He was a little older than she was, maybe ten years, maybe a little less. And he was surely no mill town boy; that was for sure.

So how did Willie match up to her list? He sure did talk a lot. But he was good looking. He sure did think a lot of himself. But he had a nice smile and he was polite. He wasn't any good with figures. But he seemed to be smart about a lot of other things. He sure was asking her family to take a big risk. But he did sound like he expected to win.

And what if they *did* win? Six thousand, six hundred, and sixty-six dollars was more money than Laine had ever dreamed of seeing in her lifetime. It would certainly be enough to get her out of Ford Crossing with or without Willie Shorter...although the idea of being with him was definitely exciting. As she fell asleep, she felt Willie Shorter's blue eyes looking at her. She smiled.

***

It was after dark by the time Willie got back to Morganton. He parked the car and went up to his room. Like most boardinghouse rooms, it was sparsely furnished. A bed, a chest of drawers, and a chair.

Willie stripped down to his boxer shorts and plopped down on top of the bedspread. The room was stuffy and the black fan blowing across his body didn't help much. Willie's mind was divided between churning out ideas about the case and fantasizing about Laine. He thought about the publicity the case would generate; the money—although he was still a little fuzzy about how he'd ended up with a third instead of half.

Then his thoughts turned to Laine. My God, those long legs and that mouth... Willie had known his share of girls, and the widow had definitely qualified as a woman, but this one was different. Not only did she have a body men would die for, she was smart. Damn! Who would have guessed a looker like that was hiding in Ford Crossing? One of the definite pluses of this case was having an excuse to see her again.

The next morning found Willie in his office earlier than usual. For the first time, he paid very close attention as he perused the law books lined up behind the glass on the shelves. He realized he was about to move up to the big time and this required real research, not just a fast mind and a quick tongue. Taking on Claxton Mills, Inc. was not like dealing with a low-level functionary for some well-digging outfit or besting some sawmill boss. This was a whole different ball game.

That idea completely overwhelmed Willie for the moment. But, rather than give in to the little-used cautious part of his brain that screamed, "Get out, get out," Willie turned his energy to a more entertaining—although equally important—chore.

He selected the latest issues of all the newspapers scattered around his office. Then he got a legal pad and began making a list. He checked each masthead for the managing editor's name and the paper's mailing address. He intended to make sure every major newspaper in the state and all the weeklies in his immediate area got a blow-by-blow account of Willie Shorter vs. Claxton Mills Incorporated.

Just to test out his journalistic skills, and to postpone the drudgery of doing research, Willie decided to write his first news release. He opened the door that covered the lower right hand side of his wooden desk, reached down and with some effort pulled up the spring-loaded shelf that held his Underwood typewriter. To be on the safe side—and to waste a little more time—he put in a brand new ribbon. Then, of course, he had to walk down the hall to the lavatory to wash the ink off his hands. Finally back in his office, he took a clean sheet of typing paper and rolled it into the machine. Then he sat back to think.

An hour and twenty sheets of paper later, he pulled the final draft out of the typewriter.

LOCAL LAWYER TAKES ON MAJOR CORPORATION

Willie Shorter, Morganton lawyer, is negotiating with Claxton Mills Incorporated on behalf of his 19-year-old client. The young man in question, JW Becker, was grievously injured through no fault of his own. There is some question as to whether Claxton Mills may be at fault...

He ended with the part about Claxton Mills plucking the feathers out of the golden goose. All in all, a good morning's work. He breathed a satisfied sigh and then he thought about the responsibility he had taken on and put the news release away.

Watch out, Boy. You're getting a little ahead of yourself there. This isn't penny-ante stuff anymore. Take it one step at a time, just go slow and do your job.

During the remaining months of spring and into early summer, Willie devoted himself diligently to the task at hand. He made several trips to Ford Crossing, always on Sunday when Laine—and her family—were home.

They didn't have a phone, so he wrote letters. At first he discussed his strategy only with Jeb. However, Willie soon realized Jeb was talking everything over with his wife and daughter. No doubt about it, Laine was a very sharp cookie. Before long she was sitting in on the discussions, which was as worrisome as it was helpful. Willie could hardly keep his eyes off her. It took all his will power, but he didn't want to give her father any reason to worry.

CHAPTER EIGHT

MORE THAN ONCE LAINE SUGGESTED that Willie needed to spend some time on the mill floor to understand what working there was really like. Finally, at her insistence, he gave in. The Becker house was much too small and there was no place in Ford Crossing where Willie could stay overnight so he left Morganton at 4:30 a.m. in order to be on time for the 6:00 a.m. shift. When he arrived, Laine disguised him in some old clothes and an old hat. He walked in unnoticed when the Beckers reported for the day shift. In ten minutes Willie was covered with a fine layer of white cotton lint, which made him indistinguishable from the rest of the workers on the floor.

Up close the deafening noise of Claxton Mill sounded much worse than Willie had imagined. It tore through his head. The moment he entered the mill, all color vanished. It was like walking into a black and white nightmare. Black machines, air filled with white lint. The particles reminded him of Georgia "no-see 'ems," the annoying gnats that always sought out the moisture in people's eyes. Breathing through his nose was impossible and breathing through his mouth was like eating cotton, but he stuck it out and watched.

He noticed the bad lighting, the slick patches on the oily floor where water sprayed into the air collected here and there. He realized people hardly ever stopped moving. Even on their short breaks to eat, they stood with one eye on the ever-whirling machines or they sat down in the aisles in front of the machines. Willie had grown up in the heat and humidity of the south, but mill heat was much more intense. It felt like being inside a pressure cooker. The hot air seemed to enter through the top of his head and force sweat out every pore in his body.

At first Laine tried to keep an eye on him, but after a while she was too busy to notice. At noon she looked for him while she ate, but didn't see him anywhere. When she got home, she found a note saying that he had given up and made a break for freedom and fresh air after a couple of hours. "How do people do that for 12 hours a day, six days a week, year after year after year?" he asked. She crumpled the note and threw it away. He made it sound like there was a choice, which showed he didn't really understand anything.

Sometime around the first of July, Willie completed his research, prepared the petition and went to deliver a copy to Claxton Mills' regional headquarters on Marietta Street in downtown Atlanta. He wore his second best suit and left his shoes looking slightly scruffy. He didn't want to look too successful or too prosperous.

It took nearly a week just to work his way through all the secretaries who ran interference for the big shots, but Willie used the time well.

Introduce yourself to those ladies, Boy. Remember their names. Get the name of the next secretary up the line. Be pleasant. Don't be pushy.

Willie chatted easily with the secretaries in each department and remembered the information they shared. He smiled and thanked each one for her help. When he walked into the next office, he greeted the secretary by name and then asked if her boss, Mr. So-and-so, was in. The ladies were impressed.

Eventually a secretary ushered Willie into the office of Mr. George Horace Alexander, Senior Manager of Claxton Mills for the Southern Territory. He wasn't an imposing man, just average height and build, brown hair with a touch of gray at the temples. His handshake was firm, but not overbearing, his manner unassuming. In spite of all that, Willie instantly knew the man standing before him was accustomed to wielding power.

The office certainly had something to do with that impression. It was bigger and grander than anything Willie had ever seen. The walls were mahogany paneling decorated with what Willie recognized as four Audubon prints, handsomely framed and individually lighted. The carpet was thick, the furniture leather. The room even smelled expensive. Willie took it all in. He could picture himself in just such an office. But the sign on his door would read "Governor" not "Regional Manager."

Willie got right down to business. He presented his petition with predictable results. Mr. Alexander didn't take him seriously. Alexander considered the whole thing a bit ridiculous. After all, he represented Claxton Mills, Inc. and nobody challenged Claxton.

Willie persevered. Eventually Mr. Alexander realized this brash young man wasn't going to go away. He agreed to discuss the situation with the company's lawyers and indicated that "someone" would get back in touch with Willie.

Of course no one did, but Willie was prepared for that. He forced himself to wait a full week, then started calling.

This time he skipped all the under-secretaries. Bright and early on Monday morning, he placed a call to Claxton headquarters and asked to speak directly to Mr. Alexander's executive secretary, Miss Faraday. When he greeted her by name, she was a little surprised and, if the truth were known, a little flattered. People wanting to speak to her boss seldom ever called her by name. Nevertheless, her job was to protect Mr. Alexander, so she told Willie what she always told unexpected callers. "I'm sorry, Mr. Shorter, but Mr. Alexander is in a meeting."

Rather than becoming annoyed, Willie assured her it was absolutely no problem at all and that he would call back. He did, every day, sometimes several times a day. By the end of the third week in July, he and Maxine Faraday were great friends.

He knew she was originally from Ohio, had moved to Atlanta to live with her widowed sister, was the breadwinner of the family, had worked for Mr. Alexander for six years, always ate lunch at her desk, drank tea instead of coffee, liked cats and hated cauliflower. He also remembered the name of her sister and the names of all her co-workers, in short, everyone in the building who might be of help later on.

That's it, Boy. Make friends with the little man…or woman. In the end, they're the ones who can help you the most.

By the beginning of August, Maxine was only too glad to help this personable young man get in to see her boss. To Mr. Alexander's surprise, Miss Faraday brought Willie's request for an appointment to his attention every morning. Evidently Willie Shorter and his petition were not going to go away.

Finally, Laine wrote to Willie with an idea that got things moving. "If the secretary, Miss Faraday, is as nice as you say she is, I'll bet she'd feel sorry for JW if she met him face-to-face. And if she liked him, then I'll bet she'd help you get in to talk to her boss. Mama thinks this is a good idea too."

Willie made one last call to Miss Faraday and convinced her to make an unofficial appointment with Mr. Alexander for the following Wednesday. "Maxine, I don't want you to get in any trouble, but I'm convinced if Mr. Alexander could just meet this young man, it would make all the difference."

Once that was done, Willie wrote to Louise Becker and asked her to have JW ready for the trip to Atlanta. Willie said he'd arrive the night before and apologized for any inconvenience saying he could easily sleep in his car.

Louise wrote back. "We can't have you sleeping in your car. Folk'll talk. I know there's an Army cot over at the church. I'll speak to Pastor Bennett and see if we can borrow it. Then I'll ask him to help me set it up on the screen porch and make sure all the neighbors see where we're putting it. That way there won't be cause for any idle gossip."

When Louise read the letter to the family, she thought she saw a flush on her daughter's face. The attraction between Willie and her oldest daughter had not escaped Louise's attention. More than once she had started to ask Laine about it, but each time she reconsidered. She'd watch and wait awhile.

The day Willie was due, Laine rushed home from the mill, took a bath, washed her hair, ironed a dress and then tried to look casual as she ran around the house dusting, rearranging and picking up things. As soon as she heard the car, she was at the screen door waiting. She let Willie in and then went into the kitchen to help her mama fix supper: fried chicken, cornbread, black-eyed peas, fried okra, and homegrown tomatoes still warm from the afternoon sun.

Supper at the Becker's was usually hurried. Everybody was bone-tired and wanted to go to bed, but that night, Laine had other ideas. She was determined to drag the evening out as long as possible. "Mr. Shorter, what are you gonna do with the Claxton Mills money if we win?"

"Finance my campaign for governor," Willie said without hesitation. He obviously intended to win, because he skipped right over the campaign and plunged right into telling them what he would do as governor. He had plans for Georgia and once he got the state fixed up, he intended to take on the whole country.

While Willie rattled on, Laine daydreamed that somehow she could go to Atlanta with him. They'd go to fancy parties, she'd have beautiful clothes and Willie would fall helplessly in love with her. He'd take her in his arms, cover her mouth with his and… She looked up and their eyes met. Laine got a jolt of electricity down to her toes. It was as if he had read her mind.

After supper, Laine sent JW to put on his good clothes so Willie could make sure he looked all right for the meeting with Mr. Alexander. While JW changed clothes, Willie casually asked Laine if she was reading the book lying on the table.

"I'm not readin' it, I'm tryin' to learn it." She showed him a page full of strange squiggles.

"What in the world is it?" asked Willie.

"It's shorthand. I'm gonna be a secretary."

Jeb laughed. "From what I've seen so far, Lainie, you oughta stick to numbers. Don't look like you got any knack for shorthand writin'."

"You like arithmetic?" Willie asked innocently, already knowing the answer only too well.

"Sure. Numbers are easy," Laine said. "They come out the same way every time and like Dad says, they don't lie."

"Past the basic stuff, I've never been very good with numbers," Willie said, "but then I reckon y'all already figured that out." Laine grinned at him.

"Tell you what, Son, if you're plannin' on goin' into politics, you better start learnin' to understand numbers," Jeb said. "A feller who don't read figures is like a blind man playing poker. You're gonna get took every time, sure enough."

Willie turned to Laine. "Reckon you'd like to come to work for me when I get to be governor? I'll take care of the politicians and you can read the numbers and tell me what they're really up to."

Laine caught her breath. "I reckon I might."

"Better be careful, Honey, I think Mr. Shorter just might be governor one day," Jeb said.

"No doubt about it, Mr. Becker. If this thing with Claxton works out the way we're all hoping, I'm definitely gonna be governor, you wait and see."

One step at a time, Boy. Don't go spending Claxton money before you get your hands on it.

At that moment, JW entered the room dressed to the nines and looking right pleased with his appearance. His arm wasn't in a sling any more, but he held it close to his body. Clearly he had difficulty straightening it out. He wore a slightly old fashioned suit with the coat buttoned all the way up. Willie had tried that trick himself. Underneath the jacket, he knew the boy had the pants riding low on his hips to make the pant legs appear as long as possible.

JW had on a white shirt but no cuffs were visible. Either the sleeves were too short or the cuffs were too frayed. His shoes were old, but they had a high shine. His tie was years out of style, but it was properly tied and knotted tightly. All in all he looked like Willie Shorter ten years ago, before he learned better.

"That'll never do," Willie said. He immediately saw JW's smile fade and his shoulders sag. "What I mean is," Willie continued quickly, "you look much too prosperous. I want you looking clean, proud, poor and pitiful. Now, Miss Becker, can you go get the worst looking clothes you got in the house? It won't matter if they don't fit, in fact it's better if they don't. We've got to make Claxton Mills feel sorry for JW, we got to...."

Contrary to his usual quiet behavior, JW spoke up. "No Siree! I ain't gonna go up there beggin' nobody for nothin'. Just 'cause I hurt my hand don't mean I'm pitiful. Hell—'scuse me Mama—but I can take care of myself just fine, even with only one good hand."

CHAPTER NINE

WILLIE TOOK ANOTHER TACK. "I know that JW. But you're looking at this all wrong. What I want you to do is look at this like...well like...like a movie. You're the star in this movie and Claxton Mills, they're the bad guys. Now what you gotta do is go up there and play-act. If you look like you can take care of yourself, they aren't gonna help you. You gotta look beat down, defeated, helpless. In fact, the worse you look the better. That doesn't mean you can't be proud. They'll respect that. Clean and proud and...."

"...pitiful," said Laine smiling. "Y'all wait here." She came back in a minute with an old shirt, an old pair of corduroy pants with the nap worn off the knees and a pair of scruffy brogans that had clearly seen a long, hard life. While everybody watched, she grabbed the ironing board, plugged in the iron, picked up a Coke bottle with a sprinkler cork stuck in the mouth and put a sharp crease in the old pants.

"Take off them clothes and put these on," she said handing the pants to JW. Unselfconsciously he took off the suit and put on the old pants. Willie couldn't help but notice that his shorts were made out of bleached feed sacks. Willie knew more about that than he ever intended to admit to anybody. The sleeves on the shirt Laine had found were a couple of inches too short. Just the thing for the image Willie was trying to create.

The effect was perfect. JW did look pitiful, no doubt about it. "Dad, gimme your hat," Laine said. "Here," she handed the old felt hat to JW. "It'll give you somethin' to hold on to." She turned JW toward Willie, "How's that?" she said proudly.

Willie and the Beckers proclaimed JW an unquestionably pitiful success. In spite of himself, JW smiled, enjoying their approval. Willie was glad there wasn't a mirror in the living room, because if JW could have seen himself, he would have backed out of the deception on the spot.

Next morning the whole family got up early enough to see Willie and JW off before they went to work. Laine gave her brother last minute instructions. "Tell Miss Faraday the truth, but don't talk too much. When you get to talk to the boss, tell him what a fixer does. Tell him how much you liked doin' it. Tell him how good you was. Tell him we're all gonna starve now."

If Jeb hadn't stopped Laine, JW and Willie would never have been able to leave. Willie started the car, but before he could pull away from the curb, Laine stuck her head inside the window. "Good luck, Mr. Shorter. We're countin' on y'all, so you and JW do good." She gave Willie a quick kiss on the cheek and was gone. It took a supreme effort for Willie not to react in any way that JW might notice. He wanted the boy's total attention focused on the task at hand, not worrying about what this fast-talking lawyer might be thinking about doing to his sister.

JW's performance for Alexander surpassed Willie's wildest expectations. He was the epitome of a young man frustrated by circumstances over which he had no control. He was forthright, honest and proud. Laine had coached him well. Maxine Faraday was so impressed she ushered them into Mr. Alexander's office even though she hadn't cleared the appointment with him beforehand. They only stayed a minute, but there was no doubt that JW had made quite an impression. From then on, Mr. Alexander couldn't treat the Becker case like just another nameless, faceless problem.

To reward JW, Willie dipped into his meager reserves and treated them both to lunch at the newly opened Herren's Restaurant on Luckie Street. The bustling, downtown eatery catered to businessmen but occasionally a woman or two dropped in. The dark walls, muted lighting, and heavy clouds of smoke made it hard to see very far. Rather than one large open room, diners were seated in a number of different rooms on several levels.

Willie followed the waiter and JW followed Willie. Once they were seated, JW admitted he'd never been in a restaurant before. Willie smiled. He suspected that so he had brought along a sports coat and a reasonable looking pair of slacks for JW to wear. As usual Willie did most of the talking, but JW participated enough for Willie to realize he was bright, ambitious and had a dry sense of humor, much like his father.

Later that day, Willie paid JW's fare and sent him home on the train, another new experience for the boy. By the time he got home the twins were already at work. The rest of the family waited up to hear what happened. JW was the hero of the hour. He told the story in detail, right down to the marinara sauce and spaghetti he'd had for lunch. Then when the twins got home the next morning, he told it all over again over breakfast.

Then they all went back to waiting for something to happen. One scorching evening in late August as Laine dragged herself home at the end of her shift, she saw Willie's car parked in front of her house. She sneaked through the neighbor's back yard and went in the back door so she could wash her face and run a rag over her arms and legs to get the lint off. Then she sauntered out on the front porch and acted completely surprised to see Willie.

Willie had brought along barbecue he said he had gotten in lieu of a fee from a nearby client. "Since I was in the neighborhood anyway, I just thought I'd drop by." Nobody questioned him because barbecue was a special treat any way the Becker's came by it.

Laine gave Willie some rather uncomfortable moments at supper as he watched her suck barbecue sauce off her fingers one by one. She seemed to be unaware of the effect she caused. To keep his mind otherwise occupied, Willie rambled on about how he spent several hours a day typing copies of the news stories he wrote and mailing them to editors on his list. Laine licked her lips and caught his eye, "I'll be glad to help you any way I can."

Willie's mind was reeling—if she only knew—and he was finding it hard to breathe.

"The only problem is, I don't have a typewriter...."

"I can take care of that," Willie volunteered, a tad too quickly perhaps.

Laine smiled to herself when he showed up the very next day carrying an old Remington under his arm. She had expected the typewriter, but she was surprised when Willie took a wooden table and secretary's chair out of the back of his car. He said he'd borrowed them from the Morganton Memorial Museum. He'd also brought typing paper, carbon paper, onion skin sheets, envelopes and stamps. Laine quickly accepted when he offered to pay her 10 cents an hour. At first she made a lot of mistakes and had to do the release over, but since she was typing the same thing over and over again, she soon built up some speed.

Meanwhile back at Claxton Mills' headquarters in Atlanta, Mr. Alexander was puzzled as to how reporters from so many little towns, to say nothing of the *Atlanta Journal,* got so much information about the day-to-day progress of the Becker situation. He even asked Willie once point blank if he had been approached by any of the papers. Willie honestly said he had not.

Laine enjoyed her new job. Typing and working 12 hours at the mill should have worn her out, but she had enough nervous energy to keep her going on very little sleep. She pounded the keys of the Remington, watched the letters appear on the paper, pulled each finished copy out of the typewriter and felt very pleased with herself.

Each week Willie sent a letter with his latest article. Once Laine got familiar enough to read Willie's scrawl, she had to laugh out loud at the lies he told. She knew nothing much was happening with Claxton Mills, but that's not the way Willie's stories made it sound. According to him, it was a constant, daily battle.

Willie's letters were always addressed to Mr. and Mrs. Jeb Becker. Laine wanted to open them, but she never did. One night after supper, her dad opened an envelope with his pocket knife and a newspaper clipping fell out. Willie's letter explained that because of the publicity in all the weekly newspapers, the *Atlanta Constitution* had called him for an interview. That meant he wasn't just local news anymore. He recounted how he went from the specifics of helping the Beckers to telling the reporter what he planned to do for all the working families in the state when he was elected governor.

"That boy's got more nerve than sense," Jeb said and they all laughed.

Alexander dragged the Claxton negotiations on for another month—secretly to Laine's delight since the longer they lasted, the more she got to see Willie and the more money she made typing stories. She saved every penny.

One Saturday night Willie showed up unannounced. After chatting a while with her parents, he suggested he and Laine go for a drive. It was all Laine could do to act normal when she asked her mama if it would be all right. "Just remember what I told you, Laine," Louise said.

Laine not only remembered, she secretly hoped Willie would try all the things her mama had warned her about. She was not disappointed. Willie drove down a narrow dirt road and parked by the Senoia River about half a mile from Claxton Mill. They got out and walked over an old abandoned railroad bridge. Willie talked about politics and how much she had helped him, but it was his hands, not his voice, Laine concentrated on. He was a lot smoother than the mill boys she'd known up to that time.

His touches were like whispers... there, but not there. After what seemed to her like an eternity, he finally put his arms around her. She expected him to kiss her, but instead he nuzzled her neck, which sent shivers down her body. She felt his warm breath as he whispered in her ear. Finally, when she could hardly wait any longer, he pulled her tight against him, tilted her head back and kissed her long and slow.

She parted her lips slightly and felt the tip of his tongue, teasing, yet holding back. He was letting her take the lead, and she wanted it all. She opened her mouth for him to explore and when he did, she felt her whole body open. The more he gave, the more she wanted.

Oh my God, this must be the way bad girls feel. But Laine couldn't make herself stop. She slipped her arms around his neck and pressed her body against him. Her mind raced. *Do it, just do it, I won't stop you.* He slipped his hand inside her blouse and touched her bare skin. She heard the clackety-clack of the roller coaster as it started up the hill and she moaned "Willie...." Then suddenly she pulled away.

"I gotta get off," she said.

"What?"

"I'm gonna...ah...I mean we gotta...we gotta stop."

"I thought you liked it."

"I did. I do, but I'm tryin' not to. No I mean...it's too fast. It's too scary."

Willie knew he could overcome her protests, but also knew if he did, there might be hell to pay. He wanted her so bad it hurt, but he also knew better than to force the issue.

Hold on, Boy. It'll happen, just take your time. Find the right time and place. The first time ought to be special.

On the drive home, Willie went back to talking about politics. Laine didn't hear a word he said. By the time they got back, she almost had herself under control. She thanked him for the ride, said good-night and watched him drive away.

Then she ran up the steps and into the room she shared with the twins. She knew her mama would be awake, but she was relieved she didn't have to talk. She just wanted to get in bed, close her eyes and go over every little detail of what happened. *Boy, mama's right. This roller coaster stuff is really somethin'!*

CHAPTER TEN

THROUGHOUT THE MONTH OF SEPTEMBER Laine hoped to hear from Willie, but he didn't get in touch with the Beckers again until the end of October – an eternity as far as she was concerned. His letter said he would have news when he arrived. When he knocked on the door, Laine knew immediately from the look in his eyes that something had happened with Claxton Mills. The family assembled to hear the verdict.

Ever the storyteller, Willie dragged the story out as long as possible. "I don't know if it was all the publicity or if they got nervous when I threatened to introduce some reporters to the twins, but something got to 'em. I'm sorry to tell you this folks, but it's over."

The family sat in stunned silence around the table. The Becker family knew there was a possibility Willie's plan wouldn't work, but he had been so sure, so positive, they convinced themselves he could pull it off.

Willie looked around the room, took his time, then casually laid a piece of paper on the table. "We won!" he yelled throwing his arms in the air. "They caved in. They paid. There it is, your two-thirds. A check for $6666! Signed, sealed and delivered."

Jeb was the first one to move. He bent over to get a closer look at the check but he didn't touch it. When he straightened up, he reached out and hugged Willie just like he hugged his boys. Laine could see that Willie was pleased even though he tried not to show it. "Hot Damn, Willie, you did it!" Jeb said in amazement.

The rest of the family had been waiting for permission to go crazy. On cue they all started laughing and jumping up and down and hugging each other. "Keep your voices down, the neighbors will think we've lost our minds," Louise cautioned. That, of course, just made matters worse. The more they tried to be calm, the sillier they got.

In spite of herself, Louise laughed until she cried. JW and Bo danced a jig and Laine threw her arms around Willie and gave him a full body hug.

Willie announced that he had a bottle of champagne in his car. He said he didn't know if the Beckers drank or not. Louise said they didn't…but that perhaps under the circumstances…. She got out some glasses and everybody, even Bo, got a taste.

Nearly a year had gone by since JW got hurt. With the check still lying in the middle of the kitchen table, they sat down to have a serious discussion. Willie explained that as part of the agreement with Claxton, the family was bound by law and forbidden to disclose any details or the amount of the settlement.

"That's probably just as well," said Laine. "I don't reckon it'd be so good for us if the neighbors knew we was richer than Midas."

"Yeah, but word'll get out that we won something, and folks'll wanta know how much. What are we gonna say?" Louise looked worried.

"Why don't we say what Willie's been writin' in the news releases?" Laine suggested. "He said it was a sizable amount. I figure most mill folks would consider $400 sizable, don't you Dad?"

"I reckon they would. Till today, I sure would have."

Then they talked about where to cash the check and where to keep the money. The Beckers shared Willie's mistrust of banks, but they agreed that having that much money in a sock under the mattress would be foolish, to say nothing of uncomfortable.

The next Sunday Willie drove Jeb to Morganton and PV made a special trip to open the bank so Jeb could deposit the check and open an official account. PV also helped arrange for the Beckers to receive $25 a month to supplement what they had lost from JW's fixer salary.

"Lord, God, I didn't know being rich was so complicated," Jeb said on the ride home.

Everybody in the family, except Bo, went back to work. JW's right arm had healed as well as could be expected. He could still use it, but his fingers didn't work well enough to allow him to pick up or handle small objects. He squeezed an old rubber ball to build up some strength.

As painful as the accident had been, JW enjoyed knowing that he had kept a secret from Willie (and therefore from Claxton Mills). He would have told the truth if anyone had asked him, but no one did. Therefore nobody outside the family knew that he was left-handed. He was pretty sure none of the supervisors or foremen at the mill had paid enough attention to him to notice one way or the other.

When it was all over and JW saw the check with his own eyes, he told Willie. It took a minute for the information to sink in and then Willie laughed until his sides hurt. That quiet, shy boy had put one over on everybody. The Becker family never ceased to amaze him.

As part of the agreement, JW was given a job in the Claxton Mill machine shop. More out of frustration than anything else, he started making small drawings of things he imagined but couldn't build. Blix Reeve, the superintendent, saw some of them and talked to Jeb about apprenticing the boy to somebody who could teach him how to develop his skill. JW was amazed that anybody could get paid for just thinking things up.

Blix had known JW all his life and he felt it was about time the boy caught a break. On his own time, he visited his friend Bartholomew Steinberg, who was a mechanical genius, and made the necessary arrangements. JW happily became Mr. Bart's apprentice with a small salary. However, there was a condition. As part of the agreement, Mr. Bart insisted JW go back to school and get his high school diploma. Louise was overjoyed and although

JW didn't think much of the school idea, he knew better than to argue with his mama.

Because every member of the Becker family had been at risk in the Claxton Mills case, it seemed only proper that each one should benefit from the settlement. Laine invested part of the Claxton money in a home-study bookkeeping course. Bessie subscribed to *National Geographic* and charged her family a nickel to read it. Callie spent her share on three new outfits, her first pair of high heels all ordered from the Sears and Roebuck catalogue. Bo got a catcher's mitt and a bicycle. Louise insisted that seeing her children happy was more than enough for her. Jeb said his reward was knowing they had money in the bank for a rainy day. "Like I always said, nothin's so bad that some good don't come out of it."

In one of their front porch discussions Willie said to Jeb, "I know you're happy holding on to the checkbook of your secret account, but the one person who didn't get anything tangible out of the settlement is Louise. Isn't there something special she wants?"

Jeb pondered that for a minute. "Well she used to talk about how she'd like to have a new living room suite, but at the time it was just a pipe dream." Then his face broke into a grin. "Her birthday's coming up the end of November; I think maybe we oughta go shopping."

Surprising Louise was totally out of the question. The family had enough trouble talking her into buying something new because the old furniture was still in good shape. Laine finally convinced her mother to give the old plaid couch, the over-stuffed chair, and the rickety coffee table to some newlyweds at the church. The young couple was delighted.

However, no sooner had they overcome that hurdle, than they ran into another problem. The Beckers had never made such a gigantic purchase before, so naturally the whole family wanted to be in on the selection. Unfortunately, Caruther's Furniture Store was never open on Sunday, their only day off. Willie had a long talk with Mr. Caruther and convinced him to let the

Beckers come look around on Sunday afternoon. Louise was clearly uncomfortable with shopping on the Sabbath until Willie pointed out that they weren't actually *shopping*, they were just *looking*. They'd make their selection on Sunday and pay for the furniture on Monday. Problem solved.

The Beckers spent all afternoon and looked at every piece of furniture in the store. Finally they settled on a blue velvet couch and matching overstuffed chair, a coffee table and two end tables with matching lamps. The whole room full of furniture cost $279.68.

"What are the neighbor's gonna think when they see Caruther's delivering all this?" Louise said.

"They're gonna think we blew almost all of our fortune on buyin' you a new living room suite for your birthday," said Jeb. For a minute Louise looked horrified and then she laughed.

On delivery day, Louise traded shifts so she could be home to supervise the placement of each piece of furniture. For the first month she wouldn't let anybody sit on the couch because it crushed the velvet. She made Bo sleep on the Army cot she had originally borrowed from the church for Willie.

Laine knew her mama still felt a little uncomfortable having all that fine furniture in the house. However every time she saw Louise walk by and stroke the back of the couch or dust off the coffee table, she knew Willie had been right to insist they spend the money.

Meanwhile, Willie took his $3334 and paid the back rent on both his office and his room at Miss Dorothy's, which he had allowed to build up while he worked on the Becker's case. Then he treated himself to two brand-new white shirts and sat down to figure out how to run a statewide campaign for governor on what was left.

CHAPTER ELEVEN

THE BECKERS WERE NO LONGER surprised to find Willie's car parked in front of their house from time to time. They came to consider him part of the family. This was a new experience for Willie. Until that point, Uncle Aubrey had been his only family. After he died, Willie became a loner.

Never look a gift horse in the mouth, Boy. Having a home to visit is like finding money on the street; you may not think you deserve it, but it sure is nice to have.

Sunday afternoons often found Jeb and Willie sitting on the porch talking politics.

Laine made a point to always be nearby. Since that night at the river, Willie had kept his distance, but it was clear a lot was going on in the silence between them. At first Laine just listened as the men talked, but eventually she joined in and Willie realized she understood a lot more about politics than he had guessed.

"It takes a lot of things to run a political campaign, Son," Jeb pointed out, "and you ain't got most of 'em. Far as I can see, you only got two things in your favor. First of all, you got more nerve than sense. Second, you got the present governor, Edward Fryer Jameson."

"I don't understand." Willie said.

"Well, Uncle Fry, as he calls himself, has been governor so long he thinks that's the natural state of the universe. I'm guessing the voters think different."

After his first eight years in office, Fry and his cronies had to stand down for one term, as mandated by the state constitution. During that time, Fry's handpicked replacement sat in the governor's office, made public appearances, and let Fry run things behind the scenes. Then Fry was elected for another two terms.

"I'm telling you, Fry don't know which way the wind's blowing. But the voters—at least the rural ones—are sure enough ready for a change."

Willie might have gone on just talking about running for governor for months if Jeb hadn't finally goaded him into actually doing something about it. "It's been nearly two months since we got the settlement. Willie, if you don't do something quick, everybody's gonna forget…what is it you called yourself?"

"The bright young lawyer who took on the biggest industry in the south and won," Laine quoted from one of Willie's press releases. "I think Dad's right. You oughta get started." Willie agreed, but for all his grandiose plans for *being* governor, he hadn't figured out the nuts and bolts of how to actually *run* for governor.

He didn't have a lot of important political friends, he didn't come from an old-line aristocratic family, he didn't have a lot of money, and he didn't have an organization behind him.

When he pointed this out for the umpteenth time, Laine lost her patience. "What's the matter with you? You just gonna go on talkin' or you gonna do something? Why don't you ask those Over-the-Hill fellers for help? Sounds to me like they got everything you need."

Willie was stunned. She was absolutely right, the solution had been right under his nose all along. As soon as he got back to Morganton, he went to the Club, told The Boys what he wanted to do and asked for their help.

It took a minute for what he said to sink in. "You're serious about running for governor?" PV inquired, trying hard not to laugh.

"Serious as a heart attack, but I haven't got a prayer without some help."

"And you want us to…to run your campaign?" This from Pappy.

"Yeah, and teach me everything you know about politics on the state level. What I need to know from you guys is how the system works at the top, what the rules are, who controls what, how to get things done. I got some big plans and I can talk to the people, but for the rest of it.... I'm counting on you." Willie waited hopefully.

"You want us to teach you all that?" They laughed. "How long do we have to impart all this knowledge?" More laughter.

"Plenty of time; the primary's still a couple of years away..." Willie said.

"Let's see. This is the first of December, so we have exactly.... eighteen months and ....27 days before the next primary in July, a year and a half from now."

There it is, Boy. Did you hear it?

There *had* been just the slightest change in the tone of PV's voice. Willie held his breath. The Boys looked to see if PV was making a joke. He wasn't.

"A political campaign is not like buying a suit of clothes, Dear Boy. You have to build it from the *ground up* and that takes time. Time, of which we *do not* have an abundance."

"Wait a minute," Pappy said. "PV, do you mean you're actually considering getting involved in this?"

"I think it has intriguing possibilities."

A long silence followed.

Bide your time, Boy. Stay silent and let the customer take the bait.

Willie waited. Finally Chauncey shrugged, "You might be right...if you think a good bar fight has 'intriguing possibilities.'" He poked Pappy in the ribs for emphasis.

"You're nuts," Pappy said. "This is crazy." He looked back and forth between PV and Chauncey several times. "You aren't actually considering this, are you?"

"Look at it this way," Willie added helpfully, "here's your chance to help me run the state of Georgia and you don't even have to run for office. Once I'm the governor, I'll appoint you to whatever office suits your fancy."

Pappy wasn't convinced. "Doesn't sound quite legal to me."

Chauncey stood up. "The Constitution only provides for four elected offices, Governor, Secretary of State, Comptroller General, and Treasurer. The rest is pretty much up for grabs." He paused and lit a cigarette. "You'll have to admit it's a tempting proposition and it sure beats sitting around here talking about what we *used* to do."

"It *does* have possibilities, indeed it does," PV said. "Our boy Willie here is a new face, a clean slate. The three of us have the history and the experience…"

Chauncey broke in, "…and we're not the only ones sick to death of Fry and his cronies. I think Willie—with our help, of course—just might pull this off."

Pappy shook his head. "This is one lame-ass idea…but I'll be damned if I'm gonna let y'all have all the fun. I'm in."

Willie breathed a sigh of relief. He was on his way. Once they got the idea, it was like somebody flipped an "ON" switch. The Boys pulled up chairs up and started tossing out ideas.

"At the outset, I might point out that the one thing *essential* to any campaign is money," said PV. They all looked expectantly at Willie.

Don't tell 'em everything you know, Boy. Just play your cards close to your vest.

"I've got $2,500 from the Claxton Mills settlement…" Like Uncle Aubrey taught him, Willie always hedged a bit when it came to specifics about money. "I'll put every bit of that into the pot."

"It's a start, but we're gonna need more, a lot more," Chauncey added. "Politics is like having a pretty, young wife. No man can make money fast enough to keep her satisfied."

The Boys hunkered down to a serious discussion; more or less forgetting Willie was in the room, which left him free to follow his own train of thought which inevitably led to visions of Laine.

PV glanced his way. "Don't be dreaming about moving in to the governor's mansion just yet."

Willie sighed. Little did they know. As he listened to the conversation around the table he realized there was one thing he could contribute. He'd need publicity throughout the campaign. He could handle the small-town papers but he'd need coverage from at least one or two of the big-city papers in the state.

The next day he had a long talk with Pappy, who overnight had done an about-face concerning the campaign. Pappy contacted a couple of his old buddies at the *Macon Telegraph* and the *Columbus Ledger-Enquirer*. They liked the idea of getting information before the *Atlanta Journal* or the *Constitution* and they agreed that win, lose or draw, Willie would be good copy.

Endorsing Uncle Fry again wouldn't get anybody's attention. He'd been governor too long. It was only good business for them to give some space to this brash newcomer, an underdog. Readers loved that kind of story. So with a nudge from Pappy, Willie got his foot in the door in Columbus and Macon.

That accomplished, Willie then approached PV about being his campaign manager. PV thought about it a while, and discussed it with Mother Ledbetter, something he always did before making an important decision. In the end he declined but recommended Chauncey.

Although Mother Ledbetter liked Willie and was willing to help him any way she could, she pointed out that her family was too prominent to be accepted by the common folks out in the counties. That job needed someone more…rural. The Ledbetter name could be put to better use behind the scenes gathering contributions from the other established families.

Chauncey was more than happy to be back in the political arena. In his time, he'd worked with a lot of politicians—good and bad. He knew the ins and outs of government and found an apt pupil in Willie who soaked up information like Georgia clay sucking up a summer shower. The more Chauncey taught, the more Willie wanted to learn. It was a political marriage made in heaven. Although Willie was a long shot, Chauncey started to think he really might have a chance.

Sol Goldman promised to put in a good word for Willie at the Temple. He also informed Willie that the Jewish community in Atlanta and throughout the state would be glad to put all their efforts into unseating the Fry administration. Uncle Fry made no secret that he disliked Negroes, Jews, and Catholics in that order.

Joe Laundry and his family were well respected in the agriculture community. In addition to being a major landowner, he had contacts in every cotton-growing county in south Georgia and knew a lot of other large landowners in the northern part of the state. He could provide valuable connections for Willie. Throughout the rest of December, The Boys continued to make plans and as the New Year dawned, things began to fall slowly into place.

CHAPTER TWELVE

IT WAS LAINE WHO SOLVED Willie's lack of a grass-roots organization. "You oughta talk to the colored folks. You helped a lot of them, right? If you just visited the churches and told 'em what you need, I'll bet they'd be glad to help."

"You mean on *Sunday*?"

"Well, they have church during the week, but Sunday'd be best."

"I can't do that. I know about pool halls and poker games, but church is mostly out of my league."

"Just talk to 'em. Black churches aren't like white ones; they're a lot more fun. The music is better and when everybody gets in the spirit…"

"How come you know so much?"

"Well, the Help for Hard Times Baptist church is right next to the mill. I used to hear 'em singin' sometimes, so on Sundays I'd sneak off over there. They'd let me sit on a bench at the back and listen. The preacher gets this rhythm going. He says something to the congregation and they answer him back. You oughta go listen, I bet you'd pick it up real fast."

Laine was right. On his own, Willie visited several colored church services over the next few weeks, showing up for Wednesday night prayer meetings as well as all-day Sunday preaching. He sat in the back, listened carefully, took notes and then went home to work on his "sermon."

When he thought he had something presentable, he asked Laine to see if he could speak for a few minutes at Help for Hard Times church. She arranged with the pastor to let Willie have some time in the pulpit. On the appointed Sunday, she sat on the second row waiting to see what would happen.

Willie wore his best suit, a starched white shirt, and his Florsheims. The pastor introduced him as "our next governor," which pleased Willie. However, when he took his place in the pulpit, there was none of the usual hum of voices from the congregation.

"Reverend, Friends and Neighbors, thank you for letting me speak to you here today. I'm not gonna lie to you, I'm not usually a church-going man."

(Silence.)

"All the religion I have came from reading the Bible when I sold them on the road with my Uncle Aubrey. I can quote some scripture but not near as well as your preacher."

(Silence.)

"I do remember one phrase that I read over and over. It became my favorite verse. Yes it did. Now here it is. 'And it came to pass…' Listen to me now. 'And it came to pass….'"

Laine heard the congregation start to hum as a few members spoke up.

(Help him, Lord.)

"That's right I need all the help I can get, Friends. 'Cause here's what I'm saying. This may be a bad time…"

(Come on now. Tell it. Tell it.)

"…but this bad time didn't come to stay. No Sir, it came to *pass*."

(That's all right. Yes, Lord.)

"You've been going through hard times…

(Amen)

"…but there's a better day coming.

(Let it come. Let it come.)

"You've been wounded…

(Wounded)

"…you've been kept down…

(Kept down)

"...but now you're gonna rise up...

(Rise up)

"...and greet that better day...

(Yes, Lord)

"...'Cause the bad days of Uncle Fry have come to pass!"

(Glory Hallelujah!)

In the best tradition of call and response preaching, Willie made it clear several times that Fry had come to pass. The congregation joined in and by the end of Willie's short speech, folks were catching the spirit of what might actually come to pass if he were governor.

With one successful sermon under his belt, Willie polished his skill and made it a point to "preach" whenever he got the chance. In the colored churches, he found an audience ready for his message.

Georgia was a one-party state which ran white-only Democratic primaries. Colored folks, therefore, had no influence in picking party nominees. Whoever won the primary ran unopposed in the general election because there was no Republican opposition.

Given that they were barred from state elections, it was little wonder the colored population wasn't inclined to register or to vote in national elections. Those who *did* try to register often got fired or thrown off the land they were sharecropping for whites. Some of them were beaten to discourage anyone else from trying to register.

As was the case across much of the south, Georgia was a state of yeller-dog-Democrats. The phrase derived, some said, from the fact that Southerners would vote for a yellow dog before they would vote for a Republican.

Willie Shorter couldn't give colored folks the right to vote in the state primary, but he offered them a way to get involved, to have a say in who the next governor would be and they jumped at the chance. They had no love for Fry, so they gladly volunteered what little free time they had to become the legs of Willie Shorter's organization.

Word spread through the churches. People contacted their relatives in other parts of the state and told them to get on board the Willie Shorter bandwagon. In no time, every fence post and utility pole in Georgia had a picture of Willie Shorter nailed to it. Uncle Fry's people tried removing all of them, but Willie's smiling face reappeared with the persistence of a kudzu vine that covered everything in its way.

Like the churches and The Boys, Laine got caught up in the excitement, too. At the end of January, she wrote Willie that the mill planned to sell an old flatbed truck cheap. "My dad says if you buy that truck, you'll have a stage to speak from anywhere you find a bunch of folks." So Willie bought the truck, left his car in Morganton and took his campaign on the road.

At one stop, three young colored men approached Willie. One carried a beat up guitar case, another had a gunnysack thrown over his shoulder and the third carried a large washtub. The guitar man introduced himself as Sonny Cunningham. The minute Willie heard the name, he remembered the case.

"How's Nelse and his mule getting along? He still doing odd jobs for Bull Rutledge?"

Turned out Nelse Cunningham was Sonny's uncle. The young man had often heard the story of how Willie tricked Bull into paying $15 for a $5 job and saved Nelse's mule in the bargain. As far as the Cunningham family was concerned, Willie was a miracle worker.

Sonny asked Willie if he and friends could ride along in the back of the truck and be Willie's warm-up band. All they wanted in return was food. They planned to find folks along the way to put them up. When they weren't playing for Willie, they'd play in local juke joints where they could make some money.

"I know that's a guitar case," Willie said to Sonny, "but what do you two play?"

"Luke here plays banjo," Sonny answered. "Show him." Luke carefully produced a well-used banjo from the gunnysack.

"Tuck plays bass." Like magic, Tuck upended the washtub and added a broomstick attached at the top to a length of rope coming up through the middle of the tub. Then he planted his foot firmly on the rim of the tub and strummed the one-string bass, which produced a deep, mellow sound.

Willie laughed. "You fellows got a name for your group?"

Sonny slapped Luke on the back. "Luke's dad calls us boys whippersnappers. What'dya think about that for a name?"

"Sounds good to me." With handshakes all around, Willie got an opening act and the band got free food and transportation around the state. Everybody was happy.

The Whippersnappers played every kind of music from hillbilly to Dixieland jazz. Depending on the audience, Willie said he had brought the band—at considerable personal expense—either up from New Orleans, down from Nashville, or over from Memphis, just for his audience's entertainment.

While Willie was on the road, he wrote "home" once a week. He still addressed the letters to Mr. and Mrs. Jeb Becker, but they knew who Willie was really writing to. Jeb opened each letter, then handed it to Laine who read them out loud to the family.

Willie told how he visited the small towns that had some kind of factory or mill just as the shift changed. That way he could shake hands with everybody coming or going. Then the band played and he made a short speech. If there were no factories, he'd visit places people gathered: barber shops, beauty shops, gas stations, grocery stores, hardware stores, offices, and always the colored churches. On the nights when nobody invited him to stay, he'd sleep in the cab of the truck under a couple of old quilts.

During February and March, Willie was moving too fast and having too much fun to take stock. But eventually he realized he had two problems. Small donations were coming in, mostly change collected by the Whippersnappers after Willie's speeches.

He had no idea where his money went, nor any idea exactly how much he paid for things.

Best place to keep your money, Boy, is in a dirty old shoebox. Tie it up with a piece of rawhide and put it under the seat of the truck. If it looks bad enough, nobody'll give it a second thought.

The method might not have been very businesslike, but it did have one important advantage. As long as Willie saw money in the box, he knew he wasn't broke. If one of his colored church groups needed more handbills, he went to the town newspaper, which was also the local printer, ordered flyers, and delivered them to the church. If there was money in the box, he paid the bill. If not, he promised to pay it the next time he came by.

But as the campaign moved into the spring, he had another problem that was completely foreign to him. "People are starting to give me folding money," he wrote. "We've been getting a fairly steady stream of nickels and dimes, maybe a quarter or two, but now sometimes somebody'll hand me a crumpled up dollar bill. I got no way of keeping track of what is coming in or going out. I need help. Any suggestions?"

Willie had a suggestion of his own. Laine. The problem was, he couldn't tell whether he was conning himself or not. On the one hand, he did need somebody who could help him keep track of the money. Somebody he could trust. On the other hand, traveling with Laine and working with her every day might be more than he bargained for.

Only one way to go with this, Boy. Plant the idea, then the next time you see the Beckers, throw the line out there again and see if you catch anything.

In the meantime, The Boys were busy with the campaign in their own ways. Willie went to them regularly for advice. Chauncey frequently joined him on the road and Joe Laundry showed up to introduce Willie whenever he spoke at a large rural gathering. If there was a community large enough to support a synagogue, Sol was always there to introduce Willie to the congregation.

Even though the crowds were small at first, Willie threw himself wholeheartedly into every speech. He moved constantly, waving his hands, quick stepping, bobbing and weaving like a prize fighter. People couldn't keep their eyes off of him. He had a deep voice that carried to the back of the crowd. He didn't want folks to miss a word.

For those who were not lucky enough to hear him in person, Willie and Laine typed summaries of his speeches and sent them to every paper in the state. Support him or not, the papers carried his speeches because they sold papers. Willie was indeed proving to be good copy.

CHAPTER THIRTEEN

TOWARD THE MIDDLE OF JUNE, Willie found himself close to Ford Crossing and decided to visit the Beckers. He took a box of Russell Stover chocolates as a gift for the ladies and hoped he would get a chance to talk to Jeb face-to-face about needing somebody to help with the finances.

He arrived a little before 6:00 p.m. one afternoon. It was a typical hazy, hot, humid day with the temperature still in the low 90s, but that didn't stop Willie from greeting folks getting off work at Claxton Mill. When Laine, Louise, and Jeb came through the gates, they were surprised but pleased to see him. "You here to make a speech?" Jeb asked.

"Yes Sir, never pass up an opportunity to talk to the voters. But after that I sure would like to talk to you. I need some advice." He was, of course, invited to stay for supper.

When they got home, Laine and Louise went in to fix supper. Eventually Willie showed up and he and Jeb sat down on the front porch hoping to catch a breeze. The house quickly filled with the aroma of home cooking. Willie explained his problem. He wondered if Laine and Louise could hear the conversation from the kitchen. "What'da think about me *hiring* Laine to come along and take care of the money?" Willie knew the answer the instant the question was out of his mouth.

"Just you and her out there on the road together?" Jeb raised his eyebrows.

"Well, no Sir, the Whippersnappers will be there, too," Willie said lamely.

"Them boys may play good music but they ain't gonna make no chaperone for my daughter."

"Yes Sir, that's true right enough, but I don't see any other way to solve this problem." Usually Willie would have tried to talk his way into getting what he wanted, but with Laine he wasn't entirely sure what that was. On the one hand, he knew exactly what he wanted, but on the other he respected and cared for the Beckers and he knew he would be in serious trouble if he did anything ungentlemanly where Laine was concerned.

He hadn't gotten off to a good start, but Willie held on to the slim hope that Jeb might rise to the bait. In the end, the answer came from an unexpected source. As they sat down to supper, JW came bounding up the steps and in the back door. The family didn't see him on a regular basis anymore because he often stayed over with the Steinberg family if he had been assigned some tricky project as part of his training.

All in one motion, JW sat down, mumbled a quick prayer and started to eat. Between bites he explained that Mr. Steinberg had been called up north for a family emergency. He was expected to be gone a couple of months, so JW was on his own.

After supper, Laine pulled her brother into the kitchen for a private word. Willie could hear them in serious conversation but he couldn't make out the topic. When Laine came out of the kitchen she whispered something to her dad and Jeb asked Willie to wait out on the porch while they held a family meeting.

Willie cooled his heels for what seemed like half an hour, then finally Jeb invited him back inside. "Laine can take over the finances for your campaign and she can travel with you…as long as JW comes along.

Willie glanced at Laine. "Well, JW needs something to do," she said innocently. "He can't work at the mill and he can't just hang around here. It just makes sense."

Jeb went on, "Don't think just because we've got some money in the bank that Laine can quit her job and run off willy-nilly."

Laine giggled.

"You know what I mean."

Willie jumped at the opportunity. Sort of making it up as he went along he said, "Tell you what, I'll turn driving the truck over to Sonny Cunningham, one of the Whippersnappers. Then we'll pick up the Ford from Morganton and JW can drive that. Lord knows, I'll be glad to get out of that rattletrap truck. And I'll pay him, of course. How about $1.50 a week?"

"I'm makin' $3 with Mr. Steinberg."

"Two dollars. That's the best I can do. And I'll pay Laine, too. Since she'll be keeping the books and typing all my press releases, she'll get $4 a week."

"Five," Laine said.

Willie's mouth dropped open. "What is this?! You guys are gonna put me in the poor house." He sighed, "OK, five."

Before Louise could raise an objection about the sleeping arrangements, Willie explained when they were in Morganton, he would arrange with Miss Dorothy for them all to stay at her boardinghouse. He assured Jeb and Louise that Miss Dorothy could be relied on to chaperone. Once they got to Atlanta, Willie would find a nice family for Laine to stay with. He and JW would find a boardinghouse. Everything would be strictly on the up-and-up.

JW could hardly wait to get behind the wheel of Willie's car. There was just one catch. "I don't know how to drive," he told Willie. Laine spoke up, "If we drive real slow, reckon Willie could teach you on the way to Morganton?"

Willie and JW simultaneously reckoned he could. Although the fingers on JW's right hand couldn't grasp small objects, shifting the car wouldn't be a problem. Even if it had been, Willie never doubted Laine would have a solution for that, too.

That night Louise came in to the girls' bedroom and sat down on the side of the bed. "Lainie Honey, I just want to remind you that you're gonna have to be on your guard out on the road and when you get up there to Atlanta." Laine pointed out that she would be living in Morganton, not Atlanta.

"Don't be changing the subject, you know exactly what I'm talkin' about. You're gonna be travelin', you're gonna be meetin' all kinds of people and you're gonna be on your own. I know JW'll be along, but you're the one who's gotta be strong, Laine. I remember what it's like to be young and to want to try new things, but you just keep in mind what I told you about findin' the right man and getting married before you go all the way."

Louise knew she had made her point, but somehow she couldn't drop the subject. "You got to protect your reputation, Baby, 'cause once it's gone, it's gone. There ain't no gettin' it back. Willie's a nice man and all, but he's older and he is *not* responsible for protectin' you. In fact, he may be the one you need protectin' from. You hear what I'm sayin' to you?"

"Yes, Ma'am, I hear."

"Well, you better take this seriously, 'cause I'm not gonna be there to tell you what to do…or what not to do. I know you're nearly grown, but when you leave here tomorrow, you've got to get serious about bein' an adult and bein' responsible for yourself."

"Yes, Ma'am. I know."

Louise saw the look on her daughter's face, half bored and half scared. She realized this might not be exactly the way she wanted to send Laine off into the world.

"It's just that I love you, Baby, and I want to make sure you're gonna be alright. But, you listen to me, any time you get to feeling' homesick or if anything ever does happen, you get yourself on the Greyhound bus and you come right home, ya'll hear? 'Cause we're your family and we'll always love you."

They hugged each other and Louise headed off to finish her chores in the kitchen. Later as Laine started to fall asleep, her dad knocked on the door. "Can I come in, Sweetie?"

Jeb assumed that Louise had already covered the important points from a woman's point of view, so his advice was much more businesslike. "I ain't got much advice, Lainie, just remember what I always said, 'Walk fast, shake hands like a man, and listen to the numbers.' They're the only thing that won't ever tell you a lie."

The next morning Louise woke up as usual and went out to chop weeds. Slowly she made her way down the rows of corn and pole beans. She and Laine never talked much during their early morning chores and Louise cherished that small window of silence without a houseful of voices or the constant roar inside the mill. However this morning the quiet felt sad, empty. She wondered if Laine would even bother with the garden. When she saw Laine stumble down the steps half asleep as usual, she smiled.

Laine was far from being asleep. Behind her half-closed eyes, her mind was racing. *I'm doing it. No more red Georgia clay, no more cotton lint, no more deafening mill noises, no more drab life. I will never have to do this again....*

Then she stopped dead in her tracks. She leaned on her hoe and looked around the back yard—perhaps for the last time—and suddenly it hit her. She was surrounded by color. A dozen different shades of green, red, yellow and purple vegetables. Blue morning glories, tiny white honeysuckle flowers and her mama's zinnias. Bright yellow, orange, white, pink. Suddenly she wanted to cry. Why hadn't she ever noticed before?

She looked at her mother bent over carefully tending to her plants and realized they would never be together like this again. Although Laine was churning with excitement to leave the mill life behind, until that moment she had not really grasped the significance of the move. On impulse, she dropped her hoe, and stepped over the rows of lettuce and radishes, "Mama...."

Louise looked up and Laine threw her arms around her. "I don't want you to think I wanta leave home. Leave you and Dad and the kids, I love you and..."

Louise held her nearly grown daughter and patted her on the back as if she were a little girl. "I know, Baby, I know." Louise was torn between being glad that Laine was getting out of the mill and knowing how much she would miss her. The two women sat down on the ground with their backs to the corn and pole beans.

With their arms around each other they cried a lot and laughed a little and the weeds got an unexpected reprieve that day.

Although the family went through the normal routine of breakfast, everything felt different. There was none of the usual chatter. They avoided making eye contact and when it happened by accident, they looked away quickly to keep from crying. Laine had hated Claxton Mill as long as she could remember and she'd dreamed of leaving, but she wasn't just leaving the mill behind, she was leaving life as she had known it. She was leaving everything.

Willie came in from his usual place on the porch and settled down to eat. He suddenly became aware of the thick silence in the kitchen. For the first time since he had explained his strategy against Claxton Mills, he looked at the people in front of him and realized he was breaking up this family unit.

Louise, Jeb, Laine and Willie left for the mill half an hour early in order to talk to Blix Reeve, the superintendent. Willie explained how much he needed Laine to work for him for a while. Jeb asked Blix's permission for Laine to leave. He was very polite. The trick was to present the situation so that Laine wouldn't actually have to quit. That way when the campaign ended, she could come back. By the time Willie finished his speech, Blix was convinced he would be a traitor to the Democratic Party if he didn't let Laine go work on the campaign.

The six o'clock whistle blew and the twins were the first ones off the line. They flung themselves at Laine, and held on to her for dear life. Reluctantly Jeb and Louise waved a last good-bye and then faded into the lint-filled air of the mill floor.

Slowly Laine walked home with the twins still holding on to her. Willie followed behind them. JW and Bo waited on the front porch. The twins were exhausted, but they refused to go to sleep. Bo, who had a summer job at the Commissary refused to go to work. To put off saying good-bye a little longer, the kids took their time loading Laine and JW's few belongings into the car.

Finally Willie volunteered to take Bo to work in his car. The twins were invited to come along, too. The children were sad to see their sister and brother leave, but weighed against the excitement of being the first Ford Crossing kids to ride in a car, they made a dash for Willie's Ford. Willie dropped Bo off, then took the long way home to drop the girls off. After one last round of hugs, it was time to go. As the twins watched, Willie and JW traded places and the driving lesson began. After a number of bucking, false starts, JW got the hang of putting the car in gear and letting off on the clutch as he pushed down on the gas pedal. The twins laughed and cheered through their tears when JW finally got the car on the road.

JW might have been a genius when it came to repairing motors, but he was a little slow to grasp the concept of driving. Once he got the car out of first gear, he stepped on the accelerator and they nearly landed in the ditch. "Slow down," Willie said. JW did... to about two miles an hour. "Not that slow. Give 'er some gas," Willie said and braced himself as JW hit the gas, then over compensated for being on the wrong side of the road. It was like riding the bumper cars at the fair.

Patience, Boy. Give the youngster time, he'll figure it out. Seems to me you didn't do so good the first time you tried it either.

With great effort, Willie stopped talking and let JW work it out on his own. Thank God there were no other cars on the road. It was clear JW needed some more practice shifting gears—and a lot more practice backing up—but after a few more terrifying moments, he settled in and drove pretty well on the straight away.

Willie glanced back at Laine who was sitting in the middle of the back seat holding on to both sides of the car. He couldn't tell if the tears on her face were because she'd just left her family or because she feared for her life. Either way, he decided to leave her alone for the moment. He kept an eye on the road, but let his mind wander.

Laine was with him now. He would see her every day. They would eat together and work together. They would sleep under the same boardinghouse roof every night. It was a dream come true...or was it?

"Don't you forget what I told you. Actions come with consequences. Whatever you do, remember a man always stands up to his responsibilities.

Admittedly, Willie knew a lot more about good-time girls and single women making it on their own than he did about church-going girls from close knit families.

His only examples of pure, virtuous girls came from reading books in which knights rescued fair ladies or cowboys rescued damsels in distress. Laine was certainly no damsel in distress. Willie knew she was smarter than he was and she had worked to help support her family since she was ten years old. In her world of Ford Crossing and Claxton Mill she was a responsible adult. Out in the real world she was a total innocent.

CHAPTER FOURTEEN

WHILE WILLIE PONDERED HIS SITUATION, Laine was having some serious thoughts about her future as well. She was excited to be free of Claxton Mill, but she had never spent even one night away from her family before. It helped to have JW close by, but she realized her mama was right; she was on her own now. She'd have to make decisions by herself and deal with the consequences, whatever they might be.

What about all those things her mama said? She'd had some experience with boys, but she hadn't been around many *men*, except her relatives and the fathers of her friends or men her family knew at church.

And what about Willie? Since that night at the river she'd kicked herself for pulling away. But what if she hadn't? Would they really have gone all the way? And then what? They'd never had a proper date. She knew he liked her…but what about love? Did she love him? Did she want to get married and start having babies? Or did she just want to ride the roller coaster to see what it was like?

Having chewed on that problem for a while, she started to worry about something else. Could she really do everything she'd told Willie she could. She had learned to type…sorta, and take shorthand…a little. She wasn't worried about the numbers; she knew she could handle that part, but she had never done anything but work in the mill. Would she be able to fit into Willie's world without embarrassing herself? She started to get scared when she heard her dad's voice, *Slow down Lainie, just remember to take it one day at a time, can't change the past, can't predict the future.*

When they finally drove into Morganton, Willie pointed, "Look at that!" A huge red and white banner was stretched across Main Street proclaiming, "Willie Shorter, Our Next Governor." "I like the sound of that, I swear to God I do," Willie said. He waved to several people as they drove slowly through town. "Turn around and do it again," Willie said. "You need the practice." JW hadn't mastered backing up, so he went around the block and then headed back down Main Street.

Laine saw things that she'd heard Willie talk about for months. Down a side street they got a glimpse of the Morganton Memorial Museum. But instead of the usual sign for the Over-the-Hill Boys Club, the Museum had been turned into the Shorter for Governor headquarters.

"JW, turn left here and stop in front of our headquarters," Willie said proudly, "and don't forget to step on the clutch before you step on the break. Stop!"

Because they had been driving down a straight road since they left Ford Crossing, JW hadn't had a chance to master the sequence needed to bring the car to a proper stop. At Willie's command, he tried to simultaneously slow down, stick his left arm straight out to signal for a turn, cut the steering wheel sharply to the left, step on the clutch, and stomp on the brakes. The car bucked twice, skidded forward a couple of feet, and finally died with the front bumper smack up against the four-by-four, which held up the right-hand side of the tin roof over the headquarters porch. The jolt brought The Boys Club out in force. They looked at Willie getting out of the passenger seat, glanced at JW and then their eyes came to rest on Laine.

Willie took a step back and watched the scene unfold. Laine wore a white blouse, tucked into a dark blue cotton skirt and a pair of black high-heeled patent leather shoes. The effect was simple, but stunning. As she stepped down from the car, The Boys surveyed her inch by inch from her trim ankles, long legs, shapely hips, slim waist, ample breasts, full lips, dark eyes, and shoulder length reddish-brown hair. She smiled. The Boys smiled back and continued to stare, open-mouthed.

Willie stepped forward. "Boys, I want you to meet Laine Becker and her brother, JW. He's gonna be driving for me and she's gonna be my…. secretary." They acknowledged JW, but they couldn't take their eyes off Laine. She looked at them with amazement. *Mama was sure right.*

Even without an introduction, Laine knew who was who. PV was round like a banker should be. His thin hair was losing its color, but it was cut perfectly and combed over his bald spot with great care. He wore a crisp summer suit, a starched white shirt and a bow tie knotted just so under his chin.

Chauncey was a little more casual. He didn't wear a coat or tie but his shirt was neatly ironed which meant some woman cared enough to make sure he looked nice. He wasn't quite as tall as Willie and although his hair was still dark, it was turning gray at the temples. Laine thought he must have cut quite a figure in his younger days.

Although she knew he had a wife, Pappy was a little on the rumpled side, his clothes looked like he had just grabbed them off the line. He was shorter than the rest of The Boys and had an old pipe stuck in his mouth. His shoulders hunched over slightly as if he had been working at a desk and forgotten to stand all the way up.

Joe Laundry wore khaki pants and a shirt to match. He was at least six-feet tall and very thin. The band on his old Panama hat was stained with sweat. The line of pale skin at the edge of his short-sleeved shirt showed his farmer's tan. He had the rugged look of a man who spent most of his time outdoors.

Sol Goldman was a compact man, like her father. His steel gray hair matched the silver spectacles he wore. Like PV, he had on a suit, a white shirt with gold cufflinks and a tie with a matching tie tack. Laine had never seen a man wear jewelry before. His hands were small and his nails were buffed.

One and all, they put on their best company manners. They practically fell over each other offering to help Laine up the steps, get her a glass of water or a Co' Cola, or fetch anything else she might want.

Willie watched the performance with great interest. He realized this was probably the reaction Laine was going to cause wherever she went. No ordinary mill-town girl, she was a diamond in the rough and with just a little polish....

The Boys Club had rescued a hodge-podge of tables, chairs, desks, lamps and filing cabinets from their collection and nothing would do but Laine—and as a second thought—JW and Willie had to take a tour of the new headquarters. The rest of the usual junk had been stuffed into two storage rooms out back.

The result was impressive. Once they got some volunteers to sit behind the desks, the place might actually look like a real campaign headquarters. Laine had completely captivated The Boys without doing a damn thing. Willie shook his head. *God almighty, I think I've got a tiger by the tail.*

As soon as he could politely do so, Willie took Laine's arm and steered her in the other direction. "JW, leave the car here and get the suitcases. I think it's safer that way. I want to get y'all settled in with Miss Dorothy at the boardinghouse without knocking the building down."

As they walked along, Willie pointed out Gold's, the Curl Up and Dye Beauty Shop, Robb's Drug Store and any other place he thought might interest Laine. She followed his gestures, but didn't respond. She was polite when he introduced her and JW to Miss Dorothy, but he got the feeling something was wrong.

He showed JW his room and then walked down the hall and opened the door to Laine's room. He put her suitcase on the bed and said, "Look, I know all this is new and you're probably missin' your family, but it'll be all right. I'll take care of you. Don't worry."

She just looked at him with her dark eyes. "Don't you like the room? Miss Dorothy thought you'd like this one 'cause it's on the corner. It just came empty. Two windows. More light. Cooler." Willie was beginning to flounder.

Laine continued to give him the silent treatment. "Alright, I give up. What's the matter? Did one of The Boys do something? 'Cause if he did I'll…"

"No," she said. "It's what *you* did."

"Me!? What did I do?"

"How come you said 'secretary' like that? I saw the way The Boys looked at me. I'm used to gettin' looks like that and most of the time they don't mean anything. But how come you didn't tell 'em I was gonna take care of the money? You told me that was what I was here for."

"It is, but what you're really here for is none of their business."

"I thought you liked them, that they were your friends. If you don't tell 'em, they're gonna think I'm just some floozy you picked up. They're gonna think I'm just here to…. well, you know what they're gonna think."

Willie smiled, safe on solid ground again. He nodded his head slowly. "That's exactly what I want them to think." Laine started to protest, but Willie stopped her. "Laine, you know I'd never do anything to hurt you, but this is politics. This is the big time. Everybody's out to use somebody to get something they want. Now sometimes that works for both parties. Like with me and The Boys. I need their knowledge and their experience. I need their connections and they need me so they can get back on top of things. Works out fine. But that doesn't mean I gotta tell them everything I know. I don't *want* them to know how smart you are.

"You're gonna be my secret weapon. As long as they think you're just another pretty face, nobody'll pay any attention to what you do. Laine, I'm gonna trust you with everything I've got. Everything I know. Everything I dream about. But you're gonna have to trust me, too. This won't work any other way."

Laine looked at him for a long time. Neither of them spoke. Neither one turned away. "I wanta think about it," she finally said.

Willie hesitated a minute waiting for an answer. Then he realized she intended to do some serious thinking. Being the kind of person who made quick decisions, he wasn't comfortable with that, but he had no choice in the matter. He left Laine alone and went back to talk to The Boys.

Laine sat on the bed and frowned at the wall for a long time. This wasn't the way she had pictured working with Willie at all. She was under the impression she would be treated the way she was treated at home where everybody knew she was smart and they asked her opinion and listened to her advice.

However, she did like the idea of being Willie's secret weapon. And being considered a floozy was kind of exciting, especially since she didn't have to actually *do* anything.

But then what about her reputation? Mama made it clear that was important…but she had her own room and the door had a lock and JW was right down the hall…and she liked Willie…a lot…and she guessed she trusted him.

He hadn't tried to push her into anything that night at the river, but what would he be like now that she was on her own? On the other hand if she did a really good job, maybe she could stay in Atlanta after the primary. Get a job…maybe even work for the new governor…

She spent a sleepless night going from being too cool with the windows open to being too hot with them closed. She tossed and turned trying to decide the right thing to do. In the morning she saw Willie and JW at breakfast. Her brother had already explored the town and chattered away while he stuffed biscuits and gravy in his mouth as fast as he could. The other borders gave her "that look" when Willie introduced her.

After breakfast she asked him to come into the parlor. "Mr. Shorter," she said in a very business-like voice, "I'll do it. I'll be your secret weapon, but if my family ever asks you, you have to make it clear this is just a business proposition and nothing more. Do you swear to that?"

"I do," Willie said and blanched at the ominous sound of those words. God forbid that he should ever have to face her parents and explain anything that was not kosher about his relationship to their daughter.

"Then I guess we've got a deal," Laine said with a smile as she stuck out her hand. Willie shook it. He was surprised at the strength in her grip. "You shake hands like a man, Honey," he said.

"I know," she responded sweetly, "and my name's Laine, not Honey."

CHAPTER FIFTEEN

AND SO THE PATTERN WAS set and Willie relaxed. Laine took charge of the money in the shoebox. She agreed with him that banks were not to be trusted, but instead of a shoe box she bought a locked box, painted flowers all over it with fingernail polish and told everybody it was where she kept her secret things. Amazingly, they believed her.

She kept the box in her room. When they were out on the road, she carried the spending cash tucked down the front of her dress. Everyone thought it was a big joke to watch her dispense campaign funds from what came to be known as the War Chest. Laine was amused at how often The Boys dropped by with requests for petty cash. Sometimes, when they assumed they were out of sight, she'd see them hold the warm dollar bill to their noses to inhale her scent. She understood and smiled.

By the end of July—one year away from the primary—Laine blossomed into a real trooper. She loved the excitement, the crowds and the attention. Willie asked her to sit in a chair on the back of the flatbed truck whenever he made a speech. She always dressed modestly, but her obvious charms were not lost on the men and boys in the audience.

They hadn't been on the road long before Laine noticed Willie was not the only one drawing a crowd. At each whistle stop, a flock of eager-looking country girls surrounded her supposedly shy brother. They smiled and giggled and she wondered what stories JW found to tell those young ladies.

About a month later, they were all listening to the radio at Miss Dorothy's. "Willie, why don't you start making speeches on the radio?" Laine asked. Chauncey and Pappy, who were sitting nearby, just laughed. According to them, not enough people owned sets to make radio broadcasts a good use of Willie's time.

Laine didn't argue, but from then on whenever she and Willie were driving from one place to another, she kept her eyes open for radio towers. When she'd see one, she'd ask Willie to stop. Then she'd go in, smile sweetly at the manager, introduce herself and ask him to please give just five minutes to her dear friend Willie Shorter, who was sure enough going to be the next governor. They never refused.

Willie couldn't sing or play an instrument, but he could talk. Lord, could he talk! He could sound as pious and religious as any hard-shell Baptist and as wild and reckless as a Good Ole Boy. On the rare occasions when the audience was a little more sophisticated, he could even sound like an educated Episcopalian.

Willie enjoyed the broadcasts and he could see that radio might be the wave of the future for politics. Several times Chauncey pointed out that not enough folks owned radios. Willie agreed that he needed to expand his audience but hadn't come up with a solution until one night Miss Dorothy came up with an idea. "Willie, why don't you tell those folks that's got radios to call their neighbors to make sure they're tuned in. And they could invite the ones without radios to come over to listen."

Willie considered that and promptly changed the opening of his speeches. "Now listen here, Friends and Neighbors, this is Willie Shorter. I'm gonna be speaking here in about five minutes and I'm gonna tell you the truth them big-city politicians ain't gonna tell you. So call your friends that's got radios and tell 'em to tune in. If your friends ain't got radios, invite 'em over. Give 'em a cup of coffee and y'all listen together."

Then he'd spend five minutes telling stories. "I ran into this ole farmer the other day who figured out a way to get around givin' half his crop to the man he was sharecroppin' for. He says, 'Boss, how 'bout you take all my crop, just pick the top, middle, or bottom.' The boss says he'll take the top, so Farmer Brown plants potatoes. When the boss got nothing but tops, he was some angry. Next time he says he'll take the bottom and Farmer Brown plants wheat. Now the boss is really put out. 'I've had enough of this nonsense, I'm taking the top and the bottom.' So Farmer Brown plants corn which just goes to show who had the brains in that situation."

Be sure to keep your stories clean, Boy. If you tell a naughty one now and then, make sure it won't offend the ladies.

When he figured he had a crowd out there in radio land, Willie began to talk seriously. He talked about how farmers needed a voice in politics. He talked about making things better for folks working hard to support their families. He told folks Uncle Fry hadn't been out of the capital in over 20 years.

"As far as Uncle Fry's concerned, Atlanta's an island and the rest of Georgia is just a sink hole. There's no way Uncle Fry is gonna get his shoes or his hands dirty. But you can count on me, Willie Shorter, to get out there and do what needs to be done because I'm sworn to be the Protector of the Poor."

A week or so later, Laine volunteered to go on the radio to give a testimony about what a great fellow Willie was. "What would you say?" he asked cautiously. Laine assured him she had listened to enough radio shows to know how to play-act. Willie had no idea what to expect, but he decided to turn the microphone over to her.

"Tell 'em my name's Abby Watson," Laine whispered. Willie introduced her and was shocked to hear an old woman's voice coming out of Laine's pretty face. "I knowed Willie and his family since he was knee-high to a June bug. He's honest as the day is long. Now friends, it's time we got rid of that worthless "uncle" up there in Atlanta. He's starting to stink like old garbage."

Her speech was short and sweet. When the broadcast ended, the guys at the radio station were laughing their heads off. Willie looked at Laine and demanded, "Where'd you come up with that?"

"I just listen to what folk're sayin' about you when you're out there shakin' hands. I guess I got a memory for words, like you do for names."

Once she got started, Laine loved being on the radio. Sometimes she'd act like a young mother. "I'm gonna vote for Willie Shorter 'cause I want a better life for my youngins'. I want some of the hard-earned money my husband and me pay in taxes to come back down here where it can do some good."

Sometimes she'd pretend to be a Sunday School teacher she'd heard back home. "It's a sin and a shame that the good people of Georgia work hard and pay taxes just so Uncle Fry can put his family on the payroll and take off up yonder to the Ken-tucky Derby. It's a known fact that he spends our money betting on horse race gambling, drinking hard liquor, and carousing with loose women."

Laine never spoke long. Just a sentence or two, but she gave Willie's broadcasts a homey touch, something he understood well. He just sat back in amazement. Laine's made-up characters were their little secret. If The Boys ever wondered where Willie found so many people willing to sing his praises on the radio, they never asked.

When she was with The Boys, or otherwise out in public, Laine was quiet, reserved, helpful, but never obvious. When she and Willie were alone, like at the radio stations, she suggested crazy ideas that somehow worked. The combination of innocence and wildness put thoughts into Willie's head that he tried hard to ignore. He was not successful. But a man couldn't get arrested—or shot by a girl's father—for his thoughts.

Keep your mind on the business at hand, Boy. You got no time to be daydreaming about that young girl with the primary less than twelve months away.

When she first left home, Laine wrote a letter every day, but gradually the letters dropped off to one a week. At first Louise felt disappointed, but Jeb pointed out that just meant the girl was getting settled in and paying serious attention to her new responsibilities. Besides, the details and descriptions in Laine's weekly letters sounded as good as any magazine story.

One week Louise opened the letter and out fell a $5 bill. "I know your old radio burned out, so I want you to take this down to Caruther's and buy yourself a new one. It's not enough for a big Philco model, but GE's got a little plastic one that you can put right on the top of a table. Miss Dorothy's got one in her kitchen that she listens to all the time. Be sure to tune in to all Willie's speeches and let me know if you can figure out who's giving testimonies for him. It sure would be nice if y'all had a phone 'cause you never know when I might need to get in touch with y'all in a hurry."

Louise's next letter back to Laine informed her that they had gotten the radio and had it sitting on the coffee table in front of the couch plugged into an extension cord. She also told her daughter that the twins recognized her voice right off. "You was real good, Laine, specially that church lady (I know exactly who you was thinking about when you did her) but Honey, I'm not sure that's exactly an honest thing to do. You know, pretending to be all those folks you really ain't. It might not even be legal. Now don't you go getting above your raisin'. I'd hate to have to come up there and get you outta jail. P.S. We're working on getting a phone."

Laine read the letter to Willie and they laughed. Willie never *asked* to hear the letters, but he soon realized that both he and Laine were anxious to get back to the boardinghouse each day to check the mail from Ford Crossing.

The campaign in the small Georgia towns was going well. Lots of those towns were laid out about 12 miles apart, the distance between water stops for the steam engines on the train lines. If he timed things just right, Willie and the Whippersnappers could hit five or six towns a day. Laine looked fresh and pretty at every stop. Willie didn't want folks to think he was too well off, but he did have to change shirts at least twice a day because of the heat. On the other hand, the temperature never seemed to bother Laine.

"Don't you ever sweat?" Willie demanded.

Laine smiled. "My mama says horses sweat, men perspire, and ladies glow. I'm just trying to do what's right. You don't want me sittin' up there lookin' like a field hand, do you?"

Willie gave up. Besides he had a lot more important things on his mind. Money, for one, but with a new twist. Now he worried about having more than he needed to get by day to day.

Laine tried to put his mind at ease. "I've got it all under control." And so she did. She created a set of books in which she accounted for all the money coming and going.

One day PV cornered Willie. "Listen, My Boy, it has come to my notice that you are now attracting attention from some of the prominent citizens in these small towns. You have made it abundantly clear that you do not trust banks—and I've never taken that personally—but don't you think it's time to find a better place to keep your campaign funds than in Miss Becker's brassiere?"

Laine overheard the conversation and before Willie could think up an answer, she handed him a blue bound ledger and said, "Here are those books you asked me to set up. You want me to give 'em to Mr. Ledbetter?"

Willie nodded, not quite knowing what he was agreeing to. He'd never seen the books before. PV took the ledgers and spent several minutes looking at them. "Well, I do declare, Miss Becker. That's as neat a set of books as I believe I've ever seen. And here we all thought you were just a pretty face. Shame on us. And shame on you, Willie Shorter for not pointing out our error." He handed the ledger back to Laine with a smile. "Keep up the good work, My Dear." Laine returned his smile.

Willie looked at Laine. She just held on to the books with her leave-it-to-me-I've-got-it-under-control smile. By now he was used to that look.

CHAPTER SIXTEEN

SO THE CAMPAIGN ROLLED INTO October. Eight months to go. Fall should have brought a welcome end to the heat, but not that year. The summer held on with bulldog tenacity. Laine had gotten used to the constantly moving sea of fluttering funeral-home fans and waving sweat-stained farmers' hats in the audience. Sweat dripped off everybody—everybody except PV and Laine. She always looked perfectly cool and comfortable; she seemed to thrive on the heat and humidity.

With PV, it was a matter of breeding. Occasionally he would remove his suit coat, but he always had on a long-sleeved white shirt with a set of flashy cufflinks and a bow tie knotted tightly under his chin. "Mother always says cultured people do not perspire, so I don't."

Willie made speeches and gained backing all over the state. Laine typed out the text of every speech. Willie wrote news releases and Laine made sure copies of both went to every paper on the distribution list Willie had originally compiled to publicize his fight with Claxton Mills. Anybody who read the newspapers in Georgia was soon aware that Willie Shorter was on the move.

For a while, Morganton served well enough as a base of operations, but Willie was anxious to get to Atlanta. He wanted the glitter and excitement of the big city. On the other hand, he enjoyed having fun with the rural voters. Deep down he was unsure about how to tackle the establishment in the big cities.

Laine had heard enough discussions by The Boys to realize the powers that be didn't like Willie. Governor "Uncle Fry" Jameson and his cronies had heard rumblings about this upstart from

Morganton. However, since they knew he had no real backing from the party leadership and no old money sources, they tended to think of him as a mosquito, noisy and annoying, but not dangerous. This infuriated Willie.

The Boys kept telling him that his main ally was still Uncle Fry himself. "Just let him go on ignoring you. By the time he figures out what's really going on, the fox will already be in the hen house," Pappy advised.

"Everywhere we go folks are sayin' the same thing," Chauncey said. "They're tired of Uncle Fry. They figure you haven't been in politics long enough to be really crooked yet. You just gotta keep telling 'em they're right." And Willie did.

So the crowds got bigger and the trickle of money became a steady stream. Laine decided on a reasonable amount to keep in cash and suggested to Willie that PV might be right about putting some of the money in the bank. Before he handed money over to PV's bank, Willie decided to spruce up the flatbed truck with a coat of paint and some new banners. Then he bought fancy shirts for the Whippersnappers. At last The Boys all agreed the time had come to take the next step and move to the capital city.

CHAPTER SEVENTEEN

FINALLY, ATLANTA! UNLIKE THE HUM-DRUM pace of Morganton or the constant throb of Claxton Mill, the city noises of car horns, jack hammers, traffic, streetcars, people going places and doing things fed Willie's soul. This was where he belonged, in the middle of things. He believed he could actually feel the power of the city through the holes in the bottom of his shoes.

Laine's first impression was color. Atlanta was like being inside a kaleidoscope. Evergreen pine trees as tall as ten-story buildings and magnolias grown fat from years of sun and rain spread a curtain of green around the city. As if flung by some careless child, splotches of yellow and red appeared where maples, dogwoods, sycamores and even an occasional ginkgo tree began to show off their early fall colors. No gravel roads, no dust, no cotton fields, no mill lint. Atlanta had more colors than a new box Crayolas.

Willie couldn't wait to find a place for his headquarters so he could show the city that Willie Shorter had arrived to change their lives. Sol located a vacant storefront downtown near the Winecoff Hotel right on Peachtree Street. Willie and JW found a nearby boardinghouse, but they didn't have room for Laine, so Willie made arrangements for her to stay temporarily at the YWCA.

PV volunteered to help find a suitable place for Laine to stay and promised to discuss the matter with Mother Ledbetter. That night as they shared an after-dinner demitasse, she tackled the problem with her usual decisiveness by sitting down to write a letter and explain the situation to her long-time friend, Mrs. Endeavor Franklin Stratham.

Mother Ledbetter had met Amanda Stratham as a young bride and the two became immediate friends. Before their children were born, Constance Ledbetter and Amanda Stratham could be counted on to be in the middle of whatever cause held center stage at the time. Now they had both settled down a bit and Miss Amanda was known as the arbiter of good taste and decorum in Atlanta society.

"Mother, I don't think we have time for all this letter writing. Laine needs accommodations now. You better call Miss Amanda," PV said as he helped himself to one last tea cake.

"I think telephones are so intrusive, practically rude. But I do understand the urgency of the situation. I'll do my best to set up an appointment so Amanda can meet this Laine girl. Now, PV, you do assure me that she is the proper *kind* of girl, refined, well mannered and polite."

PV skipped over refined and said, "You have my word, Mother. Make the call…please."

On the day of the appointment, PV picked Laine up and as they drove north on Peachtree Road, he pointed out the houses of prominent citizens—all of whom he claimed to know intimately. Each house was grander than its neighbor. PV seemed to take it all in stride, but Laine had never seen anything so beautiful.

Finally they turned into the Ansley Park neighborhood and stopped in front of a two-story house located a genteel distance from the street on a gigantic lot filled with ancient trees. The house was different from most of the others, no white columns or covered verandas here. Stratham Hall was the color of butterscotch, with an orange tile roof and a terrace that stretched across the entire front of the grand structure. Huge containers filled with exotic plants anchored the corners.

They got out of the car and Laine, in her best fall dress, hat, gloves, matching shoes, and purse—black, of course, because no one would dare wear white after Labor Day—followed PV to the carved double doors at the entrance.

A butler answered the door and greeted PV by name. After he ushered them into the foyer, he disappeared to inform the lady of the house of their presence. While they waited, PV said, "Don't be nervous. Mother would never have recommended you if she had any doubt you would make a good impression. Just remember to stand up straight and stop fiddling with that silly handkerchief. Put it away."

Laine obeyed. Just as she snapped her purse shut on the limp, crumpled handkerchief, she got her first glimpse of Miss Amanda Stratham. The woman was in her 70s, tall and slim. She seemed to float down the stairs in a long dress made of blue-black silk. She wore pearl earrings, which matched the double strand of pearls hanging nearly to her waist. Her steel gray hair was swept up in a style that gave softness to her otherwise stern appearance. She had lines in her face, but they disappeared when she smiled. The veins and tendons on the back of her hands stood out like electrical cords, but the hand she extended to Laine felt warm to the touch.

"Good hand shake. I like that," Miss Amanda said. She sounded Southern, but not the country twang Laine heard at home. "My friend, Mrs. Ledbetter, has told me about your… situation. I would like for you to tell me about yourself." She turned to address PV, "I know you must have more pressing business elsewhere. I believe I can manage things from this point. Please convey my greetings to your dear mother."

With that, she dismissed PV, who nodded slightly and left. "Come with me, My Dear. Serena has made sandwiches." Miss Amanda led the way into a room she called the lanai. It looked like a glass bubble. Outside a forest of maple and dogwood trees formed a backdrop for the windows. When the sun hit the gold and red of the autumn leaves, the room glowed. A white wicker table and four chairs with huge, cobra-shaped backs dominated the center of the room. Boston ferns spilled out of ornate planters and created lacy patterns on the terracotta floor.

Serena wore a white uniform and wheeled in a table covered with plates of small sandwiches, bon-bons, bowls of fresh fruit, a silver container of whipped cream, and a cut-glass pitcher of ice tea. Sandwiches in Laine's experience had been lunchmeat between two pieces of white bread, not the dainty little things she saw before her. She watched Miss Amanda and tried to do exactly what she did.

"Now, tell me about yourself," Miss Amanda said.

"There's really nothin' much to tell. I've been workin' for Mr. Shorter for a while now. Before that I lived with my family in Ford Crossing and worked at Claxton Mill."

"Stop!" Miss Amanda said. "I have made inquiries and I already know that you were a good student, you have continued to read on your own, you have acquired some secretarial skills, and you have a remarkable ability with numbers."

Laine started to protest, but Miss Amanda held up one long, manicured finger to silence her. "First, it is right and proper for a young lady to be modest. However, never downgrade your abilities to someone who asks you for information and who has your best interest at heart, which, you will find, I do. Your brain is quite good, your speech, however, is abominable. It makes you sound like an ignorant hick, and clearly you are not."

Again Laine started to protest, but Miss Amanda stayed one step ahead of her. "Now, before you take exception to that remark, or think that I'm casting aspersions on your family, I have nothing but respect for hard-working families. They are like my parents were. Salt of the earth. The strength of this state and this country is built on just such families. But if you intend to better yourself," she looked at Laine and raised one aristocratic eyebrow, "and I assume you do, then you will have to learn how to speak properly."

"Yes, Ma'am."

"Good."

With that taken care of, Miss Amanda proceeded to eat a substantial number of dainty sandwiches, a large bowl of fruit smothered in whipped cream and drank two glasses of ice tea. She did not touch the bon-bons. Laine ate very little because Miss Amanda kept asking her questions and she at least knew enough not to talk with her mouth full.

At the end of the interview, Miss Amanda said, "I think you will do nicely. I suppose your mother has talked to you about the importance of protecting your virginity…" Laine blushed. Miss Amanda stopped abruptly.

"Is there something you need to tell me before we continue?"

For a moment Laine didn't understand the question. "Oh, no, Ma'am! Mama and me had a long talk about…all that."

"Then what is the problem?"

Laine hesitated. "Well, I guess my mama's kinda old fashioned and…well, it's just that I never heard anybody say that word out loud before."

Miss Amanda hesitated a moment, then threw back her head and laughed. The sound was deep and carried across the room. Somehow it seemed out of place coming from such a proper Southern lady. "How old are you, Child?"

"I just turned 18," Laine said. "But Mama says I've always been old for my age. I guess that's because I been takin'…taking care of the younger kids for so long. And I've been workin'… working in the mill since I was ten."

The two women looked at each other. Laine finally dropped her eyes. Miss Amanda reached over and patted her hand. "My friend, Mrs. Ledbetter. asked me to find a suitable place for you to stay. I agreed, but I wanted to meet you and judge for myself before I went any further. With some help, I think you will do fine."

Laine waited, not sure what to expect.

"How would you like to stay here? Both of my sons are away in Switzerland at school so it's only Mr. Stratham and myself and he is often away on business. Most of the time, I rattle around in this house alone."

Laine was dumbfounded. She sat staring open-mouthed at Miss Amanda. Finally she managed to speak. "You mean I'd have a room…here…in this house?"

Miss Amanda smiled, "Oh no, Dear. You'd have a suite of rooms."

Laine shook her head. "I can't afford that. Wherever I stay, it's gotta be room and board and cheap. I'm sendin' money home every week and tryin' to save some. I could never afford to stay in a place like this."

Miss Amanda hid a smile behind her napkin. "I understand that you have limited means. How does a dollar a week sound? Room and board, of course."

Laine hesitated. She glanced around the room. It looked like something out of a movie. Then she thought about what her dad always said, "If it sounds too good to be true, it probably is." She lifted her eyes to meet Miss Amanda's. "I wanta think about it," she replied.

The girl had spunk, no doubt about that. "Whatever you say."

Hastily Laine added, "It's not that I'm not grateful, Miss Stratham. It's just that, I ain't sure…I mean I'm not…I wanta write my mama and see what she says. Would that be alright?"

"Absolutely, my dear. Would you like to call her? You could use the telephone in the library."

"We ain't got…we don't have a telephone…and everybody's at work or sleeping anyway." For some reason, that embarrassed Laine. What would Miss Amanda think if she knew Laine had never used a telephone until she went to work for Willie?

"How silly of me," Miss Amanda said lightly. "Of course not. Besides, I think letters are much nicer anyway. Where are you staying at the moment?"

"There wasn't room at the boardinghouse where Willie and JW—that's my brother—are stayin'. I've got a nice room at the YWCA." Laine hoped that was acceptable.

"Yes, I know the woman who runs it, Emily Castleberry. Please have her call me when you make up your mind. No need for you to spend your nickel." She saw the surprised look on Laine's face. "My Dear, anyone with half a brain knows to be careful with money, no matter how much of it you have. I'm sure your mother taught you that."

"My dad did. He always says we gotta be careful about the little things so when something important comes along we'll be ready."

"That sounds perfectly logical to me. Now finish your tea and I'll arrange for someone to take you back downtown." With that, she picked up a tiny silver bell, rang it once and the butler appeared out of nowhere. "Would you have Henry bring the car around, please, and tell him to take Miss Becker to the downtown YWCA."

Laine carefully refolded her napkin and put it and her plate back on the tray. Then she stood, leaned down and shook hands with Miss Amanda. The older woman patted Laine's hand. "I have enjoyed meeting you, Miss Becker. I hope to hear from you soon."

Laine followed the butler back to the front hall. She did her best not to gawk at the house, but everywhere she looked she saw more beautiful things. The hardwood floors were highly polished with exquisite carpets in every room and chandeliers hanging from every ceiling. Through one door she saw a full-length portrait of Miss Amanda as a young woman. She wore a royal blue formal gown. She still favored the same hairstyle, but in the picture her hair was jet black.

The floors in the entrance hall were pink marble. The butler noticed Laine looking at them and explained that the marble came from Tate, a small town in north Georgia. Grand staircases rose on either side of the hall and the biggest round table Laine had ever seen stood in the middle. A gigantic vase that looked like it was made of gold occupied the center of the table. It overflowed with hundreds of beautiful flowers, tulips, roses, lilies, and lots of others Laine couldn't identify. She didn't see any zinnias.

The butler walked out onto the terrace and spoke to the chauffeur. He in turn opened the back door of the car and made sure Laine was seated comfortably. The inside of the silver gray car had leather seats and little oriental rugs on the floor. Small silver vases by each door were filled with fresh flowers. At first Laine sat on the edge of the seat, but gradually she relaxed, sat back, spread out her arms and pretended to be a fairy princess in her magic coach. All too soon, the ride ended and she found herself back at the Downtown Y.

Later that evening, she described the whole experience step by step to Willie. He was overjoyed. The Strathams were one of the oldest, richest families in Georgia. The move to Atlanta was working out better than he could have dreamed.

Laine was wound up tighter than a top. "She's gonna help me learn to talk better so I don't sound like a hick. If I stay there, she said I'd have a suite of rooms. And I'd get to eat in her fancy dining room every day. And I'm…" Laine stopped. "You know, if I do good and Miss Amanda gets to like me, maybe she'll help you, too. That'd be a good thing, wouldn't it?"

"It would be a very good thing," Willie answered. Having the Strathams on his side would open doors Willie could only have dreamed about before.

CHAPTER EIGHTEEN

WILLIE FOUND HIMSELF DEALING WITH mixed emotions, an unusual situation for him. On the one hand he was delighted Laine had made a favorable impression on Mrs. Amanda Stratham and that she had invited Laine to move into Stratham Hall. On the other hand, with Laine staying uptown, he would only get to see her at headquarters. He wasn't sure how he felt about that. In the past, women had more or less floated in and out of Willie's life, a delightful diversion, but nothing serious or permanent. What he was beginning to feel for Laine was something entirely different.

However, he knew a good opportunity when he saw one. When Laine said she told Miss Amanda she couldn't agree to anything until she talked it over with her parents, he was shocked. He took a deep breath, "OK, OK I understand, but it takes too long to send a letter and get one back, send them a telegram."

"If they get a telegram, they're gonna think somebody died."

Willie said he'd take care of it and by the end of the week Laine had her parents' blessing and was ready to move.

Well, almost ready. It was PV who casually brought up Laine's wardrobe. "I don't imagine working in the mill required much in the way of fashion, but living at Stratham Hall...does. Now, since you don't know the stores here, I'll be glad to take you shopping. Oh, don't look so surprised. I go shopping with all Mother's friends. They think I have wonderful taste."

Before Laine could respond, PV rattled on, "I know you have a limited budget, but that's where my expertise will come in handy. Anybody can look decent if they spend enough money, the trick is to look fabulous without spending a fortune. We'll start at Davison-Paxon on the corner of Peachtree and Ellis. Surely in six floors of merchandise, we can find something suitable."

Shopping in a department store was a new experience for Laine and shopping with a man was just downright strange. She felt a little embarrassed about her budget, but she told PV exactly how much she could afford to spend and they set off on a treasure hunt. "Oh, this will be a challenge and I love a challenge. A few good pieces with stylish accessories, that's the key."

The week after Thanksgiving, Laine moved into Stratham Hall with a small, but well-chosen wardrobe, including a heavy winter coat, the first one she had ever owned. Willie drove the Ford and JW made sure he was invited to see his sister's new digs. On the way, he casually announced that he planned to go back to Ford Crossing.

"Now that we're not on the road anymore, y'all don't need a driver. In fact," he said with a knowing smile, "I'm not sure y'all ever did. Not that it wasn't fun, but I wanta get back to work with Mr. Bart. He said he'd help me get my high school diploma and then, well, who knows, maybe someday I could even go to college."

Willie had grown to appreciate JW's sly humor, but he could also appreciate the fact that JW wanted to better himself, and he knew Jeb and Louise would be thrilled their son wanted to go back to school.

When they arrived at Stratham Hall, Laine made introductions all around the way the etiquette book she got at the library said it should be done. Miss Amanda seemed pleased. Willie chatted easily with the older woman and Laine noticed he immediately changed his grammar and style to match hers.

"Miss Becker, would you like to see your rooms? Gentlemen," she nodded to Willie and JW, "you can come along, too, of course."

When Miss Amanda opened the double doors, the visitors were awestruck. The bedroom was bigger than the Becker's whole house in Ford Crossing. Two tall windows overlooked the back of the estate and between them was a large canopy bed covered with a pale-blue satin counterpane. Against the far wall stood a gigantic chest-of-drawers and a dresser with a beveled mirror, a large comfortable chair, and an elegant floor lamp.

The bedroom adjoined a separate study with an inlaid wooden desk and chair upholstered in silk brocade. A window seat with velvet cushions and an array of throw pillows looked out onto a small rose garden.

The final room in the suite was the bathroom. It was huge, with marble floors, a pedestal sink, mirrors along one wall, cabinets along the other, a dressing area, and a bathtub big enough to swim in.

Miss Amanda watched closely as Laine took everything in. She moved slowly around the room, gently touching things. JW stood in the middle of the bedroom obviously afraid to touch anything. However from his rapt attention, Miss Amanda had no doubt he would remember all the details and report them to the rest of the family.

Willie felt the nagging doubt again. Obviously he was pleased with the accommodations, how could he be otherwise? But clearly Laine had skipped several steps in the evolution from Ford Crossing to big-city life. This was a level of wealth and power Willie had only dreamed about. He wondered if Laine would be his entrée into this world, or if she would get bored with politics…and with him? After all, he knew the Stratham's had two unmarried sons. On the way back to the boardinghouse, Willie and JW worked out the details of his return home. Willie made it clear that any time the boy wanted to come back and work on the campaign, he would be welcome.

Bright and early Monday morning Laine took the bus down Peachtree and by 8:30 she was sitting at her desk in Willie's headquarters. Several volunteers had been recruited and were on hand to get down to work. Realizing time was running out, the campaign shifted into high gear.

At first Willie didn't have any official speaking engagements. So he went back to his usual stomping grounds. He greeted every shift at the Fulton Bag and Cotton Mills in Cabbagetown and managed to talk the WSB radio station director into giving him five minutes on the Fiddlin' John Carson country music show.

Stop waiting for the voters to come to you, Boy. Go where they are. So Willie began to haunt the aisles in the A&P and Piggly Wiggly grocery stores, talking to women shoppers, shaking hands, and handing out flyers. Women had only recently earned the right to vote and they were eager to exercise their new power.

Willie swapped stories with men in barber shops, at Standard Oil filling stations, and Western Auto Supply stores. He mingled with Christmas shoppers at Woolworth's, J.C. Penney, and Sears & Roebuck. He talked to anybody he could find. He rode the streetcars everywhere and handed out more flyers. Whether he had 30 minutes or 30 seconds, he made sure everyone got the message, "My name is Willie Shorter and I'm running for governor. I hope I can count on your vote."

Little by little, invitations to speak started to come in. Willie took them all. He met with people in church basements, cramped living rooms, school cafeterias, front porches, parks, and street corners.

Willie had no idea so many garden clubs and women's book study groups met in Atlanta. They all needed guest speakers and Willie happily obliged. He did his best to charm the ladies and make sure they made the right choice when they cast their vote. Out with Uncle Fry, in with a new face and new ideas.

No matter how hard he worked, the old guard in Atlanta still ignored Willie all together. Speaking to the Peachtree Hills Book Club, or the local Baptist church brotherhood group was fine, but Willie wanted to break into the big time: the Atlanta Athletic Club, the Capital City Club, the Daughters of the Confederacy, or the Atlanta Woman's Club. He fully intended to be the Protector of the Poor, but he needed the backing of the rich to do it.

Willie called The Boys together and explained his problem. They threw out a lot of ideas, but it was Sol who finally said what they all knew Willie did not want to hear.

"The problem is simple, Villie. Like in my store, you got a good product, but vhat you got, those big shots don't vant. To them you're a *nudnik*, a pest. On the road? Well, that's where you gonna beat Fry."

When The Boys chimed in and started quoting population figures and statistics, Willie tuned out, partially because he didn't want to think about going back to the sticks and partially because that many numbers coming at him all at once made his head hurt. "Sounds reasonable. Write it all down and give it to me so I can study it later."

When Willie had all the facts together, he stopped by Laine's desk. She looked different somehow. He took a chance. "Did you do something to your hair?"

"Miss Amanda took me to her hairdresser and got it cut. And she gave me some of her old clothes." She stood up and turned around so Willie could get a better look. "Do you like it?"

For the first time, Willie realized that while he had been campaigning, the mill-town girl had disappeared and in her place was…well, nothing short of a knockout. "You look…great. Sophisticated."

Laine beamed.

"Listen, can you stay late tonight? The Boys have dumped all these numbers on me and I need you to help me unscramble this stuff and tell me what they mean."

That night Willie suggested they go to the Winecoff Hotel for dinner. As soon as they had finished eating, he gave Laine the papers. She took her time and studied the census records and past primary returns. The numbers made one thing very clear; Willie's strength lay with the country folks. She wrote down columns of numbers, added them up, then did the math again. Finally she turned to Willie.

"OK, here's what the numbers mean. Georgia has 159 counties and it works on the county unit system. There are three different kinds: urban counties, town counties and rural counties. Eight urban ones, 30 town ones, and 121 rural ones."

She glanced at Willie who seemed to be following the explanation so far. "Urban counties get six unit votes each, town counties get four, and rural counties get two each."

Willie's eyes started to glaze over, but Laine didn't notice. She was in her element—numbers. "That makes a total of 410 unit votes. So you have to get 260 to win, understand?"

Willie looked at her, but she could tell she had lost him. "OK, forget the numbers. What it all means is that you don't have to win the popular vote, you just have to win more county unit votes—carry more counties—than Fry. Does that make sense?"

Willie took his time to process the information, but finally he nodded. "If Fry only wins the big cities and I carry the rest of the counties—or at least a lot of them—then I have a real chance of beating him. Right?"

"Right."

"I could win." The idea seemed to surprise him. "The numbers say so, and numbers don't lie. I could really win." He leaned over to Laine keeping his voice down to an excited whisper, "Hot damn, Lainie, we could really pull this off. I'm not sure I really believed it until now, but I could be the next governor of the great state of Georgia!"

He grabbed her hand, "You are a prize. Come on, I'll drive you home."

Although the temperature was dropping, Laine was walking on air. She waited on the sidewalk while Willie went to get the car which he had parked a few blocks away. Several men who had been sitting at the bar came out of the restaurant. They looked vaguely familiar; Laine thought she had seen them around headquarters. She smiled.

"Well, lookie there boys, I guess the rumors are true. She's friendly to everybody." The men approached Laine, "I've seen you

around, Honey. They say you're Mr. Shorter's 'special secretary.'"
The man nudged his friends. "He got you takin' dick-tation?"

They laughed. "I hear you lint-heads'll do anything to get
out of the mills. That what happened? He promised to give you
something really good?"

The third one patted his crotch, "Whatever he's givin' you, I
got somethin' better. You could be my special secretary any time."

Laine pulled her coat around her and turned her back. At
that point, Willie drove up and she jumped into the car. She
was seething, but Willie was too excited to notice. All the way
to Stratham Hall he babbled on about how he was going to beat
Fry. Finally he parked in front of the house, walked Laine to the
door and said good night.

Laine stormed up the stairs, down the hall to her suite,
slammed the door, threw her coat on a chair and stomped around
the room cursing. "Damn them, damn them all."

"Laine? May I come in?" Miss Amanda asked as she turned
the knob and entered the room. "Are you all right?"

Laine stood in the center of the room tight-faced, shaking
with anger. "Are you hurt?"

"No."

"Then go wash your face, blow your nose, and we'll talk,"
Miss Amanda commanded. She sat in the over-stuffed chair and
waited.

Laine went into the bathroom and splashed cold water on her
face as ordered. She looked at herself in the mirror. The angry
woman who stared back frightened her. She took several deep
breaths and splashed more cold water on her face.

When she calmed down, she walked back into the bedroom, sat
on the edge of the bed and related the incident to Miss Amanda.
"Nobody understands, nobody knows. Mr. Shorter brought me
along because I understand numbers. I'm ten times smarter than
those stupid men and I can't tell anybody 'cause Willie doesn't
want anybody to know. He calls me his secret weapon. I'm the
one who explains the numbers to him. I'm the one who keeps the

books and takes care of the money. Even The Boys don't know the way that works. Willie puts some of the contributions in the bank and I balance the books. But he keeps a lot of it in cash and I'm the only one who knows where it is, how much is there and how Willie spends it. It's not fair that people think I'm just some stupid… floozy." Laine finally ran out of steam.

Miss Amanda took her time before she responded. "You know when I first met Mr. Stratham, I was 16. His father owned the land my family sharecropped on. Dev used to come with his dad to inspect the crops. He was 15 years older than I and the handsomest man I'd ever seen. I decided I was going get that man to marry me, one way or the other. I came up here to stay with my aunt and I threw myself at Dev Stratham. I was shameless.

"Everyone assumed I was after the Stratham money, but I wasn't. I loved Dev. In six months we were married. His mother and all her friends wouldn't speak to me. My only friend in this town was Constance Ledbetter. However, I produced two healthy heirs and I made myself indispensable to Dev. He'd never had to work, had no idea how to make money. But I did. Together we started getting richer and richer until even his mother came around.

"I've outlived all those small-minded women and their stuffed-shirted husbands. Through it all, I never cared what they thought because *I* knew that *Dev* knew who I was. He has always treasured and loved me and that is enough." For a moment she sat staring off into space.

"What you have to ask yourself is whether the secret agreement you have with Mr. Shorter is enough, because it may be all you get."

CHAPTER NINETEEN

WILLIE STAYED IN ATLANTA THROUGH Christmas. Laine went home to Ford Crossing. Beginning in January everyone focused on the final six months of the campaign.

Against The Boys' advice, Willie decided to work some of the larger cities such as Macon and Savannah. Still smarting from her encounter at the Winecoff, Laine decided she might attract less attention and fewer comments at political events if she sat in the front row of the audience instead of on the platform with Willie. Now, instead of looking at the back of his head, she watched Willie's face as he spoke and she began to understand why the audiences loved him. He was magic on stage.

Willie could see the pride in her eyes. No one had ever been proud of him like that before and he loved it. When the crowds applauded and whistled and shouted, "Go get 'em, Willie," he looked directly into Laine's eyes and wondered what it would be like to have a woman like her at his side all the time.

As for Laine, she saw the look and heard a click as the roller coaster made its way slowly up the incline. It had been a long time, but in her secret heart, Laine hoped Willie would make his move after the campaign. The very thought of that took her breath away. Once that happened…well, she'd cross that bridge when she came to it. In the meantime, she threw herself into the campaign.

The Boys kept urging Willie to leave the big cities to Uncle Fry and his cronies. "You just keep talking to the folks in the rural areas and there's no way they can beat us." Willie knew they were right, but throughout February he continued to work the cities. His excuse was that nobody would stand out in the damp cold to hear him make speeches from the back of a truck. City audiences stayed inside where it was warm.

The Boys continued to urge him to go back on the road because they were afraid Willie would eventually rile up the opposition and bring out the big guns in the party. Their goal was to keep him working in the boondocks, out of sight and out of mind. If the current administration ever began to take Willie seriously, there might be trouble. The establishment wouldn't give up power easily and their money and muscle made them dangerous.

Finally Willie caved in to the pressure and reluctantly said good-bye to the cities, and Laine said good-bye to Miss Amanda for a while. "You've taught me more than I could ever have learned at any fancy girls' school. I'll never be able to thank you," Laine told the older woman as she packed her clothes.

Miss Amanda smiled. "My Dear, I love my boys, both of them. They have been the crowning achievement of my life, but secretly I have always wanted a daughter. You have provided me with an opportunity to live out that fantasy. Go do what you have to do to bring this campaign to a successful conclusion. I'll just think of this as a temporary situation, the way I did when my boys left for school overseas. This is your Atlanta home whenever you need it." Although she never would have believed it possible, Laine felt almost as sad having to leave Miss Amanda as she had leaving her mama all those months ago. Saying good bye was obviously a part of growing up, but Laine didn't like it much.

***

Willie's previous road trips had taken him to a lot of small towns, mostly in a concentrated area. Now he needed to cover the state and he realized he couldn't just run back and forth without an itinerary, so he asked Laine to work out a travel schedule. He got more than he bargained for. Laine came up with a plan that took Willie to over 200 little towns in the last four months of the campaign.

Even in the towns in the northern part of the state where he was not so well known, people still rallied to his cause. Folks were fed up with Uncle Fry and they liked what they saw in the bright, energetic young man who wasn't afraid to tell them the truth about big government. A man of the people who knew what it was to work for a living, a man who could take it on the chin and make folks laugh about hard times.

One night back at their current boardinghouse, Willie sought Laine out after a speech. "I think it's time you went home."

Laine turned on him, "You can't send me home now. It's too close to the primary. I've worked too hard to…"

"Good Lord, Laine, I'm not *sending* you home. I want you with me every step of the way. It's time we went campaigning back down toward Ford Crossing and I thought you might like to spend Easter Sunday with your family."

"Oh," Laine said. She threw her arms around him, kissed him on the cheek and ran to throw her few clothes into her suitcase.

"We'll leave in the morning…." he called after her.

"I'll be ready," Laine answered over her shoulder. She closed her eyes and savored the moment. *He wants me to be with him every step of the way. Oh, I just know it's all going to work out. I just know it is.*

So Easter Sunday found Willie and Laine in Ford Crossing…in church. Excluding the days he preached in the colored churches, Willie couldn't remember the last time he had been in a church.

Good Book says Sunday ought to be a day of rest. But with all the shouting about sin I never found church very restful. Fishing, that's the ticket.

Finally the preacher exhausted all possibility of getting anyone to walk the aisle and give their heart to Jesus, so the service ended and the family headed home.

Instead of the normal fried chicken, Louise baked a ham and as an added treat made a coconut cake for dessert. Packing eight people around the table in the kitchen was a tight squeeze but no one seemed to mind. The instant Jeb finished saying the blessing, pandemonium set in. Hands, arms and food flew in every direction. "To the right, to the right, pass it to the right," Jeb ordered. Order was restored and dishes flowed around the table until everyone was served. Then they ate…and ate…and ate. The men complimented the women on the meal and the conversation turned to politics and the mill.

After dessert, while everyone lingered over coffee, JW disappeared into the other room and came back holding something behind his back. "I've got an announcement." When he had everyone's attention he held up an official looking document. "This is my diploma. I'm now a high school graduate."

Simultaneously his family descended on him in a flood of hugs, kisses and congratulations. When everyone settled down, he said, "Now don't start lovin' on me again, but that's not all. Mr. Bart said it might take some time, but he's gonna try to help me get a scholarship to Georgia Tech." JW paused for breath. "And…and he said if that worked out, then he'd talk to some folks he knows up there in Atlanta and maybe they could help me find a job while I'm going to school." He smiled shyly and sat down.

"JW that's wonderful! I'll help out with money for books," Laine volunteered.

"And we've still got Claxton Mill money in the bank. So you just tell us what you need, Son," Jeb said. "Nobody in this family's ever gone to college before and we wanta make sure we do this right."

"I'll make you a deal, JW," Willie joined in. "If you get that scholarship and if I win this primary—which I fully expect to do—I'll be moving up to an official car and driver so I'll give you my Ford. The way I figure it, that Ford's so old it'll take a Georgia Tech engineer to keep it on the road."

It was truly a red-letter day for the Beckers. After the girls left for work, Jeb, JW, and Willie moved into the living room and stayed up late talking about the future. Even Bo was allowed up past his normal bedtime although he fell asleep listening to the drone of the men's voices.

Laine and Louise stayed in the kitchen washing dishes, drinking coffee and talking about people and politics and love. Before everyone turned in for the night, Louise explained the sleeping arrangements. She and Laine would share Laine's old bed. Bo would sleep with Jeb in the double bed. JW would sleep on a rollaway bed and Willie would have his normal Army cot— with a couple of extra quilts—on the back screen porch. Contrary to the old arrangement, Louise would not allow anyone to sleep on her new velvet couch. Finally everyone fell asleep listening to the steady noise of Claxton Mill.

The next morning Willie realized that his "speaking suit" was missing. He had hung it out on the line to air it out and now it was gone. They turned the small house upside down, but the suit was nowhere to be found. Louise questioned the neighbors to see if they had seen anyone hanging around outside. No one had.

The mystery solved itself when the twins came home from the night shift. They looked shamefaced when they came in the door. Bessie reluctantly admitted they took Willie's suit to work with them in order to prove *the* Willie Shorter really was staying at their house. "We didn't hurt it none, it's hangin' out on the back porch."

"Well go get it," Laine commanded. "We've got to get on the road or we're gonna be late getting started."

When they brought the suit in the back door, Laine let out a screech. Willie's dark blue suit has disappeared; it was now fuzzy gray, covered with cotton-mill lint. The girls apologized and promised to make quick work of beating the lint off with privet switches from the bush in the back yard. Laine watched from the back door and when they were about half way finished, she yelled, "That'll be enough. Leave it alone."

Willie was standing beside her. "Laine I can't wear it looking like that. Folk'll think I just came from workin' in the…"

Laine smiled. "Yeah," she said, "they might. It's a sure thing they won't think you've been hanging around with Uncle Fry up there in Atlanta."

CHAPTER TWENTY

FROM THAT POINT TO THE end of the campaign, whenever they loaded up to go to a farm community, Laine hung Willie's suit next to an open window so that it got a nice coating of Georgia red-clay dust. He'd make a big show of brushing off the dust when he climbed on the back of the truck to begin his speech. "Friends and neighbors, this dust is disappearing 'bout as fast as your hard-earned pay. Now ain't that the truth?" The crowd whooped and Willie revved up his speech.

Laine started traveling with a huge cardboard box, which contained both her account books——one for the bank account and one she kept for her own records of the cash that flowed through Willie's hands. She also carried the colorful locked box with petty cash available whenever Willie needed it. In addition, she had a collection of papers, pamphlets and official looking documents. Chauncey and Pappy had been helping her collect background material for Willie's speeches. No matter what he needed to know, she seemed to be able to pull any fact or figure out of the box at the drop of a hat.

The Boys finally realized that Laine had a brain as well as a pretty face. So they did the logical thing and invited her into the discussions. The outside world might not know what she was worth, but the people close to her did. For the moment, it was enough. Well, almost enough. Laine worked on Willie's campaign almost as hard as he did, but she decided to launch a little end-of-the-campaign push of her own.

As they drove between whistle stops, Laine suggested that Sonny Cunningham drive the car and that Willie ride beside her in the back seat so she could brief him before each speech. She placed the cardboard box on her left and Willie on her right. That meant he spent a significant amount of time jiggling along over bumpy, unpaved back roads thigh to thigh with Laine as she talked about farm prices and cotton yields and how the voters were ripe for a change.

The voters were not the only ones who were ripe. Overnight Willie became a religious man who prayed fervently and often. *Lord, just let me keep my hands off that woman and my mind on the campaign long enough to win this primary. Just give me strength to hold on a little longer.*

And so the campaign roared into the last three months. Willie knew the people; Laine knew the numbers. Georgia farmers north and south of Atlanta needed a spokesman and Willie was their man. He spoke their language. These were hard-working men and women, independent, honest, frugal. Before each speech, Laine told Willie the number of farms that had been taken over by the banks, the number of folks without jobs and the number of men, women and children injured in factory accidents. Armed with the numbers, Willie went into battle across the state.

"You gotta be on your guard against those big-money boys in their fancy suits who have gobbled up 14 farms right here in Gilmer County in the past three years. They're gettin' richer while you get poorer owin' your soul to the company store. You gotta watch out for the lobbyists up there in Hot-lanta talking trash and putting your jobs in danger. Why there are over 1,000 able-bodied men and women out of work within a 50-mile radius of this very spot. You gotta keep your eye on those scoundrels who don't give a damn—'scuse me, Ladies, but this just makes my blood boil—you gotta watch out for those heartless fiends who want to pay you a measly $20 like they did Leola Myers when her husband lost his arm in a sawmill accident.

"The only thing wrong is that you don't have time to fight the mill owners or city hall or in this case the state house *and* put food on the table and keep a roof over your family's head. But

I've got the time! In fact, when I'm governor, I'll spend *all* my time looking out for your interests. And I'm telling you Friends and Neighbors, the fat cats had better watch out 'cause when Willie Shorter takes over, there's gonna be some changes made!"

In every town, the audience reacted in the same way. The wild applause washed over Willie, he looked down into Laine's upturned face, winked and Laine could hear the roller coaster going clackety-clack, picking up speed.

With less than sixty days to go, the excitement of the race and the tension between Willie and Laine tinged the air with a kind of static electricity. Sparks were flying. Everything headed toward a climax.

The crowds got larger at each stop. Money came in at a steady pace. The Whippersnappers played better than ever and people danced and hollered and shouted Willie's name even before he got up to speak. At one rally, somebody yelled, "Hey Willie, why don't you dance with that pretty girl. She's just goin' to waste."

Always one to please his constituents, Willie nodded to Sonny who picked up his guitar and the band lit into *Turkey in the Straw*. Willie grabbed Laine and whirled her out into the middle of the hard-packed, Georgia-clay dance floor.

"I don't know how to dance to this," Laine pleaded.

"Just stay close and do what I do," Willie said.

Willie had his arm tight around her waist and she felt the heat of his body against hers. She was amazed to find that if she relaxed and let him lead, she could anticipate his steps by feeling the muscles in his legs. Before she knew it, they were flying around, kicking up dust, and putting on a show. Her feet moved faster and faster, her head was spinning… the crowd yelled and clapped and whistled. They loved it. They were not the only ones.

When the dance ended, everybody cheered and Willie returned Laine to her place with a most gallant bow. No girl at a fancy cotillion had ever felt anything as thrilling. *This must be like the frantic, wild part Mama talked about.* The roller coaster climbed a little closer to the top.

They had one more town to visit; the crowd was larger than usual and excitement ran high. Willie stopped by the cab of the truck and picked up the beat-up old pillow in the driver's seat he used to cover the springs that had worn through the upholstery. He laid the pillow on the edge of the stage and took his place facing the audience.

He started off slowly, talking about his plans to make Georgia the showcase of the south. Then he picked up the pillow and stood stock still surveying the crowd. "How many of you ever heard the story of the Golden Goose, the one that laid golden eggs?" Kids laughed and waved their hands; parents joined in. Willie ripped open the corner of the pillow and pulled out a handful of feathers. "Well that's what the big corporations are doing. They're pulling the feathers out of the Golden Goose." He threw the feathers in the air and the breeze carried them out over the audience.

"And do you know who that Golden Goose is? It's you, the hard-working people laying golden eggs to make the big shots rich. It's you, the men, women and children who daily endanger your health, yea, your very lives to produce cotton goods so expensive you can't afford to buy 'em even at the company store." He threw more feathers and the crowd cheered.

Then he stopped abruptly. In the total silence Willie looked into the faces of his audience. "How many of you out there have ever plucked a chicken?" Hands went up all over, mostly women and girls. "Well, I think it's time we went on the offensive 'cause Uncle Fry and his cronies are ripe for a good plucking." The men stomped their feet and whistled. The women cheered. Willie had them.

"We're gonna pluck out the blood suckers." He threw a handful of feathers.

"We're gonna pluck out the corrupt officials." Feathers.

"We're gonna pluck out the unfair tax collectors." Feathers.

Willie kept plucking and scattering feathers until the pillow was empty. "And you know what we're gonna do then? We're gonna cast Fry out of the capitol and send him down the road naked as a jay bird."

The crowd went wild. Almost as if God were getting in on the act, summer lightening flashed close by. Then the rain started and everyone ran for cover. Willie and Laine both ran for the car. As they slammed the doors, lightening hit directly above them, followed immediately by a clap of thunder so loud it made the whole car shake. Instinctively, Laine ducked and Willie put his arms around her. The spicy smell of her was exciting and when she turned her face to him, he surrendered to the inevitable. Willie kissed her and she responded.

Laine felt the roller coaster getting closer and closer to the top of the incline. The back seat was filled with boxes so they had to maneuver around the steering wheel and the gear shift. It wasn't the first time Willie had seduced a girl in the front seat of the car, but now everything got in his way. Finally he managed to unbutton Lane's blouse and slip it down to her waist.

Laine could hardly catch her breath. "Willie, I want you, I want it all…right now!"

"Me, too." Willie was desperately trying to plan his next move before she changed her mind. "Maybe we oughta trade places," he said and attempted to slide under her. Laine pulled up her skirt so she could climb over him and the sight of her bare thighs hit Willie like another bolt of lightening.

"Willie!"

"No, it's OK, don't worry, it's gonna be…

"Look!"

He turned in the seat and was shocked to see a huge oak limb lying across the trunk. "Where'd that come from?"

"I guess lightening hit it," Laine said.

"Oh my God." Willie half fell out the passenger door. The rain acted like a cold shower and jarred his brain back into place. He shook his head trying to clear his mind, *A damn limb fell on the car and I didn't even notice…. Man, I'm in bad shape.* He ran around the front of the car and got safely back under the steering wheel. He took several deep breaths to clear his mind.

Keep your hands on the wheel, Boy. Just hold on until you get yourself under control.

Laine rearranged her clothes and did her best to regain her dignity. *Damn, damn, damn. First I stop, then he stops, then God gets in on the act. It's not fair! I'm tired of riding this roller coaster up the incline. At this rate I'm never gonna get to come flying down the other side.*

Willie took another deep breath. "Listen Laine, there's nothing I'd like more than to make love to you right now, but not like this. Not all tangled up in the front seat of a car parked in the middle of nowhere in a thunder storm. You deserve better than that. Your first time ought to be really special, not like…this."

"But I thought you wanted me…I thought…"

"Oh God, Lady, I *do* want you. But, Lainie, I'm older than you and I know this is an important step for both of us. It'll change everything."

Yeah that's exactly what I had in mind.

"I'm crazy about you. You're my anchor, not just for politics, but for everything. It's just that this whole political thing we're dealing with now is a lot bigger than you and me. You've convinced me I really have a shot at being governor so I can't just do what I want to do anymore without considering all the consequences. The ride is just beginning and I want you there with me all the way. You've worked for this as hard as I have…I thought you wanted that, too."

Laine turned away from him. *Oh I want to take the ride with you all right, but we're talking about two different things.*

Willie cranked up the car and drove back to their boardinghouse in silence.

CHAPTER TWENTY-ONE

WHILE WILLIE TRIED TO KEEP his mind focused on the race, Uncle Fry confined his campaigning to the big cities where the streets were paved, the rallies were more dignified, campaign contributions slid effortlessly under the table and life continued as it always had. Uncle Fry had been at the forefront of Georgia politics so long he could not imagine the view from anywhere else. He hardly gave Willie Shorter a thought.

Just as The Boys had feared however, some of his colleagues were not so blasé. They had grown accustomed to their political jobs, their fat salaries and unlimited expense accounts. They were not going to let some brash, young upstart put that in jeopardy.

With the primary getting closer, The Boys redoubled their efforts. PV gained fifteen pounds having lunch with every person he knew who might be persuaded to contribute to Willie's campaign fund. Pappy made good use of his old newspaper buddies to keep Willie's name and picture in every small to medium sized paper in the state. No one was quite sure what Chauncey was up to, but every once in a while he'd show up with a sizable check from some new supporter.

Sol got Willie's schedule from Laine and made sure it got published in *The Southern Israelite*, the weekly Jewish newspaper. Joe Laundry showed up at rural rallies to introduce his good friend and candidate Willie Shorter. As far as Willie could tell, Joe knew every farmer in the state.

Much to Willie's surprise, Laine seemed to have put the whole episode in the car out of her mind. Assuming they were back on solid ground, he sometimes asked her to stand up and he'd introduce her to the crowd. "This is Miss Laine. She sure is pretty, isn't she (or ain't she, if the crowd was a little more countrified). My old granny, who raised me after my mama passed on, sent her along to keep an eye on me. (He'd give Laine a wink, since both of them knew Willie had never known his grandmother and could hardly remember his mother.)

"Oh yes, it's true. Miss Laine writes her every week to tell her what's going on. I can remember how hard my granny worked keeping body and soul together. She's 85 now and she still keeps a garden, but she can't travel much or she'd be right up here with me telling you what I'm telling you. She'd say it was high time we got rid of those big hogs in Hot-lanta that won't let you little fellers get near enough to the trough to get anything to eat."

Willie smiled into the eager faces so ready to believe there might be a better day coming. He saw pride when he told them the true power of the state rested with people just like them, the little people in the rural counties. He laughed with them when he poked fun at himself and at Uncle Fry. For a little while, he could make them forget the backbreaking labor, the low pay, the mounting bills, the fear of losing their jobs.

Like the rest of the crowd, Laine believed in his dreams because she believed in Willie. She got caught up in his web of words because she knew Willie planned to make Georgia a better place to live. He just needed the power to make things happen. People were drawn to him. They got a glimpse of a better day, not just for their kids, but for themselves, too. Just a little light at the end of the tunnel. Just a little hope.

Willie mixed his made-up stories with true stories about his years on the road with Uncle Aubrey selling Peruna and Bibles. Sometime he quoted his favorite Scripture, "And it came to pass…" The crowd loved that.

Another of his favorite tactics was to tell the audience that, "Life is like pouring water out of a bucket into a Co' Cola bottle. If you're tentative about it, you're not gonna do it well. You can count on the fact that when I'm governor, I won't be tentative about fighting for your rights."

Willie never let the facts get in the way of a good story. So if he exaggerated a little, to make a point, it didn't matter in the great scheme of things. If he was pressed to justify his stories, he explained, "Ancient peoples always recognized two important men – the scribes who recorded the facts and wrote the history, and the storytellers who wove the facts into the legends of the tribe. The facts have disappeared, but the legends are still remembered. Look at the parables in the Bible. People forget facts and figures, but they don't forget stories. These folks are starved for some entertainment, Laine. My stories just make it easier for them to remember the truth behind the facts."

However, the one place Willie focused on specifics was when he described the reforms he planned to institute as governor. The Boys filled him in on the issues, and Laine did her best to convince him that numbers were not his enemy.

"My dad always said if you follow the numbers, they'll tell you what the lay of the land really is. Numbers can tell you who's in charge, who wants something, what they want, and why they want it. If you pay attention, numbers'll even tell you how far somebody's willing to go to get what he wants."

Willie relied on Laine to get the truth from the numbers and explain what they meant. She encouraged him to mix local details and real figures into his stories. He refined his speeches like a composer creating variations on a theme.

Willie didn't have Laine's ability to calculate and decipher numbers, but once she wrote them down for him, his photographic memory meant he could quote chapter and verse with ease.

"There are 14 farms right here in Clayton County that have been repossessed so far this year. Taking an average of two parents and four kids per family, that's 84 people who're going hungry. Considering that the adult population of Clayton County is only 1,200, even those of us who aren't too good in arithmetic can see that's a lot of folks out of work. I mean to change all that. I mean to create jobs to get some of the things done that need doing.

"How many of you men can build a chicken coop?" Hands went up. "I'll put those hands to work building new buildings. How many of you men can handle a shovel?" More hands. "I'll put those hands to work building roads. How many of you women can sew?" Eager hands went up. "I'll put those hands to work making uniforms for state workers. And if some scraps are left over, I'll bet you can work them into a quilt to keep your family warm come winter." The women laughed and joined their men in applauding Willie Shorter. Here was a man who obviously understood what being poor was all about.

After every rally, Willie and Laine compared notes. She counted...everything. The number of men and women. How many kids, how many old people. She paid careful attention to the applause, knew which stories worked best, which promises got the best response.

The Boys decided to pull out all the stops in June. Laine figured out what it would cost to serve bar-b-cue at the rallies and suggested that to Willie. First come, first served, of course, so get there early.

"You need something to make it special and I know just the thing," Pappy said. "Cheap bourbon. Pour some over the meat while it's cooking, makes the smoke smell wonderful."

"Where do think you're gonna find a supply of bourbon in this day and age?" Chauncey wanted to know.

Pappy just grinned. "Better you don't know."

As it turned out, the aroma of bourbon bar-b-cue and the sound of hillbilly music came to be identified with Willie Shorter's rallies. Pretty soon anyone who could either smell or hear showed up. They came to eat and be entertained and they went home with a glimmer of hope that Willie really *could* make their lives better.

Willie had official strategy meetings with The Boys and Laine. Whenever he introduced one of her ideas, he gave her credit for it.

More and more they all came to recognize she had a natural sense for what would work with voters. Laine smiled and absorbed the praise like an old linen tea towel absorbed water.

Laine had always had the power to get boys to do what she wanted, but exercising this kind of power was entirely different. When she made suggestions in the meetings, Willie made things happen. She came up with the idea of serving bar-b-cue and Willie had made it happen.

If Willie wins, I wonder if I could make big things happen. Bo used to get lunch at the mill school for a nickel, maybe if I suggested free school lunches and explained how much loyalty free school lunches would buy... maybe that could happen, too.

The idea of wielding power was totally new to her. Power was something that belonged to other people, specifically men. Women didn't have power; they stayed home, raised kids, went to church, and did what they were told. Men made things happen.

But now Laine knew there were some women like Miss Amanda and Mother Ledbetter who had power of their own. She wondered how many other women out there knew the secret of how to survive without depending on a man for success.

As part of the inner circle, she was taking baby steps into that world. She got a taste of power and like a tiny bit of chocolate on the tip of her tongue, she wanted more. As Miss Amanda said, being the power behind the throne might be all she got, so she better make the best of it.

Then she thought about her mother. The only excitement in Louise's life had been to love a man. Of course, Laine wanted that, too. She wanted it all. But this political power thing wasn't like a roller coaster ride. As far as she could tell, it didn't have an end. It just kept going higher and higher and getting better and better.

As if her thoughts had taken on a life of their own, Pappy approached her about writing press releases, which Willie was now too busy to do. She jumped at the chance. He taught her what busy editors wanted; something they could use without having to rewrite it. She learned not to bury the lead, to get to the point, tell the whole story in the first paragraph, 25 words or less. She learned to include quotes, real or made up, and she watched as her writing got incorporated into articles that moved from the weekly papers to the daily papers, from the back pages to the front page to the lead story above the fold.

"There's just one thing I wanta warn you about," Pappy said. "The first time you see your words in print, you'll be hooked. Printer's ink gets in your blood and there's no cure for it. Take it from me, I know."

She laughed, but Pappy was right. When she saw her stories printed in a weekly newspaper she recognized that as another source of power. She'd read books all her life, but she'd never stopped to think about how words on paper influenced people. Now days, people read what *she* wrote. They might even quote her words to their friends. They might form their opinions based on what she wrote. The very thought of that was monumental.

Of course she continued to keep track of the numbers for Willie. Now more than ever, she understood that words could be made to say anything, but numbers didn't lie. As the rallies grew larger, the donations grew larger and Laine counted nickels and noses.

Willie always said there were two kinds of money, "talking money and whispering money." Talking money was upfront, noisy, silver coins. The loose change folks gave to the Shorter campaign at rallies was often still warm from being held in sweaty, callused hands before they gave it to Willie. Laine guarded that money with her life.

Whispering money meant folding money and checks, secret, quiet money. It arrived in the mail or in envelopes slipped under the table. Money from Fry's enemies, money that came with strings attached. Checks drawn on county-seat banks. Still not big- city banks, but that might come in time. Laine tracked the source of every cent.

"Laine, do we have enough money to take out ads in some newspapers?" Willie asked.

"I think so; I'll check the bank books."

"No, I don't want to do this with bank money; I want you to take care of it from the cash in the box. Find out how much it costs and if we can afford it, you take care of it."

Laine placed the ads and then approached PV about spending bank money to print banners and huge posters to make Willie's face as familiar to rural folks as the faces of their children. While he was at it, PV checked the latest bank statements and decided they could afford to travel by train. So Laine bought tickets to get Willie, the Whippersnappers and the rest of the entourage to more rallies faster. No more dusty old cars and flatbed trucks. They were living high on the hog and loving it, particularly the band, since none of them had ever ridden on a train before.

CHAPTER TWENTY-TWO

QUITE OUT OF CHARACTER, AS the primary got closer, Willie started getting cold feet. "It's the big cities. I'm not getting invited to speak to groups in the cities. That's where the big crowds are, ballrooms filled with people, wealthy people, powerful people. That's where I need to be and it's not happening."

Are you back on that subject again, Boy. I don't seem to remember you being so damn bullheaded.

"Willie, listen to me. Forget the cities, forget the crowds," Chauncey said.

"How can I do that? If we have 100 people at a rally, we think we're doing great. Small town support's not gonna cut it when the real crunch comes."

"You're wrong. That's exactly when it *will* count, when the chips are down." They had been over this countless times before and Chauncey was losing his patience. "Just think this through a minute. Willie, do you remember how the county unit system works?"

"Sure. Laine explained it to me."

"I mean do you really know how it works? Have you ever added up the numbers?"

"Ah.... Chauncey, you and PV lay off the numbers!" Willie groaned. "I got more important things on my mind."

"Laine! Come in here and talk to him, will you please? Now, Willie, just shut up and pay attention."

Laine smiled at Willie. "OK, remember we talked about this before. Georgia's got 159 counties, right?"

Willie nodded his head and did his best to keep his mind focused on numbers.

"OK, now whoever wins a plurality of the votes in the county gets *all that county's unit votes*. Are you following me?"

He nodded again.

"There are 159 counties...

"How about Fulton County, where Atlanta is, how about that? How many votes does Atlanta get?"

"Willie, forget about Atlanta! I know you hate doing numbers, but this is really important... and I guess it can be a little complicated. Let's start over. Now Georgia has 159 counties, right?"

"I got it. If I win a plurality..."

"You don't really have to worry about that," PV tried to clarify the point. "Since it's just you and Fry running, if you win a county, you get all the unit votes. Since there are so many rural counties, their unit votes could easily outnumber the urban counties."

"Willie, what PV is trying to tell you is this," Laine said with infinite patience. "There are more two-vote counties than any other category and they're all rural. You don't need the big towns to win. If you concentrate on the rural counties, you can take those, and if you do, you'll win."

"But there are a lot more voters in the big cities."

Chauncey lost it. "Willie, for God's sake *listen*! It's not the number of *people* who vote for you, it's the number of *counties*. Don't you get it?"

Laine shook her head. How could Willie be so smart about people and be so helpless when it came to numbers. By now it should be very clear. But Willie still didn't grasp the significance of what they were telling him. It seemed so logical to her. Why couldn't he see that?! She let out a long sigh and tried one more time. "Just trust me. It's really simple. Win where the streetcars don't run and you'll win the primary!"

Willie smiled. "Well, why didn't you say so in the first place? I can do that. I can surely do that."

Willie went back to campaigning. In the last few weeks he railed about how Fry was spending too much money. Never one to miss an opportunity, Willie capitalized on an article in the society pages of the *Atlanta Journal*.

"How many of you saw the piece about Uncle Fry in the society section of the *Journal* last Sunday?" He was reasonably sure very few of them had seen it. "There was this big spread showing Uncle Fry at the Ken-tucky Derby. I know some of y'all must have heard about his trips 'cause he goes every year. Anyway, he was wearing a brand new white suit and a big white planter's hat. And of course he took his whole family, also all decked out in brand new clothes.

"Do you know who's paying for those trips? We are! Yes sir, you and me. He's traveling at the expense of hard-working Georgia taxpayers just like us. Now maybe the *Journal* got it wrong. Maybe that car in the picture with the government plates wasn't Fry's. I can't say for sure so I'll just leave it to you folks to make up your minds about how your hard-earned money is getting spent up there in Hot-lanta. I trust you to be smart enough to figure it out."

Willie railed against big business, unfair economic conditions, lobbyists and mills...saw mills, textile mills, cotton mills, water mills, it was all the same to him when he got going, and the crowds loved it.

In one rally, Willie referred to Fry as being a sly fox. Laine made a note and called the incumbent governor "Sly Fry" in her next press release. The city editor at the *Atlanta Constitution* got a charge out of her release when it came in. He picked up the term and used it in the headline for the lead story the next day.

Power! Laine thought when she saw it. I wrote that and pretty soon half the people in the state will be calling him that.

Laine knew the number of registered voters in every county in Georgia and the number of unit votes each county had. She knew the number of important people around the state who had a grudge against Sly Fry. She knew how many votes they could swing in Willie's direction from their districts.

She kept track of the numbers. The crowds got larger for every speech. That was a good sign, but when Laine added up the numbers, she had to admit to herself, it wasn't quite good enough. She didn't discuss that with The Boys and certainly not with Willie. It was going to be a very, very close race. Way too close for comfort.

Toward the end of the campaign, Willie, Laine and The Boys were discussing ways to get more people to come to the final rallies.

"We're down to the wire, Boys and Girls," said Pappy. "What we need is something that'll knock their socks off. Something really flashy." When the room got silent, Laine looked around the table and caught PV's eye.

"Laine you got an idea, Honey, because we seem to be at an impasse."

"I've heard that some candidates give out free booze. I know we can't really do that or we'd lose the Baptist vote, and probably attract the revenuers. But why don't we say we've got white lightning and when they show up, it'll just be a singer whose name is White Lightning. I'll bet Sonny knows somebody who'd like a job singing with the Whippersnappers."

The minute she said it out loud, it sounded stupid and she wished she hadn't opened her mouth. Pappy, who was sitting across the table from her, frowned and then he laughed. "You know, it just might work. The women folks won't like it at first, but I bet once they figure out it's a joke, they'll get a kick out of it. Let's give it a try."

Everybody at the table started laughing and talking and nodding in her direction. Power! Laine smiled sweetly. It was fun being one of The Boys.

So the newly printed announcements went up. "Come Hear Willie Shorter and enjoy FREE bar-b-cue, FREE Music and White Lightning." It worked. The men came expecting free booze, their wives came expecting trouble, a law man occasionally showed up and everyone laughed when they realized the joke was on them.

The candidates weren't the only ones scrambling to get ready for the primary. Newspapers throughout the state set up a system to tally primary returns. The reporting started with stringers, a statewide network of editors or reporters on small weekly papers who filed an occasional newsworthy story with the big-city dailies. These newspapers, which usually had a couple of employees, sent stringers out to cover the polling places in their area. As soon as the votes were counted, they called their editors, who in turn called a special number at the Atlanta newspapers. One whole end of the newsroom had been set up like a war room. The wall was covered with maps showing the counties. As the results rolled in, they were posted on a tote board.

The system gave the *Journal* and the *Constitution* a leg up on all the competition. However, it had one weak spot; most small town editors didn't like the Atlanta papers very much. So Pappy had a hot line installed at Shorter headquarters in Morganton. He called in markers from his rural newspaper buddies around the state and it didn't take much effort to convince them to report the returns to Pappy first. With that in place, Willie Shorter's headquarters was the first to get primary returns.

At HQ, Laine set up a tote board and a state map showing counties. She was set to tally results moments after they were reported.

Pappy and I are going to be the first people in the whole state to know the exact numbers in this primary. Now if that's not power, I don't know what is!

CHAPTER TWENTY-THREE

AS THE CAMPAIGN HEADED INTO the final days, the tension grew, everyone worked overtime and nerves wore very thin. Willie recognized they all needed a break and insisted that each of The Boys take a day or two to spend with their families. "If we don't have it in the bag by now, another couple of days won't make any difference. Go home." Willie had momentarily fantasized about spending a day alone with Laine, but he quickly put the thought out of his head and sent her home, too.

When Laine got off the train at Ford Crossing, she was struck by the smallness of the station. She felt like Alice in Wonderland when she grew too tall to fit in anywhere. She had never liked Ford Crossing, but after seeing Atlanta, she realized how truly ordinary it was – just a dusty speck in the middle of miles and miles of cotton fields, totally insignificant to everyone except the people who lived there and whose lives were tied to Claxton Mills. No matter what happened with Willie and the election, she promised herself she would never work in another mill.

As she got closer to home she saw an old couple coming toward her. The shock of recognizing her parents nearly knocked her over. They seemed smaller, too. She had always thought they were big enough to fight off any threat that came to their family.

Her mother reached her first. "Lord, Lord, Child, what a surprise. Why didn't you let us know you were comin'? Let me get a look at you," she twirled Laine around. "When you said Miss Amanda gave you her hand-me-downs, I wasn't expecting nothing as grand as this! You look like a regular society lady.

Look at this, Jeb, did you ever expect to see our girl looking so prosperous?"

They laughed and hugged and Laine realized how much she had missed being home. As they opened the front screen door, Laine suddenly realized something was odd. The town was silent. "I don't hear the mill. What's wrong? How come y'all aren't at work?"

Her parents exchanged a worried look as they walked into the kitchen where Louise poured coffee from the pot that stayed warm over the pilot light on the stove. She put out a plate of biscuits and a jar of honey.

"Claxton's shut down for the day," Jeb said. "Some kind of special inspection they said, but I'm not buyin' that. I think they're gettin' ready to do something big, maybe sell out, maybe shut down for good. None of the bosses are talkin', but you can figure there's somethin' rotten in Denmark."

Before Laine could ask any more questions, Louise changed the subject and gave Jeb a look that said it better stay changed. "Me and your dad been campaigning for Willie," she said proudly. "We got everybody at the church all fired up about him."

"And I been talkin' to the fellers down at the mill. 'Course I done it on the sly, didn't want the bosses thinkin' I was tryin' to start trouble. How's he doing, Lainie? What do the numbers say?"

She told them stories about the campaign trail, things she hadn't put in her letters, about the crowds and how they loved Willie. She talked about all the good Willie was going to do.

"We don't want to hear his campaign speech, we wanta know if you think he's gonna win or not?" Jeb said as he poked a hole in the side of a biscuit and filled it with honey.

"It's gonna be close, Dad. No way he's gonna take the big city vote, but..."

"...he don't need to if he takes enough of the counties," Jeb said.

Laine smiled. Her dad went right to the heart of the thing; the one fact Willie didn't completely understand even yet.

Before long word spread that Laine was home and the twins, JW, and Bo came bursting into the house. A day off and Laine home all at the same time was like Christmas. They laughed and talked and told Laine everything that had happened since she left. The one exciting story was that Brother Bennett, the Baptist preacher—whose wife had died six months before—had run off with the president of the Women's Missionary Union. Unfortunately, she still had a husband who was very much alive and very much put out about the whole thing.

The couple came back after a wild weekend in Savannah and the preacher made an impassioned plea to the congregation to forgive his trespasses... which they reluctantly did. However, the gossip was that when he tried to take the WMU president home, her husband said, "You took her, you can keep her." The matter was still to be resolved.

All too soon the time with her family was over. Laine walked with them down to the railroad station where they said good-bye. On the train ride back to Atlanta, Laine thought over the visit. It had been both wonderful and scary. Things had really changed. She was so happy to escape the mill that she hadn't taken into account that Claxton Mill was what held the town together. It held her family together. If Claxton Mill closed, what would they do? If Willie lost, what would she do?

***

Meanwhile, with a little free time, Willie was doing some soul searching, too. He had a general understanding of the county unit vote, but what if The Boys and Laine were wrong? What if he didn't carry enough of the rural counties? What if he lost? When he allowed himself to think about it, Willie realized he couldn't go home again either. If he didn't win, there was nothing in Morganton for him. The law practice was just that, practice for bigger and better things.

He had no family to go home to. If the primary election didn't go his way, where would that leave him with Laine? He knew she could make it on her own, but what about him? Could he make it without her? Could he run again in four years? Would he leave the state and try his luck somewhere else? Would he ask her to go with him? Would she want to go? Everything was up for grabs and everything hung on the outcome of the primary.

By the time she got back to Atlanta, Laine had come up with a plan. "Pappy, can I talk to you a minute?"

"Sure, Honey, what's up?"

"Well, I was just thinking, you've got all your newspaper friends lined up to call in results from each polling place. What if we paid them a little something and asked them to call the nearest radio station with those results, especially if Willie's ahead? The *Journal* and the *Constitution* think they're the only place folks can find out what's happening. But, if the local radio stations got the returns first, they could report the local results long before the papers had time to get everything tallied and put out an Extra. What do you think?"

Pappy considered the idea a minute. "We got enough money to do that?"

Laine smiled and nodded her head.

"Well… I'll be damned if I don't like the idea of twisting the *Constitution's* tail. 'Course it's gonna take a lot of time to get that lined up…."

"I have all the names and numbers; I'll take care of it. It kinda makes up for the fact that I'm too young to vote."

That took Pappy by surprise. He shook his head as he walked away mumbling, "Lord, God Almighty, was I ever that young?"

And so it came to pass that Willie Shorter bought himself a statewide radio hookup. Along with Willie's original list of newspaper editors, Laine had made a note of every radio station and every station manager she and Willie had visited along the campaign trail. Willie taught her the power of using people's names and she made sure each letter was addressed to a specific person.

In her letters she included exactly what she wanted the station managers—or their announcers if they were big enough to have an announcer—to say on the air. "Ladies and Gentlemen, as a way of showing his appreciation for your support, Willie Shorter has made it possible for you to be the first to get your local primary returns through this station. Now listen closely, here are the figures."

If Willie didn't carry the county, there was to be no announcement.

The last days of the campaign were like being caught outside in a Georgia thunderstorm. Sudden flashes of electricity, lots of crashing noise, people running in every direction, and no place to hide.

All The Boys and Laine were back in Morganton and Shorter headquarters was a madhouse. Pappy had insisted Willie have three phones installed. He said three was the absolute minimum but Laine couldn't get over seeing three phones in one room. Not even Stratham Hall had three phones in one room!

The day of the primary, Willie was on hand to vote early at his local polling place. Of course, Laine had given every newspaper in the state Willie's schedule and more than a few of them sent photographers to catch the auspicious moment. Willie wore his Florsheims. He sported a new haircut, a new white shirt and a bright red, white and blue tie.

"You're looking mighty stylish this morning, Willie. Any reason for that?" one of the reporters asked.

"Gentlemen, I want you to bear witness to the fact that I'm so sure I'm gonna be Georgia's next governor I have begun to dress the part already," Willie said as he happily posed for pictures.

CHAPTER TWENTY-FOUR

AS THE DAY WORE ON, volunteers started filing into Shorter headquarters. With the help of a lot of local supporters and the purchase of every red, white and blue balloon and roll of crepe paper in town, Shorter headquarters was ready for a victory party. Miss Dorothy and two of her friends were working the phone bank. They had also supervised the decorating and were quite proud of the final result. Of course none of the polls had closed yet, so there was nothing for anybody to do but keep the coffee pots full and ashtrays empty.

The Boys had wandered in and out all day. Late afternoon they sauntered in with bar-b-cue and gallon jugs of sweet ice tea. Even with nothing to report, the tension was as dense as the clouds of cigarette smoke that floated up to the ceiling.

More people arrived. Men milled around, talking loud and slapping each other on the back. Women stayed for a while and then went home to feed their families. The polls closed at 7:00 p.m. and then the votes had to be counted.

Willie found Laine busy checking numbers at one of the desks. "Laine, why don't you get some rest and come back around 9:00 p.m? I can promise you one thing – no matter how the vote goes this is going to be a long, bumpy night."

She knew he was right, and when Miss Dorothy also suggested she go back to the boardinghouse and take a nap, she left. Much to her surprise, she fell asleep two minutes after her head hit the pillow.

Sonny, White Lightning, and the rest of the Whippersnappers ate their fill of bar-b-cue, then stretched out in a back room to take a nap. When the time came, they planned to be ready to play *When the Saints Go Marching In,* Willie's victory song. But for the moment, there was nothing to do but wait.

When Laine came back about 8:30, she expected to see Willie shaking hands and telling stories, but she didn't see him anywhere. According to Pappy, he was in Atlanta.

"Atlanta? You mean he's gonna wait up there for the returns to come in?" How could he do that, after all their hard work together? How could he *not* be here to share this moment with her?

"Don't look so upset, Honey. He left this afternoon. Once he voted here, there really wasn't any reason for him to stay. Right now he's exactly where he should be, hobnobbing with the hoy-paloy. He's going with PV to some fancy, society party. All the bigwigs with their big, fat pocketbooks will be there. Yes sir, Willie's gonna be doing a lot of that once he gets to be governor. Just wait and see."

Laine turned away quickly so he wouldn't see the tears in her eyes. She hadn't even considered the possibility that Willie would be in Atlanta. He was supposed to be here with her. This was their moment. She had even hoped that maybe after the victory announcement they might finally…

About that time, a phone rang. The room immediately fell silent. No one moved. The phone continued to scream for attention. Finally, Laine picked it up. It was Willie.

"Hey, Laine. Just wanted to check on everybody. You havin' a good time yet?"

Laine wanted to scream at him. Instead, she was all business. "We're fine. I'll get Pappy for you."

On the other end of the line, Willie frowned. He had expected a warm reception, he couldn't figure out what he had done to make Laine angry.

Laine took her time finding Pappy. "You can just sit there in Atlanta and wait for somebody to talk to you," she muttered to herself as she stormed around the edge of the crowd. "Sit there and wonder why I'm mad. Shoot! You've been so wrapped up in yourself lately, you probably didn't even notice. Well, you just try reading the numbers without me, Buster, and you'll see who's important around here." She spotted Pappy. "Willie's on the phone," she pointed to the desk and stomped off in the opposite direction.

Along about midnight things started to pick up and despite herself, Laine got caught up in the excitement. The numbers were coming in. This was it. The hard fast truth that would determine what happened to them all. Laine knew the magic number, 260. She chalked up the county votes each time the results came in from a new polling place. Then she slowly and carefully added the figures. It was a senseless exercise since her mind automatically calculated the numbers the instant she heard them.

At 1:30 a.m. Willie came striding through the door. Laine didn't notice. A cheer went up. Laine looked surprised; it wasn't time to celebrate yet. The city returns were the first to be reported. Those polling places were better staffed and better run than the rural ones. To no one's surprise, Sly Fry was leading with a wide margin of the popular vote. Willie was running a poor second. Laine just waited, counting up the county unit votes. Those were the numbers that really meant something. The *only ones* that were important...

Willie watched as she posted the latest tally on the board and stood back to look at the figures. He finally had to tap her on the shoulder to break her concentration. For a moment she stared at him then her face broke into a smile of such innocent delight that it took Willie's breath away. He had seen the same smile the first day he looked at her through the screen door and wondered what in the world a beauty like her was doing in a dirty mill town. With that smile she had just given him his victory...even if he didn't win.

"You didn't think I was gonna stay up there in the big city all night did you? Not with all those stuffed shirts and empty-headed women. They may look fancy on the outside, but I swear they can't think of a single interesting, important thing to say. Tell me, Miss Laine, how are we doing? What are those magic numbers of yours telling you? We're running way behind. You think we'll make it?"

Laine smiled again, but a different kind of smile this time. Willie had come to appreciate that look, her I-know-something-most-folks-don't-know look. Her "numbers" look.

"It's way too early to tell…but we might just make it."

Willie looked at the board where the popular vote was being tallied.

"Don't go looking at that. Look here," she held out a clipboard with the number 260 circled at the bottom. "That's the total county unit votes from all the two-vote rural counties. If we can just take those…we'll do it. We'll win."

Willie wanted to believe Laine's calculations, but every fiber in his body drew his eyes to the numbers showing the popular vote. No matter how hard he tried, he couldn't get over the fact that he was more than 50,000 popular votes behind Fry.

***

Shorter headquarters in Morganton wasn't the only place people were waiting and watching. Hugh Gandy, the city editor of the *Atlanta Constitution* and most of the *Constitution* staff had been working through the night. The morning paper was made up and ready to go, except for the lead story on the front page. That was being held until the very last minute. Huge charts lined one wall of the newsroom, with numbers being updated as votes were counted and returns came in.

Even this close to deadline, typewriters clattered, reporters shouted across the newsroom, ashtrays overflowed, got emptied, and overflowed again. "Lord God, I've never seen a primary like this!" Gandy kept repeating as he walked back and forth watching the slow shift of votes. Fry was still way ahead in the popular vote, but old-time political watchers knew not to count their chickens before they hatched.

Finally at 3:00 a.m., Gandy made the decision to roll the presses with what they had and put out an Extra as soon as all the returns were in. With an eye on his own calculations of the county unit vote, he could smell a story coming. A dream story, a money-making story, a career-making story for the reporter, the editor, and the paper that got it first and got it right. "Hot Damn, I think this is gonna be the big one, it's gonna go down in history!"

As usual, once the big presses began to roll, the noise in the newsroom dropped to a dull roar. Reporters milled around, drank more coffee, smoked another cigarette, and talked.

"Listen up boys! Better grab a bite then get back here on the double. This story is just gettin' started."

Hungry reporters don't really need to be told to eat. They marched out the door into the pre-dawn heat, rounded a corner and settled like a flock of blackbirds in their favorite café. Two waitresses appeared with coffee pots at the ready. They didn't take orders, they just brought breakfast: eggs, biscuits, grits, bacon, sausage, grape jelly, and more coffee.

As soon as the newsroom emptied, Gandy summoned the nearest copy boy. "Get me a copy of the Georgia Constitution."

"Where?"

"Initiative, Boy! Use some initiative. Find me one. Now."

Gandy positively salivated as he called the publisher and discussed the follow-up Extra. In the end, they agreed on the largest press run in the paper's history. Whichever way the final tally went, it was gonna be newsworthy. Everybody was gonna want a copy of this one.

If she could have seen it, Laine would have been gratified to know that her totals matched Gandy's figures to the last digit. Throughout the early morning hours, and into the long day ahead, while everybody else watched the popular vote climb for

Fry, Laine checked off the counties and tallied up the county unit vote.

The final results dragged on into the next day. Reporters, campaign workers and candidates alike managed to catch naps whenever and wherever they could. They drank cold coffee, smoked more cigarettes, splashed water on their faces and waited. Finally, more than 30 hours after the last poll closed, the final votes were all counted and reported.

By 2:00 in the afternoon, Laine turned the attention of everyone in Shorter headquarters from the growing popular vote for Fry, to the long narrow column of single digit county unit votes that were beginning to mount up. The Fry column included all the major cities, which had anywhere from three to six unit votes, and a few of the more populated counties. Willie's column had only the two-vote counties, but he had a lot of them.

When it was all over and the dust settled, Sly Fry won the popular vote 123,115 to Willie's 66,569. Fry carried 20 counties with 132 county unit votes. Willie carried 139 counties with a total of 278 county unit votes.

Willie Shorter had won the primary!

CHAPTER TWENTY-FIVE

PANDEMONIUM! AT SHORTER HEADQUARTERS THE Whippersnappers played *When the Saints Go Marching In* as supporters hoisted Willie on to their shoulders and marched around the room. Whiskey bottles appeared out of thin air and got passed around with abandon. People hugged and kissed and shouted and laughed. They repeated the magic number, 278, and whooped and laughed some more. Miss Dorothy didn't miss an opportunity to tell everyone, that *Governor* Willie Shorter lived in *her* boardinghouse.

Back in Atlanta, in an unprecedented move, both the *Atlanta Journal* and the *Atlanta Constitution* simultaneously hit the streets with Extras. The *Journal* announced "Shorter Upsets Fry" in a banner headline across the front page. The *Constitution* was more succinct. WILLIE WINS! Just in case there was any doubt, a sidebar with the relevant passages from the Georgia Constitution accompanied the front-page story in the *Constitution*. The antiquated county unit system had paid off—at least as far as Willie Shorter was concerned—and Georgia had a new governor.

At Fry headquarters, stunned silence reigned. Like many other citizens reading the headlines, and the sidebar quoting the state constitution, they couldn't believe their eyes. Most ordinary citizens and a fair number of politicians had never read their Constitution before. How could this have happened? Two years ago nobody had ever heard of Willie Shorter. He was an upstart. A nobody. He had no power base. No political connections. No machine. It had to be a huge, horrible mistake. But try as they might, they couldn't make the facts go away.

They had completely forgotten what life was like away from the state capitol and far from the halls of power. They had no idea what to do or where to go. Fry had lived at the governor's mansion so long he couldn't even remember the address of the house he owned in Inman Park.

The news of Willie's victory traveled like wildfire throughout the rural areas of the state. People who had no access to radios, telephones, or big city newspapers got the news almost as fast as those who did. For the first time, rural folks had "their man" in the governor's office. Willie was going to be living in the governor's mansion and the little people were celebrating. Even the colored people, who hadn't been allowed to vote, knew they had played an important part in getting governor Shorter elected.

Working folks couldn't afford to take the day off, but they celebrated in their own ways as they plowed fields, milked cows, operated mill machines, picked cotton, tended children, washed clothes, or cut timber. The most visible thing was color. Everybody found something bright to wear even if it was just a piece of cloth pinned to a sleeve or on a collar. Something small, but significant. They smiled, waved to each other and looked to the future with hope for a change.

People who saw Willie that day said he looked more like a kid with a new bike than a seasoned politician. He stood for numerous pictures holding the newspaper in front of him with the headline in 72-point type, "Willie Wins!" The story carried the usual phrase, "…won the Democratic primary which is tantamount to winning the election." An unnecessary explanation, considering the Republican Party did not exist in Georgia. In fact, there were probably not more than half a dozen stray Republicans in the whole state and they were all from Up North.

Well, you pulled it off, Boy. Damn, but I'm proud of you!

Willie knew his victory was a miracle. He was virtually unknown, with comparativley little financial support and with no political organization to speak of. However, with a lot of help,

he'd done it. Jonathan William Shorter, Protector of the Poor—
black and white—had won the primary.

After a week or two, the adrenaline level in the Shorter
camp settled back down to normal. Having won the primary,
now all they could do was wait three months for the election in
November—which was just an official blessing on the results of
the primary—and then on to January 2 when Willie would be
officially sworn in.

The crepe paper and deflated balloons were cleaned out and
the door to Shorter headquarters was closed for the time being.
Later in the week, Laine and several volunteers packed up all the
important papers and stored them in locked files. As Willie was
packing up papers and books in his law office, he discovered a
serious deficiency in his library.

"Laine, before you take off for home, I need your help and this
has got to stay just between us. Truth is, I know a lot more about
campaigning for governor than I do about *being* governor. I've
gotta understand exactly how this state runs, but I can't take a
chance that somebody might see me looking up facts I'm already
supposed to know. I want you to get me a copy of the Georgia
State Constitution. I'm not sure where to tell you to get one, but
you'll figure it out.

*You got it, Boy. You wanta know the answer, get a book. Look it
up. Go straight to the source. That way you'll know what's what.*

It took some doing, but Laine eventually delivered the State
Constitution to Willie, concealed in a grocery bag. Shortly after
that, she made plans to go home to see her family.

Eventually The Boys took a brief vacation to go home too, get
reacquainted with their families, and make some serious plans
about taking up residence in Atlanta for the next four years at
least. Laine took the train home to Ford Crossing and Willie
found himself alone with no family and nowhere to go.

After everybody left, he walked back to his upstairs office.
Sure enough, the July heat had warmed up the lingering odor of

horse manure. Willie smiled. Who would have thought the smell of horse shit would feel like home?

Willie took the heavy volume out of the grocery bag and settled in to read every word of the Georgia Constitution. "Par. XI. The governor shall be commander-in-chief of the army and navy of this state, and of the militia. Par. XII. He shall have power to grant reprieves and pardons... Par. XIII He shall issue writs of election to fill all vacancies in the Senate or House of Representatives... Par. XIV. When any office shall become vacant, by death, resignation, or otherwise, the governor shall have power to fill such vacancy...Par. XVII Every vote, resolution or order, to which the concurrence of both Houses may be necessary, shall be presented to the governor and approved by him..." It was tedious reading, but once Willie uncovered the meaning behind the aforementioned's and the hereinafter's, he had a solid understanding of what he could do, what he couldn't do, and what he could get away with. Timing, he discovered, was often critical.

Sitting in his rump-sprung chair with his feet propped up on the desk, he reminisced about what he'd learned and the two years it had taken him to get where he was. Since he first read about JW's injury and met the Beckers, he'd felt an urgency to get things moving, to confront Claxton Mills, to get the settlement, to win the primary. Now what? Three months until the election and then another month until the inauguration...an eternity for someone like Willie.

And as often happened, he found himself thinking about Laine. Willie had a hard time separating the man from the politician when it came to her. She had initially agreed to work behind the scenes, but would she still want to do that? He knew it was unusual for a bachelor to get elected to office, and some advisors had suggested he get married to bolster his image. After all, he had five months before he moved into the governor's Mansion, plenty of time to find an "appropriate wife."

But getting married was the last thing on his mind at the moment. His first priority was to expand The Boy's Club to include enough powerful men to support him and help him get things done. Men he could trust the way he trusted Laine.

More importantly, he needed to line up enough votes in the House and Senate to get his bills passed. That was going to be a chore, because although the voters loved him, his fellow politicians, for the most part, did not. But he didn't doubt that he could get the job done. After all, what good was power if you couldn't use it? In one of his front-porch chats with Jeb, Laine's father had reminded him that there's more than one way to skin a cat. To that end, Willie did some research to determine the exact number of appointments and state jobs he controlled. It was an impressive list.

Beginning the first of August, Willie deputized The Boys to get on the road to drum up political support with members of the general assembly. Working on the principal that the enemy of my enemy is my friend, they ignored the Old Guard and made their pitches to the younger members of the legislature and to those who were biding their time to see which way the political wind was going to blow. Professional politicians followed one rule: stick with the winner.

Lining up support before the legislature reconvened proved to be a wise move. According to capitol scuttlebutt, Fry's cronies were consoling themselves with the fact that they still controlled both the House and the Senate. Without their votes, all Willie's campaign promises would go up in smoke.

One project near and dear to Willie's heart was the idea of providing free books to school kids. He accidently stumbled across some interesting facts in a stack of legislative papers he read to fill the time after the primary. The State Department of Education had issued a list of "approved" books that all the schools were required to use. A central distributor bought the books on consignment and shipped them—usually to local drug stores—which handled the books for a commission. Every year or so the DOE issued a new list, which meant parents had to buy new books instead of being able to pass them down in the family.

Without Laine around to calculate figures in her head, it took Willie a while to unravel this complicated supply chain. However, he stuck to the task and in the end he could prove that the average cost of books per child was $5.99. Most rural families had from three to five children and having to replace books for every child every two years was beyond their ability.

The next time The Boys were all together, Willie brought the situation to their attention. "I did some checking and Texas is buying school books cheap and giving them to kids free. I'm going to appoint Sol as head of the Department of Education…

"No, no, Villie, you cannot do that. It's plain *mishegoss*," Sol said.

"What?"

"It's crazy," Pappy answered. "You can't appoint a Jew; you'd never get away with it."

Willie's research began to pay off. "State Constitution says I can appoint anybody I want. I'm the governor."

"Maybe, but you don't want to start out with a fight you can't win."

"OK, I'll put Sol on the state payroll as the Textbook Commissioner," Willie said.

Pappy lit a cigarette. "Georgia doesn't have a Textbook Commissioner."

"It will come January. Sol, can you go straight to the publishers and get us a good price on books?"

Sol beamed. "Sure, sure I can do that. Of course. I get the books for you wholesale. That's a good thing you do, Villie. A really good thing."

Willie smiled. Being governor was going to be fun.

The Boys went back to work extracting promises of support from legislators and making promises they hoped they could keep. The summer heat finally broke and by election day in early November, Atlanta was once again bathed in the reds and golds of fall. Because there was no opposition, most residents considered voting in the general election a waste of time so the turnout was always very slim. Willie, of course, made a big show of voting and Louise and Jeb voted again, just to be on the safe side.

The holiday season began and PV insisted Willie have Thanksgiving dinner with the Ledbetters. "Mother will be furious if I don't guarantee your appearance. She has her heart set on being the first one of her crowd to host a dinner party for the new governor-elect." Willie assured him he would be there.

CHAPTER TWENTY-SIX

IN THE WEEKS BETWEEN THANKSGIVING and Christmas, Willie attended a round of parties and speeches and meetings with the up-and-coming movers and shakers in Atlanta. He was living the high life and enjoying every minute of it. Well, almost.

After all the excitement and the hand shaking and well-wishers, Willie still went home to his room at the boardinghouse. The truth was, he missed Laine. That day in the rain they had come so close to stepping over the line. And what if he hadn't stopped. Would making love to Laine make her what most people had already decided she was…the governor's kept woman? Maybe he ought to marry her.

But that would change everything. She wouldn't be able to continue working for him and he needed her now not only to interpret the financial side of things, but she was the only one he trusted with all his secrets. Still he found it harder and harder to keep his hands off of her.

One morning as he was shaving, a realization that had been sneaking up on him for months finally hit him with the force of a body blow. "Damn," he said and nicked himself, "I love that girl."

Finally! Took you long enough to figure that out, Boy. Now, whatcha gonna do about it?

The question so unnerved Willie, he lit a cigarette. Willie was a social smoker who hardly ever smoked when he was alone. "Holy Christ! What do I do now, Unk? If I make my move, and she takes it the wrong way, she'll leave. If I ask her to marry me and she says no, she'll leave. If I do nothing, there's a good chance she'll leave." He stopped talking to himself and paced around the room several times. "Well, damn it, she can't leave. I'm the governor and I need her."

***

Had he been a fly on the wall at the Becker house, Willie would have realized Laine was also trying to figure things out. She had always assumed she would get married, everybody did. In her old world, marrying a man with a steady job was considered a good match. Well, Willie had a steady job…more or less. But she didn't want to just sit home being a wife…not that he had asked her to. If he wanted her to be his secret lover, could she live with that? Could she strike out on her own without Willie?

Jeb and Louise realized after the inauguration their relationship with Willie would change, too. Willie had become part of the family. But Governor Shorter was someone altogether different. Realizing it might be their last opportunity to do so, they decided to invite him to share Christmas with them.

When the invitation came, Willie noticed Louise—not Laine—had signed it. Disappointing, but either way, it sure beat sitting alone in his room in Atlanta. He lost no time in accepting and telling Louise he would be glad to bring the turkey for dinner.

Louise wrote back saying that the twins had each bought a five-cent raffle ticket at the mill, and lo and behold, Callie won a 20-pound turkey. It was the second time Claxton Mills had provided the Becker family with unexpected riches. Willie enjoyed being in on the family joke.

When he arrived in Ford Crossing, he realized things were changing already. Practically the whole town was waiting in front of the Becker's house to welcome him and wish him well. From inside the screen door, Laine listened as he accepted their congratulations and good wishes. He seemed older, more sophisticated, and she heard a new tone of authority in his voice.

Once he walked into the house, however, the old Willie was back. "You know, Miz Becker, spending Christmas with a real family and having a home-cooked dinner is a first. Me and Uncle Aubrey used to eat at some diner. One time we tried baking a ham, but it didn't work out so good. After he passed on, I spent my holidays at whatever boardinghouse I was living in."

Laine smiled. Even after all this time, she couldn't tell if this was just one of Willie's stories, or if it were true. One look at the smile on her mother's face, however, convinced her it didn't matter. With Willie, the truth was whatever he said it was.

With the uncertainty of the mill's future, the Beckers stuck to their tradition of only giving each other one present. Willie made sure his presents were discreet, but he brought something special for everyone: an Irish linen tablecloth and napkins for Louise, an atlas of the world for Jeb, a portable record player and records for the twins, a new baseball glove for Bo, a set of fancy drawing pencils for JW and a silver comb and brush set for Laine.

In return, he received small thoughtful gifts from the family. The twins had each decorated a cigar box with posters from Willie's campaign—"It's to keep private stuff in." Bo gave him a flashlight—"To find your way around the governor's mansion." JW gave him a cigarette lighter—"Mama said not to, but I couldn't think of nothing else." Laine gave him a leather billfold—"To replace that sad looking thing you have in your pocket."

"Willie, Jeb and me don't exactly have anything to give you, but we're loaning you this," Louise handed him their family Bible. "We thought you might want to use it at the swearing in ceremony and we'd be mightily proud if you did."

After the presents were distributed, JW set a large cardboard box down in front of his mother. When she opened it, she found a smaller box inside. Everyone laughed and gathered around as Louise opened one box after another. Finally she found an ordinary white envelope. She opened it and let out a shriek. "You did it! Lord have mercy, you did it!"

"It's my scholarship to Georgia Tech," JW said. "I'm going to college."

When the excitement over JW's announcement died down, Willie pulled the keys to the car out of his pocket. "Well, I promised you the car if you made it, so it's yours. Of course, now either I have to take the bus or you're gonna have to drive me back to Atlanta."

The Beckers may have skimped on presents, but they went all out for Christmas dinner. Jeb put a board in to extend the kitchen table and Louise used her new table cloth to cover it. Even so the table was barely long enough to hold not only the prize turkey, but a ham, green beans, butter beans, black-eyed peas, sweet potatoes, fried okra, cornbread dressing, carrot and raisin salad, biscuits, and three desserts: pumpkin pie, pecan pie, and a huge pan of banana pudding. It was by far the best Christmas Willie had ever had.

The next morning he and JW left for Atlanta. Laine couldn't help but think about the last time Willie and JW had gone to Atlanta to confront Claxton Mills. Things sure had changed since then.

Several days later a Southern Bell truck showed up at the Beckers to install a telephone. As soon as they left, the phone rang. Laine answered it. "Your dad told me about the trouble he had getting a phone installed, so how do you like my last Christmas present?" Willie asked.

"It's wonderful, I guess. How did you do that?"

"I just called and said, 'This is Governor Willie Shorter and I want a phone installed at the Becker residence in Ford Crossing.' Tell your family not to worry about paying for it. Turns out utility companies like doing favors for the state."

Laine was glad she didn't have to worry about the long distance charges, because Willie rambled on for half an hour telling her about preparations for the swearing in on the capitol steps January second. Instead of a lavish inaugural ball, he had decided to hold an open house at the governor's mansion and invite anybody who wanted to come. He had asked Miss Amanda to make the arrangements and act as hostess. She had graciously accepted.

"Now here's the real reason I called. I've reserved a special place for you and your family on the platform for the inauguration. They said I could invite my family, and y'all are the closest thing I've got."

On New Year's Day, all the Beckers took the train to Atlanta. The next day they attended the parade through downtown Atlanta with JW driving the governor's official car. It was cold, just above freezing. Willie didn't seem to notice. He had all the windows rolled down and shifted back and forth in the back seat, sticking his head and shoulders out first one side and then the other, waving to the crowds.

In the rotunda of the capitol, the Georgia Tech Band, the Rotary Boys Band and the choir from Atlanta Girls High School entertained. The program also included the requisite number of guest speakers.

Finally, Willie put his right hand on the Becker's family Bible and took the oath of office. "I do solemnly swear (or affirm as the case may be) that I will faithfully execute the office of governor of the state of Georgia, and will, to the best of my ability, preserve, protect and defend the Constitution thereof, and the Constitution of the United States of America."

At 32, Jonathan William Shorter became the youngest governor in the history of the state.

CHAPTER TWENTY-SEVEN

THE WHOLE STATE WATCHED IN awe as Willie Shorter went into action. The day after he was sworn in, his picture appeared on the front page of the *Constitution* with his sleeves rolled up washing out a big frying pan. Readers could hardly miss the symbolism.

Willie never moved into the governor's mansion. Instead he turned a suite of rooms on the second floor of the Henry Grady Hotel on Peachtree Street into an office. The hotel was a brisk walk from the state capitol. He also arranged to eat his meals—when he actually took long enough to sit down—at the hotel and to occupy a single room on the top floor where he slept.

Before the Boys could question his decision, Willie called a press conference to explain. "If I'm in the capitol, folks can't see me. The people who made me governor think that place is just for politicians. They won't go near there and most of 'em don't even know where the governor's mansion is. Close the place up, save some money. I need to be visible. I need to be easy to reach. So I'm gonna run the state from here at the Henry Grady, just one floor up from the lobby. Y'all drop by anytime, my door's always open." It may have been an unorthodox move, but the press and their readers loved it.

Privately he told The Boys, "Now I'm counting on y'all to settle in down there at the capitol where you can keep your eyes and ears open. Report to me and together we're gonna get things rolling here in Georgia." Without calling too much attention to the fact, Willie had a room adjoining his office set up for Laine's office.

Although there was no Republican opposition in the state Senate or the House, the Democrats were split into a number of warring factions, each one determined to amass the most power, make the best deals, stay in office, line their pockets, and, oh yes, get a little something for their constituents in the process.

Willie called a meeting of the General Assembly early on and made an impassioned plea to both houses to work together for the good of the state. In a move unprecedented in Southern politics, the Georgia legislature did just that…for a while.

Nice work, Boy. You're off to a good start.

Willie backed up his pleas with some sophisticated political footwork. Because of the support The Boys had built up in the months after the primary, as soon as the legislature came to order, a number of Willie's resolutions were offered and quickly passed. Fry's old cronies were shocked. They were under the impression they still had control. Clearly Willie was not limited by the old rules. If those rules didn't work to his advantage, Willie made up new ones. Political reporters now actually spent time at the capitol because with Willie in charge, something big could happen any minute. As he got bills passed, the press reported and the masses cheered.

The honeymoon lasted about half of the session. Willie had done his homework and he knew the historic pattern of legislative infighting. He had therefore hoped for the best and prepared for the worst. If some of his new supporters reverted to their previous loyalties he would hit a road block. He also knew if he took drastic action while the General Assembly was in session, the opposition could still gather enough support to undermine him. So he backed off. He made a note of those who opposed his proposals and when the session ended, he fired every last person appointed by the Fry administration. Then he appointed his own people, called an emergency session and proceeded to push through several appropriation bills.

That completed, he fulfilled his promises to The Boys. He created a new office, Assistant to the Secretary of State, and put

PV in that position so he could keep an eye on the Secretary of State which was one of four elected positions set forth in the Constitution. He made Chauncey Attorney General. Pappy became head of the Department of Transportation with the State Police under his jurisdiction. He appointed Joe Laundry Public Service Commissioner and made Sol Goldman head of the Department of Education along with his job as state Textbook Commissioner.

Paragraph XIX of the Constitution gave Willie the "power to appoint his own secretaries, not exceeding two in number…" so he appointed Laine as the official Executive Assistant to the Governor and told her if she wanted a secretary of her own, he could easily appoint one for her, too.

Willie had said he would be a hands-on governor, but right from the beginning hands-on clearly meant hands on the wheel, controlling every department. If someone disagreed with him and threatened to turn in their resignation, Willie took them up on the offer. Before they knew exactly what was happening, they found themselves on the outside looking in…generally at the newly-appointed, more-cooperative person occupying their former position. In essence Willie took over the boards and agencies that administered the state's business because each one provided a number of juicy jobs. Willie needed every reward he could lay his hands on because by controlling state patronage, he could control the state.

Willie had promised to clean out some of the deadwood in the state so he consolidated and streamlined the alphabet soup of independently functioning state departments. He'd also promised to balance the state budget, lower utility rates, and reorganize the State Highway Board.

When Joe Laundry couldn't convince the elected members of the Public Service Commission to lower utility rates, Willie dismissed them and appointed a new board to get the job done. He put the State Highway Board under Pappy's control, and when some members objected, Willie declared martial law and appointed members who could be counted on to vote his way. Willie knew his constitutional rights and he exercised them at every turn.

Although some legislators and people in power thought he was playing fast and loose with the law, other politicians looked past that and actually caught a glimmer of long-forgotten goals and aspirations to do good, to make things better. Life in Georgia was looking up. It seemed the more Willie did, the more he wanted to do.

Nobody can accuse you of being subtle, Boy, but I have to admit you're getting things done.

When it came to budget questions, he consulted Laine. He came to rely on her judgment even when she reigned in his more elaborate ideas. However, sometimes she surprised him. "Willie," she said as she came into his office, sat down and crossed her long legs, "I know you've pushed a lot of bills through the legislature. That's all well and good, but people can't *see* those things. You need to start doing things folks can see."

Reluctantly he raised his eyes to her face, "I went to a lot of trouble to get their utility rates lowered; can't they see that?"

"No, they can't. They need to see something they can point to. Something tangible. Something that will make their lives easer right now."

"OK, like what?"

"Roads. You could get a lot of mileage out of that. Driving on those dusty gravel roads is enough to choke a saint. And the dirt roads are worse. Whenever it rains, they turn into mud thick as wallpaper paste. Pave the roads."

"I'd love to do that, but it takes too damn long to get anything done around here. What I need is a source of money I can use to make things happen. Something I don't have to account for."

"What about the cash box?" She shuffled through the papers on her lap and pulled out a slim account ledger. "There's $2,347.26 in that."

"No, no, I'm talking about lots of money, enough to pave a road or build a clinic or a school, something like that. I know I'm not quick with numbers the way you are, but I do understand one thing. Money's like water; it needs to flow and I intend to see that it flows in the right direction to make Georgia an example of how this country could be run.

"While we're on the subject," Willie continued, "I've been wanting to talk to you about this idea I've got. It just came to me like God speaking to Moses out of the burning bush." He handed her a tablet. "Here, you do the math. How many people are there in this state?"

"I'm not sure. About two million, I guess."

"How many can I put on the payroll working for the state? One percent? Five percent?"

"Try maybe half a percent."

"Doesn't sound like much. How many is that?"

"10,000 people."

"Alright! Put that down. Now, 50 times a year the state of Georgia hands employees a pay envelope with cash in it. The church says they owe ten percent as a tithe to the Lord. From now on, whenever I put someone on the state payroll, I'm going to give them an opportunity to pay *me* a tithe. Asking for another ten percent would be way too much, so I started out thinking I'd let them tithe the tithe, that would be one percent, right?"

Willie was off on a tangent, talking so fast Laine had a hard time keeping up. Besides, his logic with numbers didn't always track.

"Anyway, when I got to thinking about it a little further, I realized working with percents might be a little complicated for normal people. So, here's what I've decided. I'm gonna take a dollar out of everybody's pay envelope every payday. How much would that be?

"Ten thousand dollars a payday, $500,000 a year."

Willie was genuinely shocked at the figure. "That much with just a buck? Well, damn! All right then, $500,000 a year. I'll be able to do a *lot* of good with that much dough and still have some left over to start my national campaign. I'll get a safe for the cash and put it in your office, 'cause nobody would think to look for it there. You keep the books."

Willie was practically dancing around the office. "Hey! How about this? We'll call it the bread box…you know, dough. I'll tell The Boys about it in my own good time, but until then, mum's the word.

"I probably can't do everything I want to do in one term, but I can sure do it in two. Once I start improving things, getting elected the second time will be a snap. I'm going to put Georgia on the map and when the big boys in the state party and up there in Washington start to take notice, that's when I'll start my *national* campaign. If I were in the White House…."

Aren't you getting a little ahead of yourself, Boy? You haven't even got the roads paved yet.

"The White House?!?" Laine was shocked. "Willie I don't think…

Willie ignored her. "It may take me another term as governor, but once I fix things up here in Georgia, the people that count will take notice and they'll see that I can do it all over the country. It just takes money, that's all.

"No more flatbed trucks and shoeboxes under the seat. The national campaign will be first class all the way. I'll have a special train made up. We'll go all across this country. I'll tell folks there's no need to wait forever to get things straightened out, there's a shorter way…" His energy revved up another notch. "That's it, Lainie, that'll be my campaign slogan, "Don't wait, Do It the Shorter Way."

And so it was that on an ordinary Monday night, in a small, unimpressive office at the Henry Grady Hotel, The Bread Box came into existence.

After Willie's initial show of strength and cunning, the General Assembly was somewhat reluctant to oppose him… at least publicly. With his new source of funds to fall back on,

Willie wasted no time putting his plans into effect. The next day he called Pappy into his office. "Laine and I have been talking and she's come up with an idea. We've got to do something big, something the voters can see, like roads. Now the way I figure it, those will be the easiest bills to get backing for because they'll make the local politicians look good back home. So go back to the DOT and get me a list of the worst roads in the state. Building roads means jobs. I'll put hundreds of men on the state payroll to put gravel on the dirt roads and blacktop on the gravel ones."

Willie was right. The politicians jumped at the chance to get roads in their districts paved and put their constituents to work. The bills sailed through the House and Senate and Willie put hundreds of men on the state payroll. Jobs in Georgia were scarcer than hen's teeth so nobody questioned the dollar each payday earmarked as a "tithe." With thousands of people throughout the country out of work, men and women in Georgia thanked their lucky stars they had a steady job paying good wages. Working for the state was considered a plum.

There should have been enormous logistical problems collecting the money, but mysteriously there never were. The money, in large bills, was delivered to Laine's office by a rough-looking, silent man on the Monday after every payday.

After the first round of collections, Willie decided he better take The Boys into his confidence. They met in Laine's office. "You're doing *what*!?!" Chauncey demanded.

Willie explained the system. "The money's just flowing through here back out to the state doing good. In fact, I don't want to hear any of you referring to this as *our* money. Every dollar belongs to the people of this state. We're doing just what the church does, taking up a collection to help folks out."

The Boys were not convinced.

"Don't worry about it," Willie said. "I've got it under control. I'm doing good and the people of this state are making it possible. I don't use one dime of that money for myself. Laine keeps the books, she can show you that. Every bit of it goes back to the people."

"And where do you keep this '*tithe*' money?" PV asked.

"Right here," Willie said and he showed them the safe hidden in Laine's storage closet behind a stack of filing boxes. "Just think of it as a cigar box…like we used to have in the truck. I call it The Bread Box." Willie saw their worried faces. "Relax Boys, everything's gonna be fine. Just remember to keep this under your hats. It's our secret."

But a secret like that was bound to get out sooner or later.

CHAPTER TWENTY-EIGHT

WILLIE TOOK POLITICS SERIOUSLY, NO one doubted that. However, he wasn't above having a little fun in the process. One of his campaign promises had been to lower the cost of license tags for cars, trucks and buses from $13 to $3. Uncle Fry had consistently kept the cost high which Willie considered an unnecessary burden on the poor.

After the election, Willie called for a reduction, but for some reason the Fry supporters in the General Assembly dug in their heels on that issue and refused to pass the resolution. So Willie took another tact. Just for the hell of it, he wrote a short poem which the newspapers, of course, printed for all the world to see.

I'm a Shorter man from my head to my toes
I'm a Shorter man and everybody knows
It don't make sense, it's a crime by far
To buy a $30 tag for a $3 car.

The figures might not have been correct, but Willie just considered that poetic license. In short order, the fee was reduced to $3 which won Willie not only the gratitude of the poor farmers, but the undying support of the truck and bus companies.

Two years into his first term, Willie looked back with pride at all the projects he had underway: roads, bridges, schools, and clinics. The Boys had slipped back into the mainstream of politics so smoothly it was hard to believe they had ever retired.

And Laine. Not a man in the capitol or at the Henry Grady could resist turning to look when she walked by. Willie smiled to himself. If they only knew coupled with that gorgeous body was an equally impressive mind. Time after time she had seen through the political crap to the heart of a problem. Having her around was a key to his success. How in the world had he gotten so lucky?

To most people, Laine was a nice distraction, nothing more. She opened the mail and answered general inquiries, sat in on meetings to take shorthand notes, and moved freely about the capitol and Willie's hotel office. However, the papers on Laine's desk that everyone dismissed without a thought were budget reports from every state board and commission. Laine pored over them with the intense concentration of an archeologist deciphering an ancient text. The figures talked to Laine and she talked to Willie.

Not even Willie realized that Laine's main source of information was the simple task of opening the mail. She logged in letters and made careful notes about who received what from whom and how often. She not only read every piece of mail addressed to the governor, she often drafted the replies that Willie approved and signed. She knew more about what was going on in Georgia politics outside of Atlanta than anybody else in the state. Nothing got by her. It took a while, but patterns and alliances began to emerge.

Another source of Laine's information—and gossip—was PV. The two of them had lunch once a week and as PV was fond of saying, "Mother and I know where the bodies are buried and in most cases, we know who did the *burying*."

"Really?" Laine said as she smiled at him across the table and offered him her full and undivided attention. PV was hooked.

"Oh my goodness, yes. Mother may be 94, but she has a mind like a steel trap and a memory that goes back to when *God* was young. She knows everything!" He touched the corner of his mouth with his napkin. "For instance, did you know the only reason Sly Fry was *ever* accepted into society was because he married Lou Ann Rollins? *His* daddy owned a *filling station*.

Her family's money financed all his political campaigns. And her family only put him in politics because he couldn't do anything else."

PV leaned a little closer. "Way back when Fry and Lou Ann were first married, he had a fling with some little piece of trash from up in Ellijay and Lou Ann found out about it. Well, she told her *daddy* and he told Fry if he ever caught him doing anything that stupid again, he'd make sure Lou Ann divorced him and cut him off *without a dime.* Fry must have believed him too because they're still married...although I understand Fry makes regular trips down to New Orleans and *everybody* knows what goes on down there."

PV's stories were a wealth of information which might prove useful someday so Laine started a file on people in high places doing low-down, dirty deeds.

With everyone in place and functioning well, Willie's political life was running smoothly. The only thing he hadn't been able to do was to break into the ranks of old money and power in Atlanta. And then like manna from heaven, an opportunity dropped into his lap.

Automobiles and trolley cars crowded downtown Atlanta, a sure sign that the city was growing by leaps and bounds. One of the main causes of congestion was the railroad lines that bisected the downtown business district. Citizens alternately cursed the tracks as dangerous and inconvenient and boasted about the outstanding architecture of Terminal Station and the fact that Atlanta was the rail center of the southeast. Even so, times were changing and some city leaders were looking to the future of air travel.

The new lucrative air mail route contracts the United States Postal Service was giving out caused a lot of political gossip. The mayor was determined that Atlanta be chosen for a Federal contract. The only difficulty was Atlanta didn't have an airport. Pilots used an abandoned automobile race track near Hapeville to land the occasional military or barnstorming plane. However, the site didn't have enough level space for a proper landing strip.

So the race was on to find an appropriate piece of property. No one in Atlanta city government asked for Willie's help, but of course he got involved in the hunt, too. He dispatched Laine to check foreclosure records and land office property deeds.

One night she brought up the subject at dinner with Miss Amanda. "From what I can find out, a couple of civic organizations are looking for a place, but so far no luck. It's too bad because Willie says an airport would be good for Atlanta. It would create a lot of new jobs."

"I suppose they've looked at the old racetrack."

"Yes, Ma'am, but I guess it won't work."

They dropped the subject, or so Laine thought. Two weeks later she opened the *Atlanta Journal* to find that "Mrs. Amanda Stratham, on behalf of her husband Endeavor Franklin Stratham who is traveling overseas, has made a very appealing offer to the city. For a nominal fee, she has offered to lease a tract of land near the old racetrack in Hapeville to Atlanta for five years providing the city government will pay the property taxes."

Of course the announcement was the prime topic of conversation at Stratham Hall that evening. "Miss Amanda, I think what you're doing is wonderful! Now Atlanta's going to have an airport and there'll be lots of new jobs and…."

"Yes, one would think the problem was solved, wouldn't you?"

"Isn't it?"

"Not according to the mayor. He says a group of old fuddy-duddies in his administration don't think air travel will ever catch on. They don't think the city should take on the burden of paying the property taxes. So they've formed a committee to discuss the situation. By the time they finish talking about it, the contract will have gone to Savannah or worse… to Birmingham. God, men can be so short-sighted."

Laine couldn't wait to get to work the next day. She made a quick stop by her office where she picked up the ledger for The

Bread Box. Then she burst into Willie's office. "I've got it. I know how you can get all the big boys in Atlanta on your side. Miss Amanda told me that…" and she explained about the taxes. "I've already checked on how much the taxes would be and there's plenty of money to cover at least three years. I'll bet if you offered to pay the taxes even for that long, you would be the hero of the day."

"I'll be damned if you haven't turned into a political genius. Maybe you ought to run for governor. All right, we need to strike while the iron is hot. Can you type up something that looks official—but don't mention The Bread Box—something I can take to the mayor?"

Bright and early the next morning, Governor Willie Shorter called on the Mayor of Atlanta. Willie calculated that the significance of his making the trip to the City Hall would not be lost on the mayor. He explained how fervently he agreed with the mayor and the forward-looking businessmen who could see Atlanta's future as the southeast hub of air travel.

To that end, the state was willing to pay the taxes on the Stratham property for the first three years, if the city could take care of the other two. On top of that, the state was willing to hire one-third of the new employees needed to build and run the airport. Having them on the state payroll would take some of the financial burden off the city, a way to further guarantee that the airport would be a success.

"That's a very generous offer, Governor, but how can you guarantee the bill to fund this project won't get stuck in your legislature the way it's currently stuck in my city council?"

It's just like selling Bibles and Peruna, Boy. Anticipate the question, have an answer ready.

"Mayor, I have a discretionary fund at my disposal which does not require the approval of the General Assembly. It is there for just such opportunities and I am honored to offer this assistance to the City of Atlanta."

Like Laine had predicted, it did the trick. Business leaders who previously would not give Willie the time of day, began vying for his attention. Work on the airfield began immediately and eventually the Atlanta Municipal Airport opened, the city received the Federal contract, and the first air mail flight took off.

To commemorate the occasion, the mayor organized a banquet in the Main Ballroom of the Henry Grady Hotel to honor Governor Willie Shorter for his partnership with the city. Everyone who was anyone in Atlanta was invited. Laine wore a simple smoke-gray satin dress, but one that accentuated every curve of her body. Willie saw her enter the room and she took his breath away. He had never seen anyone so beautiful, or anyone he wanted so much. Every eye in the room followed her as she walked across the room to join The Boys and their wives at their front row table.

Willie sat next to Mrs. Stratham at the head table and listened graciously to the praise from all the speakers. Uncharacteristically, he did not make a speech. "I accept your thanks as your servant and look forward to a long and prosperous partnership." He was the epitome of decorum and good manners.

Willie gave Laine a signal to wait for him. He shook hands and accepted congratulations until the room finally cleared out. Casually he came to her side, "Come with me," he said and smiled.

Without touching, they took the elevator to the top floor and walked down the hall toward his room. However, Willie didn't stop there. When they came to the last door on the right, Willie opened it and stood back for Laine to enter.

She stepped in and saw a small sitting room with a comfortable couch, several chairs, and a table set for a candlelight dinner for two.

"Is this yours? Do you live here?"

"No, my room is down the hall. This is something special to celebrate our grand victory." With that, Willie became the perfect host. He went to the table where a bottle of champagne was chilling. With practiced ease, he popped the cork and filled two glasses. "You know me, I never drink in public and banquet food is awful. Besides, I was too nervous to eat. I hope you are at least a little bit hungry."

Even if she hadn't been, Laine would never have admitted it. Very faintly she heard the final click, click of the roller coaster nearing the top.

"Did you see them, Lainie? I know better than to believe all that speechy stuff, but afterward, they shook my hand and they actually talked to me. For the first time I think they really saw me. And you made it happen. I could kiss you...." he paused, "and I think I will." As he leaned toward her, there was a discreet knock on the door.

"Who knows we're here?" Laine asked anxiously.

"Nobody," Willie said. A waiter entered pushing a serving cart. He placed the food on the table and left. Laine had eaten many meals with Willie, but usually they were hurried, eat, run, and get back to work. This was different. The portions were small, the seasoning perfect. "Do you want wine, or will you stay with champagne?"

"Champagne, definitely champagne."

After dinner Willie asked, "Do you want to see the rest of the suite?"

Laine nodded eagerly. Click, click. Willie took her hand and led her to the door in the far wall. He opened it and they walked in together. It was surely not what she expected.

Apparently the room was being redecorated. The walls had been stripped, exposing the patina of countless paint colors and layers of ancient wallpaper. Floor to ceiling windows, uncluttered by curtains, looked out to the south. Candles everywhere cast the room in a soft, golden light. The only furniture was a gigantic double bed in the middle of the room. Above it a huge ceiling fan turned in slow circles, moving the air just enough to make the candle flames waver slightly. The bed was made up with sparkling white sheets and more pillows than Laine had ever seen on one bed, even at Miss Amanda's.

"I'm sorry the room's not finished, but I couldn't wait any longer." Willie slowly turned her to him and kissed her gently on the mouth. He put his arms around her and pulled her close, but not as close as she wanted. She snuggled against him. "Slow, Laine, we have all night," he whispered as he kissed her again. Feather touches at first and then deeper.

"I told you your first time should be special and it will be," he said and then stepped away from her.

Laine closed her eyes and definitely heard the click, click, loud and clear. Then she heard music. She squinted at the shadows and finally made out the orange dial lights of a record player sitting on top of two old suitcases. Willie smiled as he walked across the room. "May I have this dance?"

Easily she slipped into his arms. It was like making love to the music. She could feel his body through the satin of her dress and the more she felt, the more she wanted.

Finally he danced her close to the bed, stepped away from her again, took off his coat and loosened his tie as he kicked off his shoes. She sat on the edge of the bed and Willie removed her shoes. Then he ran his hands up her legs to the top of her stockings and removed them, too. When he finished, she looked up at him and whispered, "My turn."

She stood and as he watched, she unbuttoned and removed his shirt and undershirt. Then she ran her hands over his bare chest. In one fluid movement he unzipped her dress and slipped that and everything left underneath it to the floor. Finally she stood naked before him. Although he had pictured the moment a thousand times, the reality took his breath away.

Before he could touch her, Laine gave a wicked little smile and reached for his belt buckle. As she undid it, her eyes never left his. This time he didn't stop her.

He picked her up, and laid her in the middle of the bed surrounded by all the pillows. Seconds later he slid naked into bed beside her.

Willie had to force himself to go slow. He was determined to use all his experience to make it a night she would never forget. When he could stand it no longer, he lay back against the pillows and pulled Laine on top of him. Willie *had* planned to take it slow, but the minute he felt the weight of her body, he rolled her over and as gently as he could parted her legs and entered her. With a force that surprised him, Laine pushed up to him, taking him in, moving with him.

He counted to a hundred and tried to name every baseball player he knew. He needn't have worried. Their bodies moved in sync. Then Laine threw her hands over her head and let out a yell that could have been heard half way to Savannah. Willie rose to the occasion and rode with the raw excitement of the sound. Never in all his life had he made love to a woman like this.

When their breathing finally returned to normal he asked, "Lainie, not that I didn't appreciate it, but what in the world was that scream about? Was that all for me?"

Laine snuggled close to him and sighed. "Oh my mama told me about it."

"Louise told you about...that?"

"Yeah, she said it was like coming down the first big hill on the roller coaster sittin' in the front car with your hands in the air." She gave a pleasant little shudder. "She said there's nothin' like it and she was right."

CHAPTER TWENTY-NINE

LATER THAT NIGHT, WILLIE WOKE up and realized Laine was sitting up in bed. "What's wrong?"

"Nothing's wrong…or maybe everything's wrong," she hesitated. "Willie, what are we going to do now? We can't just go on like nothing happened…"

Willie sighed. He knew this moment was going to come sooner or later. He had played it over in his head a dozen times, always with a different ending because he had yet to come up with the right one. "I guess we have some hard decisions to make Lainie, but I know my responsibility and I want you to know I'm willing to do the right thing."

He waited. Laine just looked at him without moving. He could tell by the look on Laine's face he was off to a bad start. "I don't mean that I think of you as a responsibility… but I *am* responsible…I mean I don't take this—us—lightly." He decided to take a different approach.

"Laine, of all the women I've known, you are the only one I can imagine spending the rest of my life with. It's just that you and I aren't ordinary people anymore. I'm not sure what the right thing is in this case. If I marry you, I lose you and I'm afraid if I don't marry you, I'll still lose you."

Her expression softened. "Why do you think you'll lose me?"

"As my wife, you couldn't continue to work for me. You'd be in the governor's mansion. You'd be the First Lady and you'd be expected to entertain, and to give teas for garden-club ladies, and church women's groups. We'd be expected to start a family. Is that what you want?"

No response.

"I love you and I want you in my life, but we have a lot to consider here. I don't see how we can have it all. I'd be the luckiest man alive to be married to you, but then I'd lose you here. There's no one else I trust like I do you and there's surely no one else who can take your place. I honestly don't know what I'd do without you."

Laine had longed to hear those words, but now they made her sad. She loved Willie, but she had to admit she loved her new life at the capitol, too. "I don't know what to say. I didn't think it would be like this. The way I was brought up it was just automatic. You worked in the mill, you dated somebody, you got married, you had kids and eventually they went to work in the mill. You didn't have a lot of choices, especially not if you were a girl."

This time Willie waited.

"I love being part of the excitement, knowing things no one else knows, watching plans unfold…but I always thought I'd get married and have a family too…" Her eyes filled with tears, "Oh Willie, why do I have to choose?"

He pulled her back into his arms. "I'll do whatever you want me to do, but we don't have to make that decision right now."

The next morning a gentle knock on the hotel door woke Laine. Willie was gone. Before she could make up her mind what to do, he walked in carrying a garment bag. "I just ran over to Davison-Paxton to get you something to wear. You can't very well go to work in what you had on last night. I hope this is alright."

The dress was fine and Laine had to laugh. As usual, Willie had taken care of everything. In the end, neither of them made a decision about their future. They postponed doing anything and eventually things settled into a new kind of routine.

Monday nights Willie told everyone he would be working late and didn't want to be disturbed. He left the light on in his room, and then met Laine in the suite down the hall. Sometimes they ate dinner and talked. Sometimes they plotted strategy. Sometimes they discussed budgets. Sometimes Laine told Willie the stories she heard from PV. Sometimes they made love. Sometimes they did it all.

Little by little, Laine realized that although on the surface her life in Atlanta was drastically different from her life in Ford Crossing, on a more basic level it hadn't changed much at all. She still lived "at home" although now that was with Miss Amanda at Stratham Hall. And she still depended on a man to determine her future. She needed to make a change.

Toward the end of the summer, Laine announced she had found a furnished apartment on Spring Street and planned to move out of Stratham Hall. Willie offered to pay the rent but she declined. Laine had never had anything in the world that was just hers and being able to pay rent on the little apartment was important. It represented something far more significant than just a place to live. It was her Declaration of Independence.

The last morning she had breakfast with Miss Amanda, she dissolved into tears halfway through the meal. "Shoot! I promised myself I wasn't going to do this."

"Let's go into the study," Miss Amanda said gently, 'it'll be easier to talk there."

When they were comfortably seated, Laine tried again. "Miss Amanda, when I left Ford Crossing I was running away from the mill, something I hated. But now…" she looked around and gestured helplessly. "This is the most beautiful place in the world and in a way I don't want to ever leave…but I hope you understand that I need to do something on my own…"

"Of course I understand. It makes me sad, but I understand completely. However, I trust you will come back to visit, I would hate to think that I will lose touch with you all together. I've come to treasure our friendship."

Laine thanked her for everything she had done and promised to stay in touch. Then she went upstairs to get her belongings. She planned to call a taxi, but before she finished dialing, Miss Amanda came to the door and said the chauffeur would take her wherever she wanted to go. As the Silver Cloud Rolls Royce pulled away from Stratham Hall for the last time, Laine realized that having choices wasn't all fun and games.

She continued to meet Willie at the hotel, but she only invited him to the apartment when other people were present and she never invited him to stay all night.

One Monday night at the hotel Laine was lying in bed with Willie, her arms stretched over her head and a satisfied smile on her face. Suddenly she sat up and said, "Willie, I've got something to tell you."

Willie froze.

Seeing the stricken look on his face, Laine burst out laughing. "Oh it's nothing like that. It's about the mail. You keep getting letters, mostly from women, thanking you for the free text books, but saying lots of mornings they have to send their kids to school with nothing to eat for lunch. Why don't you do something about that?"

Like waving a magic wand, Willie had kitchens installed in schools. Then he put women on the state payroll to work in school cafeterias cooking and serving free lunches to kids all over Georgia. Without much education and no special training, women were proud to be earning money doing what they knew how to do…cook. The state bought produce from local farmers and the women made the budgets go farther than anyone dreamed possible. They had plenty of experience feeding a family of six on $5 a week. More people on the state payroll meant more funds in The Bread Box.

Next Willie struck a deal with the paper mills to get newsprint tablets produced free. The quality wasn't much, and Georgia school kids quickly became experts at drawing interesting faces and designs around the lumps of wood pulp stuck in the paper.

Willie was in his element. Just to keep things on the up and up, he continued to meet with members of the legislature. He slapped backs, pumped hands, told stories and got more bills pushed through the House and Senate. Sometimes Willie met with opposition, but he didn't care. He usually got his way and his projects made him a God in the rural counties where he could do no wrong.

Building clinics in rural areas was Willie's most ambitious project. When The Boys asked if he put the projects up for bids, Willie just laughed. "That takes too long and it's a stupid system. The way it's set up, the state has to take the lowest bid, even if it's not the best one. I'm not going to build something half way when I can get it done first class."

Makes sense, Boy, but be careful you don't get in too deep.

When Laine or The Boys raised concerns that he was not being held accountable, Willie went on the offensive. "What do you mean I'm not accountable? I'm accountable to the people of this state. They're the ones who voted for me and I don't have to answer to anybody else. I'm not going to let you or the General Assembly or anybody else hold me back. Nobody understands what I'm trying to do here."

Willie's outbursts were few and far between and over almost as soon as they started. For that reason—and perhaps because they didn't want to consider the alternative—those closest to him ignored them. After all, Willie was accomplishing things far quicker than anyone had expected.

He used The Bread Box funds to pay farmers for land that was used as the sites for state-run clinics. Then he recruited doctors and nurses and hired local folks to fill all the staff positions. More people were added to the state payroll and The Bread Box funds grew fatter.

At the opening of every medical facility, Willie told the story of JW's injury and pointed out there wasn't a hospital or a clinic of any kind within fifty miles of Ford Crossing. "In the past, folks could die trying to get to a hospital in the city. Well, you folks in Henry County don't have to worry about that any more. Welcome to your new clinic." The plaque he unveiled read, "Henry County Clinic Built by Governor Willie Shorter." He wanted JW to go along to the openings, but Laine drew the line at pulling JW out of classes to make Willie look good.

One of Willie's other favorite activities was to visit in homes and sit and talk to rural folks. He was always welcome and he made sure he had a box of $5 bills in the car and one bill in his pocket. When someone told him a particularly sad story, Willie would make a show of turning his pocket inside-out and giving the man or woman his last five dollars.

After watching him repeat this several times, Laine said, "Willie, that's just plain dishonest. How can you do that?"

"Laine, if I pulled out a wad of cash and gave that family one bill, I'd make them feel small and unimportant. But when I give them everything I have, I've made a friend for life and they have a story they'll be telling folks for years to come. If you don't believe me, ask anybody in these small towns, they'll tell you I'm God's gift to Georgia."

Willie never bothered to look at The Bread Box ledgers Laine kept and she never pressed him to know how he managed to collect the money. She simply learned to push her doubts to the back of her mind and convinced herself there were some details she didn't want to know.

She could, however, show figures to back up the fact that in his first term in office, the Shorter administration created more state-funded work programs than any other administration in Georgia's history. She knew who got favors and who was owed favors. She knew who supported Willie on every issue and the few who opposed him.

The Boys knew in a general way what Willie was up to with The Bread Box, but wisely they didn't press him for details either. It was sufficient to know the funds were available whenever the Shorter camp needed them.

Despite their efforts to keep it quiet, rumors about The Bread Box began to surface: everything from a cigar box under Willie's bed, to a secret bank vault in New York City. The amounts varied widely too, anywhere from a few thousand dollars to over a million.

When PV asked Laine about the ledger, she said Willie had it. When he asked Willie, he always sidestepped the question. PV insisted, "I don't mean to pry, Dear Boy, but I need to know how much is in there so I know how worried I ought to be about this."

"Oh, about $250,000, more or less," Willie finally admitted.

PV was astonished. Little did he know. Even after all the payments Willie made both under and over the table, the total of The Bread Box funds had grown to over $750,000.

The Boys did convince Willie that they needed some kind of cover story for The Bread Box. PV gladly took on that assignment and concocted a story, which he told over dinner, to a few well-chosen associates—in strictest confidence, of course. "Now this must not go any farther than the edge of this table." He lowered his voice to a horse whisper, "It is strictly *entre nous.*"

He checked side to side to make sure no one was eavesdropping. "Locked in the safe, at the Henry Grady Hotel, is a box—not with money, mind you—something *much more valuable.*" His dinner companions leaned in, anxious to hear every word.

"In that safe, are enough incriminating documents to put Willie's enemies behind bars for a long, *long* time." PV sat back and watched the rumor take hold in fertile soil. He had no doubt the word would be circulated all over Atlanta by morning and all over the state in no time. PV knew his audience. If there was anything people loved more than money, it was discovering other people's dirty laundry.

Although PV didn't realize it, there was some truth to his story. Since she first came to work for Willie at the capitol, Laine had kept a secret file on businessmen and politicians and their unsavory activities. She called it the hanky-panky collection.

Laine continued to watch the state employment rolls grow. Putting people to work was a good thing. She had seen what being unemployed did to a man's sense of pride. She knew the state was full of men and women who wanted to work, wanted to support their families, and she encouraged Willie to see that as many of them as possible were gainfully employed...by the state, of course.

Willie put them to work by the thousands. They worked for the state of Georgia and they were grateful to Governor Shorter for their jobs. The money flowed through The Bread Box back to the people in the form of state improvements. It was a great system and it worked like a well-oiled machine.

Businessmen from up north had long seen Georgia as a source of cheap labor. Now instead of working for outside interests, the laborers worked for the state, which in turn improved the towns and counties where they lived. They saw things change before their eyes, things they could point to with pride.

"I helped build that bridge."

"I helped pave that road."

"I worked on that clinic."

With every new road, every ground-breaking for a clinic or ribbon cutting for a bridge, Willie made sure reporters covered the event. He particularly enjoyed getting his picture taken driving along a new stretch of blacktop with a car-load of local folks, all having a great time.

Willie truly believed in his idea that money, like water, needed to flow freely. As far as he was concerned, he had set up the perfect system. The money flowed in and he saw that it flowed out into good works.

Not everyone, however, was equally impressed. In smoky back rooms, and large corner offices, men who had ruled the party and the state for years looked at Willie Shorter and saw something completely different. They didn't see a savior; they saw a firebrand, a rebel who didn't understand the rules of power. They saw trouble and they began to formulate plans to teach the interloper a lesson.

If Willie had any inkling of their intentions, no one would ever have guessed it. From all indications, Willie Shorter considered himself invincible.

CHAPTER THIRTY

IN FEBRUARY WILLIE WAS IN high spirits as he made plans to go back on the campaign trail. It began as a three-man race, just Willie's cup of tea. As was normal in Georgia politics, all three contenders, Willie, Sly Fry, and another old line politician named Jess Goodnight, started out going at each other hammer and tongs. Not long into the campaign, Willie decided to drop back and let the other two candidates exhaust themselves. Then he planned to step in, dictate surrender terms to Goodnight and send Fry packing…again.

However, because of all that was at risk this go-around, Willie decided he should give up his Monday nights with Laine. He dreaded the discussion, but as it turned out, he needn't have worried. Laine came to the same conclusion. Their relationship was getting too dangerous and she agreed they shouldn't take any unnecessary risks. She assured Willie she didn't want to give Fry any ammunition.

That night as they lay in bed, it started to snow. By morning Atlanta was paralyzed by an ice storm. For two solid days, sleet, snow, freezing rain and temperatures below freezing kept the city in its grasp. Streets caked with ice were impassable, people were without electricity, trolley cars couldn't run, telephone and telegraph wires were down; for all practical purposes, Atlanta was cut off from the rest of the world.

Not everyone considered that a hardship. Snow meant schools closed and every kid in town searched for something to use as a sled. An old piece of cardboard, an inner tube, a large metal tray, a piece of tin. If nothing else was available, they simply put on three or four pairs of pants and went sliding downhill on their bottoms. Snow days were holidays and they intended to take advantage of the rare opportunity.

So did Willie and Laine. They considered the two days a gift. Little did they know how long it would be before they were alone together again.

Eventually the city thawed out and Willie hit the campaign trail again. This time it was first class all the way. Just like he promised, he had a special train equipped with every possible luxury. Defying the prevailing laws in the south, the Whippersnappers traveled in the same cars as the rest of the campaign workers. Laine had her own stateroom.

In a variation on the theme of handing out his last five dollars, Willie liked to have cash available in his old shoebox to hand out on the spot to solve problems. People approached him like subjects seeking an audience with their king. If they won his favor, he used money from the shoe box to make things right. Pay a month's rent here, or a doctor's bill there, repair an old tractor or get a roof fixed. No waiting around when you did things the Shorter Way.

At each stop Willie alighted from the train and walked through town shaking hands with folks, while the band set up. Sometimes he asked Laine to tell the crowd how he went to bat for her brother. Occasionally he danced with her to the delight of the audience.

Because he liked showing off, when Willie drove to towns that were not on the rail lines, he always traveled with a police escort of at least two highway patrolmen on motorcycles. Now, for no reason that Laine knew of, he insisted on six State Troopers who traveled with him wherever he went.

In all the small towns, Willie still reigned as king. Mothers actually handed him their babies to kiss. Men waited in line to shake his hand. Pretty girls flirted with him and respectable married women brought him home-cooked offerings or handmade gifts.

Willie accepted all this as his due. He deposited the gifts in a box, washed his face and changed into a sparkling clean white shirt, ready to begin the show all over again.

During the first campaign, Willie had insisted The Boys stay close. He sought their advice, bounced ideas off them. Now, he encouraged them to stay in Atlanta, which made a certain amount of sense, but they had an uneasy feeling they were being shut out of things.

Laine saw Willie on a day-to-day basis and she noticed the difference, too. The first time around it had all been exciting, loose, and fun. Willie was truly one of the people. Now he was someone else, someone pretending to be one of them.

On the train, he kept his distance from her, stayed to himself or played cards with his body guards. They were mostly good boys from small country towns. However, putting them in uniform and giving them side arms gave them a sinister air. They watched over Willie like a mother hen with her chicks. Clearly they worshiped him and were prepared to do anything necessary to keep him safe.

On a rare occasion when Laine got a chance to talk to Willie alone, she mentioned her concerns.

"I've got to be careful, Laine. I've got more to lose this time. Fry is watching my every move, just waiting for me to make a mistake."

"It's not that. I know you've done great things, but Willie, you've made some serious enemies. I read the papers. I know what some people are saying."

Willie just laughed. "That proves I'm getting things done. If I wasn't making somebody angry, I wouldn't feel like I was doing my job for the people of Georgia. Maybe I should just use the money in The Bread Box to buy the primary and save us all a lot of time and effort."

He meant it as a joke, but Laine was worried. Willie had gotten used to having his way. He was so convinced he was the only one who could bring prosperity to Georgia he started to believe his own press releases. As he saw it, he was on a mission. He had a God-given mandate to do good…whatever the cost.

Turns out, Laine wasn't the only one who was worried. Back in Atlanta, Chauncey called a meeting of The Boys. "All right, we've got some important things going for us this time. Willie's the incumbent. The favorite. He's got an impressive record and the rural counties are behind him one-hundred percent. But there are rumblings in some very high places."

"Yeah, I've been keeping up with coverage in the papers," Pappy said. "Not just here in Georgia, but I read *The New York Times*, the *Chicago Tribune*, the New Orleans *Times-Picayune* and the Houston *Chronicle*. Willie's gotten to be national news and reporters are taking a much closer look at his tactics now that he's headed into his second term…and maybe into national politics."

"The thing that worries me the most is The Bread Box," Chauncey said. "If Fry or anybody else finds out there really *is* a Bread Box with money in it, there will be hell to pay. All we need is for the newspapers to say that Willie is stealing money out of the pockets of every state employee…"

"Which, strictly speaking, is exactly what he *is* doing," PV pointed out.

"Yes, but he does these things only to make life better for everyone, no?" Sol asked.

The ethics of the situation notwithstanding, they reminded themselves of the importance of keeping The Bread Box a secret and vowed never to mention it outside their inner circle. Earlier in the year, PV had planted the rumor that the Bread Box contained damaging reports on the shenanigans of state politicians. Now, Laine began to read the same information in newspaper articles. She didn't know whether the information came from one of PV's "confidential" sources or whether Pappy had decided to spread a little misinformation, too. Either way, the papers claimed the information came from an unimpeachable source.

One source, who preferred to remain anonymous said, "I've seen some of the reports in the vault with my very own eyes and

I can tell you the whole idea of a safe full of money is ridiculous. It's not hard cash, it's hard evidence that'll put folks behind bars. That's what those crooks ought to be worried about."

Laine shook her head. How could anybody read that and put any stock in someone who wouldn't even give his name? But she also knew if you said something often enough, people would believe anything, especially if they read it in the paper. "I read it in the *Constitution*, so I know it's true." If only they knew what she knew.

***

Like a freeloading relative who overstays his welcome, the unusually cold winter showed no signs of moving on. Southerners tend to cope better with long hot summers than they do with long cold winters. March should have held the promise of spring, but snow covered the northern counties and penetrating, damp cold hung on in the south. Daffodils and azaleas were blooming, but the continuing overcast skies put everyone's nerves on edge. But true to the old adage, when March comes in like a lion, it goes out like a lamb.

By the middle of April all of Atlanta burst into full bloom. Out of the blue, Willie knocked on Laine's office door one afternoon and asked her to go for a ride with him. Instead of taking a state car and driver, Willie got behind the wheel himself. They drove up Peachtree Road, past Ansley Park, and on farther north. Just after they crossed Peachtree Creek, Willie turned onto a wide street between two gatehouses.

"Know what they call this neighborhood?" Willie asked. "Peachtree Hills, real original, huh?"

Eventually they stopped in front of a well-built, white frame house. It sat on a double lot which backed up to a wooded area. A large screen porch ran across the entire front of the house. Two big sugar maples in the front yard were just starting to put out new leaves. "I'm thinking about buying this as an investment. Chauncey said it was a good idea. Makes me look more respectable, if anybody cares to check."

The house had obviously been well taken care of and although Laine liked it, she couldn't picture Willie ever living there. It was too large for one person and it had to be at least six miles from downtown.

CHAPTER THIRTY-ONE

ON HER 23RD BIRTHDAY, WILLIE took Laine out for lunch—he did that for all the secretaries on their birthdays—and presented her with the deed to the house.

She was speechless.

"Laine I just wanted you to have something you could count on. Who knows what may happen. You can live in it, move your family up here, rent it, sell it, do whatever you want with it… There are a lot of things I can't do for you, not publicly. But you know I wouldn't be where I am today without you…and your family."

Laine smiled. Willie tended to talk a lot when he got nervous. "I just want to make sure if anything should ever happen to me, you have a home of your own so you and your family don't have to worry if the mill closes or something like that."

Laine wondered if he knew something about Claxton Mill she didn't know.

"The house is yours. Just in case things ever turn ugly."

Later as they walked back to the Henry Grady from lunch, she said, "What did you mean, 'If things get ugly or something happens to you?' Is there something you're not telling me?"

"No, but you know I've been stepping on some toes and I'll probably step on a lot more before I'm done. This is just my way of taking care of you. Better to be safe than sorry…or something like that." He laughed. When Laine told her family about the house, Louise cried. Laine knew her mother was torn between being disappointed that she and Willie weren't getting married and being impressed with Willie for doing something so generous. Although her family was still working, Claxton Mill had laid off a lot of folks. Other mills in the area had closed down completely. Her dad said it was just a matter of time until they all closed.

As might have been expected, the Fry camp soon got wind that Willie had bought Laine a house. With predictable malice, they accused him of using state funds to buy his mistress a big house. The story ran on the front page of the Sunday *Journal.*

Never one to hide from his accusers, bright and early Monday morning Willie called a press conference…at the new house. He took the reporters on a walk-through. The house was unfurnished except for a refrigerator in the kitchen. Willie said he had installed the icebox and stocked it with Co' Cola just in case anyone was thirsty. They all were.

Back out on the front porch, he introduced Laine. "Uncle Fry has made some unkind remarks about Miss Becker and I want to give y'all the true facts and clear this misconception up right at the get-go. Miss Becker has been working for me since the beginning of my campaign. She will be glad to show you bank statements documenting every pay check she received, first from my personal account and later when she went on the state payroll.

"If you check the amounts, no doubt you will agree that in the years *I* employed her, she was seriously underpaid, considering she kept me on a tight budget all that time and made sure I accounted for every last nickel and dime I spent on my campaign. And she's still at it. That's right. I'm the Governor of the Great State of Georgia, but I get an allowance every week. I'm sure some of you know what that's like."

The reporters laughed and scribbled notes.

"I'll bet she can tell you exactly how much I've spent today and what I have in my pocket right now. How 'bout it, Miss Becker?"

Laine held up several receipts. "According to my records, you started out this morning with two $10.00 bills in your pocket.

You spent $2.50 for breakfast and a ten cent tip for the waitress. You got a shave and a haircut .50. Then you spent $1.50 for a new tie and you bought a case of Co' Cola for $1.20."

"And I had to pay a deposit on the bottles, so y'all remember to put 'em back in the case."

"So far, you've spent $5.80 which means that right now you should have one ten-dollar bill, four one-dollar bills and two dimes in your pocket," Laine said politely.

The reporters gathered round as Willie turned out the contents of his pockets to confirm Laine's facts. "Now, about this house. Through a special arrangement with the Henry Grady Hotel, they provide the space for my office absolutely free. I do maintain a single room at the hotel, which I pay for out of my salary from the state. I don't have time to eat much; I'm still wearing the same suits I owned before I became governor, and the same shoes." He held up his foot and pointed to the holes in his soles. The photographers moved in for close-ups.

"I did splurge on one thing. I bought a new tie this morning so I'd look good for this press conference. You've already seen the receipt for that. Now, if I decide to use the money I earn as governor to make an investment in the City of Atlanta by buying a house to reward a loyal employee and her family by giving it to her, it's nobody's damn business. I just wanted you boys to get the facts straight."

Never one to let an audience go to waste, Willie launched into a story.

"This whole situation with Sly Fry reminds me of a yarn my Uncle Aubrey used to tell about a farmer down in south Georgia who owned this sorry old dog. When they'd go hunting, the dog would commence barking up a tree, but when the farmer got there, and chopped down the tree, he never found anything. He pretty-near cut down every tree on his land before he figured out that old dog was just *barkin' up the wrong tree.*"

More laughter, more pictures, and more publicity for Willie. The next day Barkin'-Up-the-Wrong-Tree headlines appeared

first in Atlanta and eventually as far away as New York and
Houston. No further questions were ever raised about the house
in Peachtree Hills.

Laine was still a little uncomfortable about Willie's methods,
but he dismissed it. "It's just politics, don't worry about it."

Willie continued to supply good copy for the reporters with
stunts and stories guaranteed to entertain readers and hopefully
divert attention from more serious issues. Still an undertone of
trouble lingered and despite his show of unconcern, The Boys
were aware Willie was getting a little paranoid, seeing enemies
behind every tree.

Pappy kept up with the news coverage Willie got and although
the small weekly papers were four square behind him, in the larger
cities, words like "dictator" and "demagogue" began to show up
not just on the editorial pages, but in news coverage as well.
When The Boys attempted to discuss this with Willie, they were
met with his standard response. "It's like I've told you before, if
I'm not making somebody angry, I'm not doing my job."

They decided to send Laine campaigning with Willie both to
keep an eye on him and to be on the lookout for any signs of
unrest in the rural areas. At first she reported that even more than
the first time around, people in the country treated Willie as if he
were the next best thing to the Second Coming.

Ordinary folks obviously weren't concerned with *how* Willie
got things done. They had jobs. They could see the roads and
clinics in their counties. Their kids got free lunches and free
books. Their attitude seemed to be "the guy in the saddle is
always the one getting shot at" and they chalked the accusations
up to sour grapes and continued to worship their hero.

Then one rainy afternoon in early April, Willie and Laine were
riding in his official car, coming back from opening a rural clinic.
Willie had never gotten over his love for speed and he often urged
his driver to get out in front of the State Patrol. They knew about
Willie's quirks, so they hung back and let him have his fun.

"Open it up, George, let's see what this baby'll do." They roared down the newly paved road north to Atlanta. When they got to McDonough, the driver slowed down only to find the main street blocked by a logging truck that had lost his load. George followed the detour signs and ended up driving down a narrow back alley. At the end of the street, several men in overalls and well-worn work hats were unloading bags from the back of a pickup truck.

As the men turned and walked toward the car, Laine reached out to stop Willie who started to get out of the car to shake hands. Just then, one of the men threw something at the car. The rotten egg splattered as it hit the windshield. Instantly George pushed Willie down. "Lock the doors!"

The men pelted the car with more rotten eggs and beat on the windows with their fists. "Go home, nigger lover. Stay in Atlanta, you dirty kike!"

In two minutes the State Patrol arrived with sirens blaring and lights flashing. The attackers jumped into the back of their pickup and took off.

For a moment, Willie was paralyzed. Then one of the Troopers tapped on the window. It took a moment for Willie to get his bearings. He made sure Laine was all right then jumped out of the car waving his arms and screaming.

"Where were you guys? We could have been killed. Who the hell were those bastards? For God's sake don't they realize all I'm doing to make their stupid lives better?"

The Troopers eventually calmed him down and the convoy finally got back on the road. Willie shook his head. "I don't understand, Laine. Why are they mad at me? I'm just trying to do right for everyone."

Both the State Troopers and Laine reported the incident to The Boys. They were initially upset, but in the long run no one was hurt so they advised Willie to ignore it. It might have been a politically motivated attack, but without an official report, Fry couldn't admit he knew about the incident or turn it to his advantage. No one wanted any kind of negative publicity so close to the primary. They decided to continue to present Willie as being universally loved.

Later that evening in his office Willie went over everything that had happened. "Laine, I still don't understand. Why would folks in McDonough do something like that to me? I mean, I opened a school down there not more than two months ago."

"Willie, I didn't say anything in front of The Boys, but I don't think those men were from McDonough. I've been thinking about it. This afternoon something struck me as not quite right and I just realized what it was. When those men started walking toward the car, they had on overalls and old hats, but they were wearing city shoes... shiny polished shoes."

Willie's expression changed from puzzlement to anger. So, it wasn't just local boys. Up until that moment he had assumed his opponents were just playing politics, now he realized they were playing for keeps.

CHAPTER THIRTY-TWO

THE FUN AND GAMES ENDED there. From that point on, Willie added two unmarked cars filled with plainclothesmen to his police escort and body guards surrounded him inside every building.

Boy, the voters are gonna wanta know what's going on. Best thing to do is lay it on the line.

And that's just what he did…at every rally. "I want y'all to look around at all the State Troopers and body guards traveling with me. They're fine men with wives and families and I'm proud to have them in my service. But, Friends, I'm also ashamed. Ashamed that the actions of my opponents have made this necessary. Ashamed that our political system has fallen this low. Ashamed that we all live in such troubled times.

"I'm told my opponents want to get rid of Willie Shorter; that they don't think what I'm doing is on the up-and-up. They want to erase me? Well, I can tell them exactly how to go about it. They can start by tearing up that new road that runs through this county. Then they can tear down that new clinic over yonder. Next they can snatch up all the free books and free lunches your kids get in school. And while they're at it, they can tear down the school. They can stop all the state improvement programs and put thousands of you hard-working folks out of good jobs. Yes, Sir, and when they're done, they think Willie Shorter and the memory of what I've done for the people of this state will disappear. Let me tell you something Folks, they're dead wrong."

The murmurs from the crowd told Willie he was on the right track. "They're wrong, Friends, because I don't think you want to get rid of Willie Shorter. I think you want me to serve as your governor another term. So I'm not backing down. No Sir, I'm going forward and if you give me a chance, I'm gonna finish what I started."

Now Willie was on solid ground and he preached the familiar sermon of how he would continue to make Georgia a shining example for the whole country. He was the scrappy kid standing up to the bully in the schoolyard.

As long as he was working the crowds and drawing energy from them, he was fine. But alone, he was gripped by a nameless fear he didn't understand. Willie considered himself a good man, people liked him, and he liked people. He had been through some hard times in his life, but he'd always believed in the basic goodness of his fellow man and up until the incident in McDonough, he'd had no reason to doubt that belief.

PV, who fancied himself an expert on human nature, declared that Willie needed something to restore his confidence. Pappy interpreted that to mean the best defense was a good offense. The consensus among The Boys was that Willie needed to focus his energy on *doing* something, not waiting for something else to happen. The attack might have been an isolated incident, but if it was the beginning of an anti-Shorter movement, it needed to be nipped in the bud.

"A scandal, that's what we need," PV said. "Something on Fry, something *huge,* a very large can of very nasty worms. I'll talk to Mother. I'm sure she can come up with something."

All the talk of attacks and counterattacks made Laine uneasy. Since she wasn't part of the strategy, she decided to take a couple of days off and go to Ford Crossing. Things were pretty much the same as always. Talk around the kitchen table was about slowdowns at the mill, the weather and crops. Louise complained that a late frost had destroyed blossoms in her garden that should have turned into vegetables.

"Good thing we don't depend on raisin' crops. I got this letter from your Uncle Mickey last week and he said up around

Cherokee county they're into a three-year drought with no relief in sight. Banks were foreclosing on farms all over the place.

"They thought they might lose their farm 'cause they couldn't pay the taxes. Then like some fairy godmother, along comes this man who offered to buy the land and let them live there rent-free for five years. Said after five years, they'd have an option to buy the land back."

Jeb shook his head. "Turns out right off, that deal wasn't quite as sweet as it sounded. Mickey and Emma had to sell the farm for 50 cents on the dollar...."

Louise broke in, "Jeb, it's not like they're *sellin' it for good*. Way they figure, they're *buying time*. Without having to pay rent or taxes for five years and a couple of good crops they oughta be able to buy it back. Besides, Mickey's not the only one. He knows a bunch of folks made the same deal."

"Yeah maybe, but I'm tellin' you, it don't make sense," Jeb said putting his cigarette out on the bottom of his shoe and dropping it into the ashtray. Laine didn't want to worry her mother, but she had to agree with her dad. It sounded to her like Uncle Mickey had made a deal with the devil.

The visit was over too soon. When Laine got back to her office, the first thing she did was to go down to the title office and check recent land sales in Cherokee County. Sure enough, more than a couple of farmers had made the same deal as Uncle Mickey. Twelve parcels of land running along the Etowah River had been bought by one corporation, Estes Enterprises, Inc. The same signature appeared on each document. When Laine brought that to the bored clerk's attention, the woman explained the signatures probably all belonged to the lawyer who filed the papers.

"You'll have to search the Articles of Incorporation filed with the Secretary of State," the clerk said. "When you get that information, then go look for the corporation's annual report. It'll list the officers and the registered agent with his name and address."

Laine hadn't counted on the process being so complicated. Just to clear her head, she went back to her office and played with numbers for a while. She added up the prices paid for the different sections of land. A total of $6,573. The next day she looked up the Articles of Incorporation for Estes Enterprises, Inc. The president of the corporation was William Franklin McCoy. Several days later, she mentioned what she'd found to PV and Pappy. "Have y'all ever heard of Mr. McCoy?"

"Billy Frank? Sure I know him," said Pappy. "He's one of Fry's flunkies. Strictly a small-time crook," he said between bites of his club sandwich. "Sounds like he took advantage of your uncle, but that's not illegal. Although with Billy Frank, you never know. There might be something bigger going on. Keep digging. Let us know what you find out."

"So far Mother hasn't come up with anything juicy," PV said, "but I'll ask her if she knows anything about Estes Enterprises." He lit a cigarette. "I'm telling you, the woman knows every businessman worth his salt. And when it comes to finding dirty laundry, do *not* let her Southern charm fool you. She's got a nose like a *bloodhound*."

Later that week Laine sat in her apartment going over some government documents when the phone rang. After 6:00 a.m. long distance rates went up, so it had to be bad news.

"Mickey and Emma are gettin' kicked off their land!" Louise's voice was high and strained.

"What happened?"

"Some man from the Army Corps of Engineers told 'em the United States government owned that land now and everybody had to be gone in 60 days. They don't understand. They didn't sell their land to the Federal Government. Your dad says they should have expected something like this, but how could they? Do you think there's anything Willie can do?"

"I don't know, Mama, but I'll talk to him."

Instead she talked to The Boys. PV was gleeful. "Oh, I think we may be on to something. Mother checked the annual report from Estes Enterprises, and Billy Frank is indeed the president, but—oh you are going love this—Sly Fry and four of his close friends actually *own* the company."

"Does your uncle have a contract or something?" Chauncey asked.

As it turned out, all Uncle Mickey or any of the other farmers had was a bill of sale, nothing in writing guaranteeing their right to stay on the land five years. That part was just a "gentlemen's agreement" between buyer and seller.

"Without something in writing, it'll be hard to prove Estes did anything illegal," Chauncey said. "But let's keep digging."

Further research showed that Estes Enterprises, Inc. had sold the land—at a considerable profit—to the Army Corps of Engineers. Furthermore, the Fry administration knew the USACE had plans to flood the area in question and turn it into a recreation lake. The worms were crawling out of the can one by one.

The one thing that continued to bother Laine was that number. Something about it was strange. $6,753. It was too precise, too specific. It wasn't until she went back five years that the number turned up. In a budget passed by the previous administration, she found an addendum that earmarked funds for the "Cherokee County Riparian Project." The amount allotted was $6,753.

She hurried over to Chauncey's office at the capitol. Chauncey lost no time in calling the rest of The Boys. Laine recapped what she knew then showed them a copy of the budget figures. For a moment no one said anything. Then Chauncey let out a Rebel yell and slapped his hand down on the desk. "Hot damn, I think we're got 'em by the short hairs now."

"Yes *indeed!*" PV said. "Last night Mother remembered one of her friends telling her in *strictest confidence, of course,* that her husband was about to make a killing in a land deal. But since it was Billy Frank she was talking about, Mother didn't take it seriously. Everybody knows the man is a *third-generation* loser and he's always *about* to make a fortune. I can't wait to tell Mother the news."

The Boys agreed the information was too good to keep, so off they went to the Henry Grady to find Willie and lay out the facts for him. "Let's hope this takes his mind off that dumb episode with the rotten eggs," said Pappy. "Since then he's been as nervous as a virgin in a whore house, excuse my French."

"On the other hand," Chauncey said seriously, "if Fry has decided to play dirty, then this may just be enough to bring him down…for good.

They found Willie in his office. Without preamble, Chauncey launched into his explanation, "Fry used one of his flunkies to buy a bunch of farms up in Cherokee county. Got 'em dirt-cheap. Then his corporation sold 'em to the Corps of Engineers for a big profit. Fry and his boys walked away with a tidy little profit.

"Now, long as both parties agree, cheating someone out of their land's not illegal, unless…" here Chauncey cast his eyes to heaven, "Oh, thank you Jesus…. unless they used *state funds* to buy it and… *and* had prior knowledge that the land was going to become valuable. And that is exactly what Fry and his buddies did and we have the documents to prove it."

"Oh yes, and Mother will be glad to testify—if it comes to that—that one of her friends told her Fry and his associates walked away with about $25,000 each. Not a bad return on $6,753 that wasn't theirs to begin with."

"I can't believe Fry didn't have sense enough to cover this up," Willie said.

Pappy grinned from ear to ear. "More like they didn't have time. They never counted on losing the primary. My guess is they thought you were just a temporary inconvenience and after the primary, they'd cover their tracks. Funny how things work out." He was clearly enjoying himself. "When this hits the papers, Fry can kiss this primary good bye!"

"What about the farmers? Are they still going to lose their land?" Laine asked.

"I'm afraid so," Chauncey said. "They sold it willingly… but since the purchase itself was illegal…"

Willie sat very still behind his desk, deep in thought. Then he smiled, "What if *I* took control of the land?"

"Willie, what are you talking about?" PV said.

"I'm talking about justice, Boys."

Willie began searching through his bookcase. "The history of Georgia law can make very interesting reading. Amazing what you pick up in law school. There's a statute from a couple hundred years ago…." He pulled a well-used volume off the shelf and started turning pages. "Ah, here it is. It's called the Headright Law. It was passed back in 1777, and it says that the leader of the executive branch can acquire disputed land and give it to individuals to 'strengthen the state.' I think giving the land back to its rightful owners would be a good way to strengthen the state, don't you? Besides, what's Fry gonna do? He and his boys got the land illegally, so none of 'em actually has a right to it."

"I know you're all fired up about this, but Son what you're proposing is like being locked in an outhouse poking at a hornets nest," Pappy said. "We defeated Fry, that was bad enough, but it was just politics. They probably figured to lick their wounds and get back into power in this primary."

Always one to avoid a *public* confrontation, PV joined in. "If you publically expose Fry *and* prosecute his administration on top of *that,* it's a declaration of war and wars have casualties, Willie. God knows we Southerners know about *that.*"

Willie stood up with such force he knocked over his desk chair. Laine and The Boys automatically took a step backward. "So what do you want me to do? Overlook the whole thing? They had me running scared, but no more. You think I'm sitting in a locked outhouse? I'm about to kick the door open and let the hornets out."

The silence that followed Willie's outburst was thick as Jell-O. His face was blood red, his eyes blazed.

Boy, you got to calm down. You're liable to give yourself a heart attack.

Then very slowly, Chauncey stood up and lit a cigarette. His voice was quiet and the corners of his mouth turned up in just the hint of a smile. "You know...I think we're going at this backward. Willie, you don't need to confront Fry. When you reclaim the land, the *Feds* are going to protest because it's their land now. You give them all this proof," he indicated the papers scattered around the office, "explain the fraud happened under Fry's administration and it's *him* they should go after."

Laine burst out laughing. She turned to Willie. "That's brilliant! The farmers get their land back, you let them keep the money they got paid for it, the Federal Government makes the case against Fry. Chauncey, it's beautiful."

As the genius of the plan dawned on the rest of The Boys, they laughed, slapped Chauncey on the back and generally acted like school kids who find out the test they didn't study for has been called off.

Somehow the information was leaked to the newspapers and reporters stormed Willie's office at the Henry Grady. "Governor, is it true that you're taking on the Federal Government to get the land back for the farmers?"

"As much as I would enjoy taking on the Feds, I don't have a dog in this fight. It's a little complicated, so I've prepared some background information for you." Laine handed out several typed sheets neatly stapled together. "When you read through these, you'll see how this terrible fraud was conceived and carried out by the previous administration. We gave copies to the government boys that show how state funds were used to defraud the Army Corps of Engineers who thought the land they bought was theirs to do with as they pleased."

"So will the state be bringing former governor Fry and his accomplices up on charges?

"No, I have no wish to add insult to injury. I think Sly Fry is going to have his hands full dealing with the Feds."

The reporters filed their stories with all due speed and the morning papers carried the headline, "Fry Administration Cited by Feds in Land Swindle." Like thousands of other folks, Fry received the news when he sat down with his morning coffee.

The Associated Press picked up the story and in moments it went out on the wire service to every major newspaper from New Orleans to New York. Fry was going down in flames as Willie stood quietly in the background and continued his fight for the little people and working folks. All across the south, voters were beginning to think Willie might just be the person they wanted to see in the White House. Willie agreed. Why should he stop with Georgia when the whole country needed him?

CHAPTER THIRTY-THREE

WEEKS LATER THE FRY LAND Scandal was still big news. As the Federal investigation proceeded, more shady deals came to life. Fry had been milking the state for years. Willie was riding high. Without any effort, he was getting national coverage, and the Fry organization was in shambles. Like the proverbial rats leaving the sinking ship, long-time supporters put as much distance between themselves and Fry as possible.

As if making up for the harshness of the winter, the calendar skipped spring and went directly to summer. By July temperatures were hitting 98 to 101 degrees every day. The primary saw voters turn out in record numbers, casting their ballots as soon as the polls opened to avoid having to contend with the stifling mid-day heat.

Laine had not been old enough to vote in the previous primary, but she was the first in line to cast her vote the second time around. As everyone expected, Willie won hands down, and although they'd all been working toward that goal, Laine and The Boys admitted it didn't live up to the excitement of a close, hard-fought race.

Throughout the next four months, Willie sauntered in and out of the House and Senate chambers talking to folks on both sides of the aisle. Everything was running smoothly; no need for him to get involved. With no opponent to fight against and no cause to fight for, Willie was seriously bored. Thanksgiving came and the inauguration was a month away.

You better find yourself something to do, Boy. You know what they say about idle minds being the devil's workshop.

At lunch one day, Willie overheard two legislators arguing about Ku Klux Klan activities in Georgia. With nothing better to do, he grabbed a handful of books out of the library and decided to do some research.

It was fairly common knowledge the original Klan was organized in 1866 shortly after the Civil War in response to Reconstruction. Its national membership fluctuated from high numbers early on then dropped significantly. However, in 1915, it reappeared in Georgia. Two events fueled the fire.

In 1913 the trial of Leo Frank, a Jewish factory manager accused of killing Mary Phagan, began in Atlanta. Because Frank was convicted on such slight evidence, the governor commuted his sentence to life. This brought about a wave of anti-Semitism and in 1915 a mob broke Frank out of jail in Marietta and lynched him.

In December of that same year, W. D. Griffith's film *The Birth of a Nation* opened in Atlanta. It portrayed the Klan as a noble organization that saved the south from the evils of Reconstruction. Willie found copies of front page stories showing a big Klan parade down Peachtree Street following the premiere. These two events sparked a resurgence of the Klan in Georgia that lasted nearly a decade.

That gave Willie an idea. "I think I'll write a series of exposés for the *Constitution* reporting on Ku Klux Klan violence in Georgia," he announced to The Boys. "In my opinion, the paper ought to publish the names of any and all public officials who are or who have been Klan members."

"Willie, have you lost your mind?" Chauncey demanded. "There's hardly any Klan activity left in Georgia. Why stir up old hatreds?"

"When I was a little kid," Pappy said, "my dad took us to the Baptist church around the corner from where we lived on Whiteford Avenue. I remember the front pews filled with Klansmen, all dressed up in their long white robes with hoods. I figured they must be some kind of rich kings or something because each one of them dropped a whole dollar bill in the collection plate."

"What exactly does that have to do with today, Pappy?"

"I'll tell you what it has to do with now," Willie broke in. "The Klan wants to confuse folks. They want people to believe they're for law enforcement, honest government, better public schools, traditional family life…but they forget to mention that's only good for white, American-born, Protestants. No immigrants, no Jews, no Catholics, no colored folks."

Chauncey stubbed out his cigarette. "Willie, the last thing you want to do is to antagonize those crazies. You don't know what they might do. Just let sleeping dogs lie, for goodness sake."

With the inauguration only weeks away, Willie finally agreed to listen to reason. However, he couldn't resist stirring things up a little, just to see if anyone would rise to the bait. He proposed hiring Louis Armstrong and the Fletcher Henderson Orchestra to play at the Inaugural Ball. Willie had been a fan of Satchmo since his early days playing in New Orleans. Much to Willie's disappointment, those in charge of the ball vetoed the idea.

Unlike the first inauguration celebration, Willie's second round of public appearances and victory celebrations was closely controlled. All functions were by-invitation-only and all went off without a hitch. By the end of January, the Shorter administration breathed a collective sigh of relief and got back to the business of running the state.

In the spring, shortly after baseball season opened, Willie called Laine into his office. "Call The Boys and tell them to get up here. I think we all need a break, so we're going to see the Atlanta Crackers play. What's more American than that? The governor and his friends watching their hometown baseball team?"

Laine hesitated. "Willie, do you think it's a good idea to be out in the middle of a crowd?"

"Now who's sounding paranoid? Laine, just between you and me, it's not regular folks I worry about. It's those candy-assed politicians, the party bosses, who have never done a day's work in their lives. They're the ones that'll get me, if anybody ever does. But it's not going to be today. Look out there. It's perfect. For once, the temperature and the humidity are down. There's even a breeze. We're simply going to have some fun. Now stop worrying."

Of course nothing Willie did was simple anymore. By the time Laine rounded up The Boys and all the State Troopers and bodyguards were loaded up, they formed a small parade. Willie rode along Ponce De Leon Avenue with the windows down and waved to people along the way. The governor had a special box in the new concrete and steel stadium. Although Spiller Field replaced the old wooden stadium, most people still called it Ponce De Leon Ball Park.

The Boys got a kick out of the fact that Laine never played baseball as a kid. "JW played for Claxton, but they didn't have girls on the team." Keeping her voice low, she leaned over to Pappy and asked, "What's that magnolia tree doing out there in the middle of the field?"

Pappy laughed. "The way I heard it, Mr. Spiller, who gave money to build the stadium, just liked it. It's way out there, not really in the middle, but if a ball lands in it, it stays in play…just adds something to the game."

The afternoon turned out to be just what Willie said it would be. Fun. In the bottom of the ninth inning, Atlanta was in the field and they were one out away from winning the game. Then the batter hit a high fly ball to left field.

Just as the Atlanta outfielder caught the ball, the wood behind Willie's head exploded. The crowd was on their feet, yelling and having a great time. None of them heard the sharp crack. But standing next to Willie, Laine recognized the sound. She'd heard too many hunting rifles to mistake it. The Boys heard it, too. Chauncey instinctively pushed Willie down. The Atlanta fans never knew anything happened; they were too caught up in the excitement of the Cracker victory. It was Pappy who carefully pried a .22 slug out of the splintered wood just inches to the right of Willie's head.

That was a close one, Boy. Looks like they really might be out to get you.

The shooter was never found and once again, The Boys decided not to make an official report, but Willie took the incident to heart. Before the day ended, he had everything moved out of his office at the Henry Grady Hotel and into an office at the capitol. He instructed Laine to move her office, too, and to clear out their corner suite on the top floor. "I'm also moving The Bread Box out of your office to a safer place."

From then on, Willie had State Troopers posted on 24-hour guard outside his office door. He kept the single room at the Henry Grady, and there too the police provided protection in rotating eight-hour shifts.

Even with all the added protection, Willie's paranoia kicked into overdrive. He ordered the windows in all his official cars replaced with bulletproof glass. He scheduled trips at one time and purposefully arrived or departed at a different time. He instructed his drivers to take different routes every day. He hired new bodyguards who were little more than armed thugs and they accompanied him everywhere. He was never alone.

The shooting at the ballpark had unnerved them all. Laine finally came to believe the danger to Willie was not exaggerated and the extra precautions were necessary. Clearly some powerful men were determined to silence Willie Shorter and end his political career.

Willie had other ideas. He settled into the beginning of his second term, but instead of the sense of wonder and possibility evident the first time around, Willie was just biding time. He still served the people of Georgia, but his focus changed. Everything he did now was calculated to draw national attention to himself and his accomplishments. Whatever the cost, he had turned his eyes toward Washington.

CHAPTER THIRTY-FOUR

AS HIS SECOND TERM GOT under way, Willie faced increased opposition to his programs. When some board or commission got in his way, his first response was to fire them and replace them with his own men. When that didn't work, he used threats and intimidation. He applied the tactic often. If the legislature opposed him, he ignored it and ruled by executive decree. In a few extreme cases, he threatened to declare martial law to insure that what Willie wanted, Willie got.

Sadly, his initial plan to do good for the people of Georgia had turned into an addiction to power. Laine and The Boys watched helplessly as Willie slipped from an I-can-do-this attitude, to an I-*will*-do-this compulsion. He used The Bread Box money to buy sheriffs, judges, and politicians. It was as easy as buying a sack of potatoes. Willie was above the law and its consequences.

Laine loved Willie and believed that deep inside he still had the greater good in mind. However, the evidence didn't support that. When she was honest with herself, she saw Willie was being corrupted by the very power she had helped him create.

At first, the change only manifested itself in Willie's public dealings. In private, Laine could almost convince herself he was still the same man she had met six years ago. Once in a while he slipped away from the State Troopers and the bodyguards to visit Laine at her apartment. Since they had no other place to meet, Laine relented and allowed him to stay overnight.

Their lovemaking changed, too. He had always been a seducer, a practiced lover. Now he was always in a hurry. Wham bam, thank you ma'am. Laine tried to talk to him about it, but Willie dominated every conversation. It was always the same subject — power and control. Anyone who disagreed with him now was his mortal enemy, someone to be destroyed. Even The Boys came under suspicion. When Laine defended them, Willie accused her of taking their side in a plot against him.

Things grew worse. Whereas Willie had started out persuading people to help him, now he used force to get his way. When he wanted something, he got it and he cared less and less about how it happened. If he decided to build a clinic and a farmer refused to sell his land to the state, Willie took it by eminent domain. It was the very kind of thing Laine had watched him fight against so courageously in the beginning. Like seeing a sand castle being washed away by the waves, Willie's friends watched him self-destruct and were powerless to stop the process.

In desperation, PV came up with a possible solution. In the same way he considered a scandal good for politics, he considered a party good for morale. "We absolutely *must* lighten things up around here. It's as gloomy as a morgue. Depressing. So, mark your calendars for Valentine's Day. I'm going to throw the most elaborate gala this town has ever seen to celebrate Mother's 96th birthday. The affair will be held at the Piedmont Driving Club and I guarantee it will be *the* social event of 1929. Get your tuxes out of mothballs, Boys."

"PV, the Piedmont Driving Club won't admit Jews, even as guests," Pappy said. "What are you going to do about Sol?"

"That will *not* be a problem on *this* occasion. I have taken care of it, or rather Mother has," PV said. "She spoke to the Board of Directors and made it *clear* there will be hell to pay if *anyone* makes a fuss. And Amanda Stratham backed her up. I can assure you *nobody* is going to take on those two pillars of Atlanta society."

PV's announcement seemed to have the desired effect. Even Willie got caught up in the excitement of a grand event. After all, there would be lots of reporters and lots of publicity.

Out of the blue one morning, Willie came into Laine's office and gave her an exaggerated courtly bow. "Miss Laine, I am here to request your presence at the ball celebrating Mother Ledbetter's birthday."

Laine laughed. It was a relief to hear the old Willie again. "Of course I'll be there."

"Madam, you wound me. I did not mean to imply that I was simply requesting your presence at this event; my intention was to have you accompany me. I am presenting myself as your escort. That is, if you will accept my invitation."

"You mean to go with you...as your...date or something?"

"Yes indeed, as my date.... with a little "something" later on perhaps. Will you do me this honor?"

Laine stood up, came around the desk and gave him her best courtesy. "Yes, kind sir, I would be delighted to be your date..."

"And later...?"

"And later I thought perhaps we might go for a roller-coaster ride," she said with exaggerated sweetness.

Laine felt a little like Cinderella finally going to the ball, but she wasn't quite as naive as she used to be. She knew when Willie walked into the Piedmont Driving Club with her on his arm he was flaunting his power in front of the cream of old Atlanta society. In other words, "This is what I want and if you don't like the way I live my life, to hell with you!"

Another wild card was Sly Fry and his cronies. Although they were under Federal indictment, they were still free to come and go as they liked. That caused some concern in the Shorter administration. However, there hadn't been any sign of trouble since the incident at Spiller Field so maybe they were worrying too much.

As it turned out, Fry was no longer the real danger. The threat went much higher than that. In his years in office, and with the Cherokee County land scandal, Willie had indeed generated a lot of support not just in Georgia, but across the entire south. The national party bosses now saw him as a real threat.

In the Deep South, Democratic candidates slugged it out during the primary and the last one standing claimed the victory. On the national level, it was a different ball game. The last thing the Democratic Party needed was some upstart from the south attending the National Convention and splitting the party vote to win a place on the national ballot. The party needed every single vote firmly behind their favorite. They needed a candidate they could control, and that definitely was not Willie Shorter. Their political lives depended on winning and they were prepared to go to any length to see that nothing and no one upset their chances.

However sometimes ignorance truly is bliss. Under the impression that things had calmed down, Laine turned her thoughts to getting ready for the ball. "Miss Amanda? I'm sorry to call so late, but I need some advice. Willie, Governor Shorter, has asked me to be his official…date for Mrs. Ledbetter's birthday party. I know all the really important people will be there. Of course I want to go…but I don't want to embarrass anyone… especially myself. What do you think I should do?"

"My Dear, if your parents were going to be attending this party, would you be embarrassed for them to see you with Governor Shorter?"

"No, Ma'am. Well, maybe a little. A while back, Mama asked me what was really going on between Willie and me. I told her I wouldn't lie to her, so not to ask me questions unless she wanted to hear the truth. She dropped the subject and we've never talked about it again. She and Dad both like Willie, but they're old fashioned about some things."

"The question then becomes what you think of yourself. If you have made peace with your relationship and you can live with that, then by all means go and have a wonderful time. However, if you are going to be escorted by the governor, I must ask if you have something appropriate to wear?"

Laine planned to take the trolley up from the capitol to Davison's on her lunch hour, go through the racks and find some gown to wear. Maybe something on sale.

"That will simply *not* do, "Miss Amanda announced. "Off the rack is not acceptable. We will go shopping," she continued. "I'll pick you up tomorrow at 9:00."

The next morning the Silver Cloud was waiting in front of Laine's apartment. First Miss Amanda directed the driver to drop them at the Regency Salon at Rich's. Nothing met Miss Amanda's approval.

Back in the car, the next stop was Regenstein's where they sat and drank tea while an elegant saleswoman brought out selections. Again, nothing pleased Miss Amanda.

Next it was off to Froshin's. Here they sipped sherry in a private sitting room and finally Miss Amanda chose a long, black dress. Nothing special as far as Laine could tell.

"Try it on, Dear."

The dress didn't have a price tag and Laine was afraid to ask the cost. Oh well, she had saved the rent money from her house and she would probably never be invited to the Piedmont Driving Club again.

The dress hadn't looked like much on its padded satin hanger, but the transformation from hanger to body was magic. Tiny silver and gold threads were woven into the fabric and they reflected the light as Laine turned from side to side. The saleswoman brought in satin shoes. With two shiny combs, she pinned Laine's hair away from her face. Sparkling earrings and a necklace completed the ensemble.

In a daze, Laine walked out to show Miss Amanda. "Ah yes, I believe that will do." She finished her sherry and turned to the saleslady. "We'll take the dress, the shoes, and we'll need a pair of evening gloves. I will, of course, replace the jewelry with something from my collection when I get home."

As the chauffeur drove them back to Laine's apartment, Laine said, "Miss Amanda if you tell me what the dress and everything cost, I'll pay you back."

The older woman smiled. "I don't think so, Dear. Consider it a gift."

Laine started to protest, but Miss Amanda raised her index finger…a gesture Laine remembered from her first meeting. She simply nodded and said thank you.

So it was that at the birthday party of the decade, Miss Catherine Elaine Becker, wearing an original Coco Chanel, and Governor Jonathan William Shorter, in white tie and tails, made their entrance at the Piedmont Driving Club.

Damn, if you don't clean up nice! I'm proud of you, Boy.

The photographers loved them. Everyone applauded when they walked into the main ballroom. For the first time, Laine got a taste of what it was like to be adored. It wasn't half bad.

Mr. and Mrs. Stratham also made a handsome couple, but it was Mother Ledbetter who was truly the belle of the ball. She wore a bright red chiffon concoction, which she admitted, was much too young for her. "But it's my birthday. I'm 96 and I've earned the right to wear anything I damn well please," she announced after copious amounts of champagne.

While attention was focused on the Birthday Girl, Laine finally got to live out her fantasy of dancing in Willie's arms, in a Technicolor setting filled with beautiful people, laughter and music. It was better than any cotillion she had ever imagined standing in the dust and noise of Claxton Mill.

At midnight, everyone sang Happy Birthday. Then Mother Ledbetter took a deep breath and blew out all 96 candles on the first try. She received a thunderous round of applause. At her request, the orchestra played several Viennese waltzes and she danced in a haze of red chiffon with a number of distinguished men, both young and old. Willie waited his turn to dance with her and finally she danced with PV. After their dance, she acknowledged the applause, breathlessly thanked her guests, then turned the festivities over to PV and bid the assembled group *adieu.*

Like the wind changing the leaves on an olive tree from green to silver, the energy in the room shifted. Now, it was Willie's turn and he quickly became the center of attention. Laine, who had no wish to be in that spotlight, stood with The Boys watching the long line of people waiting to speak to the governor.

PV fanned himself with a handkerchief. "I swear Mother will be the *death* of me yet. I do not know *where* that woman gets all her energy. It has to come from *her side* of the family. Dad and I could *never* keep up with her."

"Hell of a party, PV," Chauncey said. "The governor seems to be having the time of his life. Nice to see him that way again."

And he was. Willie loved seeing the amazed look on people's faces when he shook their hands, called them by name and asked about their families. He hadn't lost the touch. He was surrounded by an adoring crowd. He told stories, laughed at jokes, patted men on their backs, and kissed women on their cheeks. It was Willie at his best.

Pappy glanced around the room. Willie's bodyguards were slouching by the door looking like cheap overstuffed furniture in their formal suits. PV shook his head, "Useless, totally useless." The room was full, the music and cigarette smoke floated up to the chandeliers, glasses clinked. God was in his heaven and all was right in Willie Shorter's world.

Chauncey stifled a yawn. "He's gonna be here 'till dawn shaking hands with everybody. I've had enough celebration for one night. I'm going home."

Pappy agreed. "It's been a long night. I'll be glad to get home and get out of this monkey suit. Laine, you want us to drop you off at your apartment?"

"No, I'll wait. My mama always said, 'Go home with the one who brung you.'"

"Entirely proper, My Dear," said PV. "However, I'd find myself a comfortable chair if I were you. Looks like this could go on for some time. Good night boys, I'm off to have a word with the kitchen staff."

Laine said good night and watched as The Boys made their way through the crowd, gathered up their wives and then went to say good night to Willie. She also saw the tall, red-haired man standing in line with the other well-wishers waiting to speak with the governor.

Willie looked the man in the eye, smiled and extended his hand. But instead of taking the governor's hand, the man leaned forward, his face contorted with rage. Then Laine saw the gun in his right hand. He fired. Two bright flashes. Two shots point blank into Governor Willie Shorter's body.

CHAPTER THIRTY-FIVE

FOR A MOMENT, TIME STOPPED. All sound ceased. The Boys froze. Willie looked puzzled. Like a wild animal's cry, they heard the gunman snarl something about getting even. Still nothing moved except the bright red blood stain that spread slowly across Willie's white shirt. The governor put his hand to his chest, pulled it away and watched as a drop of blood dripped from his fingers to the floor.

Then, as suddenly as it had stopped, the world came chaotically to life. "Gun!!!"

Men ducked, women screamed.

"Governor's shot," Chauncey shouted.

The crowd scattered in every direction. Some people tried to get out, others ran toward Willie.

"Stop that guy." But nobody knew who the shooter was and in a crowd of men all wearing tuxes, they all looked the same.

"Red hair, there. Don't let him get away."

Finally the gunman came into focus. He pushed his way through the startled crowd seeing nothing but the French doors that led to freedom. Everything and everyone in his path was knocked aside. Tables fell, dishes shattered.

The noise and excitement woke the bodyguards from their stupor and they reverted to their rural roots. They were hunters, concealed, waiting for a chance to make the first kill of the day. Clear-eyed now, they identified their prey, exposed and trying to escape. They pulled their weapons, aimed and fired. The assassin crumpled and fell forward.

The State Patrol in their dress uniforms had been invited more for show than for protection, but they immediately converged on the fallen gunman and emptied *their* weapons into his body.

On the other side of the room, the crowd around Willie expanded and contracted like a living organism.

"Move back."

"Give him air."

"Get a doctor."

Laine was the first to get to Willie. He seemed to be surprised that his hand was covered with blood. Still on his feet, he reached for Laine to steady himself. "He shot me, Laine," he said in a voice that sounded like a child who had been unjustly chastised for an unknown sin.

You hang in there, Boy. You're a fighter, you'll make it. Just hold on.

Laine supported Willie the best she could as they slowly sank to the floor. She sat and cradled his head in her lap.

Willie looked up into her eyes, "Why'd he do that? I just wanted to make things better…"

In the background Laine heard The Boys shouting orders. "Get back, give him air. Is there a doctor in the room? Someone call an ambulance."

Dr. Lawrence T. Williams, one of Atlanta's top surgeons, and an old friend of Mother Ledbetter, was waiting for his car to be brought to the entrance when someone rushed him back inside. The crowd parted like the Red Sea to let him through. He dropped to one knee beside the wounded man. At the same moment, a waiter appeared with a stack of white linen napkins. When he saw the front of Willie's shirt covered in blood, he turned away and retched. Some quick thinking person rescued the napkins. Another club employee handed the doctor a first aid kit.

"Does anyone have a knife or a pair of scissors?" Dr. Williams asked. Men fumbled in the pockets of their tuxes, but came up empty. Wiping his mouth with one of the napkins, the young waiter pulled out a pocketknife. "Will this help?"

Using the small, sharp knife, the doctor cut away Willie's shirt and examined the wounds. One shot had gone through his right shoulder. It didn't look too serious. That could wait. The other bullet had entered his body just under his rib cage.

The doctor grabbed the linen napkins and pressed them over the chest wound. "Keep the pressure on here," he said to Laine. She obeyed. "We need to get this man to a hospital immediately," he quickly bandaged the wound in Willie's shoulder. With one wound taken care of, the doctor stood and looked over the crowd. "Where's the damn ambulance?" he demanded.

Willie still didn't seem to grasp the seriousness of the situation. He watched as his blood slowly seeped through and soaked the monogrammed napkins. "Thanks, Doc. Glad you showed up." Then he turned to Laine. "Why'd the fellow do that, Laine? Don't even know the guy. Never saw him before…" His words were a little slurred but he was conscious. "What'd I ever do to him?" Laine had no answers.

It seemed like an eternity until they heard the sirens. The medics burst through the door and quickly lifted Willie onto a stretcher. Normally Dr. Williams practiced at Piedmont Hospital, but for some reason, the ambulance driver took Willie to the much smaller Davis-Fischer Sanatorium at Peachtree and Linden Avenue. It was perhaps easier to reach, but not nearly so well equipped.

The Boys and Laine all tried to get into the ambulance with Willie. Laine stayed by his side, Pappy bullied his way into the passenger seat opposite the driver and the rest came behind with the State Police. Dr. Williams followed in his own car. When he realized the ambulance driver wasn't headed toward Piedmont Hospital, he swore, but there was nothing to be done about it. He followed the ambulance to Davis-Fischer.

As the ambulance pulled up to the emergency entrance, the crowd traveling with Willie converged on the emergency room.

They found a very nervous young resident, Dr. David Sinclair, on duty. The police had sent word ahead and the young man did his best to take charge, but his experience did not cover dealing with a governor who might very well be dying.

"Put him in here," he indicated a small treatment room. The Boys and Laine crowded around Willie as he lay on the narrow table. A quick examination told Dr. Sinclair the first order of business was to remove the remaining bullet and make sure there was no serious internal damage.

"You can't all stay in here," he said.

"Listen, Son, we'll give you room to do your job, but we're staying," Chauncey announced in a voice that brooked no disagreement.

Trying to establish his authority, Dr. Sinclair said, "Family… it should just be family…"

With none of his usual Southern politeness, PV fairly snarled, "We *are* his family. Now get on with it."

Although his pulse was weak, Willie was conscious and he seemed to be enjoying the exchange. He smiled at Laine who was holding his hand. "They're a pretty stubborn bunch, Doc."

The doctor ignored Willie. Very slowly he said, "If you want me to save this man, get out!"

That finally got their attention. Laine kissed Willie on the cheek and they all cleared the room. She watched helplessly as Willie was rolled down the hall toward the operating room.

"What happened to the doctor from the party?" Pappy asked. No one knew.

Not more than half a mile away, Dr. Williams' car had been hit by a drunk driver. The doctor wasn't injured, but the damage to his car made it impossible to drive. He finally hitched a ride to the hospital, but the delay was to have unforeseen consequences.

Minutes after Willie was wheeled off to surgery, the corridors outside the emergency room began to fill with reporters, loyal supporters, and dissenters. Once the reporters were told the governor was in surgery, they made a dash to find phones and call in the news to their editors. After that, they settled in to await the outcome.

It took Dr. Williams nearly fifteen minutes to get to the hospital. He was not happy to learn that an intern was attending to the governor. He quickly explained about the accident then strode off in the direction they had taken Willie.

Nearly an hour later, Dr. Sinclair and Dr. Williams reappeared. Sinclair's surgical gown was limp with sweat, his face was drawn, but his step was confident. "He made it."

A jubilant shout went up from the assembled crowd. Reporters demanded details, but that was all the young doctor would say. Finally Dr. Williams added, "We are cautiously optimistic. The next 48 hours will tell."

That became the official word. Reporters ran back to telephones to file their stories. Within the next four hours, Extras from newspapers all over the state were printed and newsboys were selling them as fast as Georgia boiled peanuts on a hot summer day.

When she first heard the doctors' report, Laine whispered, "Thank God." Then she looked at the doctors' faces and knew that wasn't the end of the story. They ushered Laine and The Boys into a small office. "He's out of danger at the moment, but make no mistake about it, he's not out of the woods yet," Dr. Williams said. "He's lost a lot of blood. As we told you, the next 48 hours are crucial. If he makes it past that, I think he'll pull through."

"When can we see him?" Pappy asked.

"He's in intensive care and he's resting right now. My advice is go home, get some rest, try to eat something. You can see him in the morning let's say 9:00. There is absolutely nothing you can do here tonight. Go home! Tomorrow is going to be a long day."

The word spread fast and the crowds slowly began to disperse. Several reporters refused to leave just in case something happened. This was the story of a lifetime and they weren't going to take a chance on missing it.

The State Troopers made sure that everyone who came with them got a ride back to the Piedmont Driving Club. They took Laine directly home.

In the pre-dawn hours, people who rose early turned on their radios to the startling news. They called others and within no time people all over the state were huddled around radios. They were shocked and outraged. When news came that the governor was out of danger, the state seemed to breathe a collective sigh of relief.

Of course, not everyone felt that way. There were some people in Georgia and others outside the state who heard the news and hoped that Willie's condition might change and fate would find a way to remove the blight of Willie Shorter from their lives.

The *Atlanta Constitution's* regular edition carried a front page, three-column picture of Laine holding Willie's head in her lap. The blood-soaked napkins were clearly visible. The banner head stated, "Governor Shot. Unknown Assassin Killed." The details were sketchy. There was no identification on the killer's body and no way of knowing what his motive had been. Most people were shocked. Some were not.

As the State Troopers let Laine off at her apartment, she saw JW sitting on the front steps. He stood up and wrapped her in his arms. She hadn't cried until that moment, and once she started, she couldn't stop. "He looked so helpless, so confused. He asked me why and I couldn't tell him anything. I couldn't do anything." JW gave her his handkerchief and waited. Eventually she dried her eyes and they went into the apartment together.

"Is he gonna be alright, Laine?"

"The doctors said we just have to wait and see. They sent us all home. I guess we'll know more tomorrow."

"Can I do anything?"

"Not really." For the first time Laine seemed to be fully aware of JW's presence. "Aren't you in the middle of exams?"

He nodded.

"Look, I'm really glad you came, but don't do anything that's going to mess up your education. Willie's in good hands and all we can do is wait. I'm going to try to sleep a little and then go back to the hospital. I'll call Mama and Dad. Now you better head back to school." She hugged her brother once more and sent him on his way.

CHAPTER THIRTY-SIX

AS SHE TURNED AROUND, LAINE caught a glimpse of herself in the hall mirror. There was no trace of the Cinderella girl she had been the night before. With a deep sigh, she unzipped the dress and left it on the floor where it landed. The blood hardly showed on the black dress, but Laine knew it was there. She shuddered when she remembered the warm, sticky feeling as the blood soaked through the thin material onto her skin and she would never forget the sharp, metallic smell.

She put on her bathrobe and before she did anything else, called her parents. Since they always got up early, they might have already heard the news, but she needed to talk to them anyway. Other than the fact that Willie had been shot and was being treated she didn't know what else to say.

When Laine hung up the phone, she went to take a shower. For the next half hour, she stood under the stream of hot water trying to wash away her weariness and the strain of the night's events. Willie was going to be all right. He was strong enough to get through this. He was a fighter, he would make it. He was much too young to die. She repeated all the right things to herself, but try as she might, she could not rid herself of the tight knot of fear lodged deep in her chest.

She was bone tired, but couldn't sleep. After her shower, she dressed in her normal work clothes and turned on the radio. The announcer on WSB was talking about the shooting and although she knew more than he obviously did, Laine sat down to listen. Following the doctor's orders, she grabbed a bowl of cereal, which she forced herself to eat. Several hours later she was jolted awake by a knock on the door.

She opened it to find Pappy looking tired, but more at ease in his usually baggy pants and tweed jacket. "The rest of The Boys are down in the car. You want to ride to the hospital with us?"

She took five minutes to get ready. Then she grabbed her purse and coat and followed Pappy downstairs. PV's big Packard was parked by the curb. Pappy held the front door open for her and she got in between him and PV. Chauncey, Joe Laundry, and Sol Goldman were sitting in the back seat.

No one said much on the ride to the hospital. "I can tell you one thing," Chauncey finally said, "I'm sure glad he's gonna be OK. He really had me scared last night. It wasn't till I got home and tried to go to sleep that I realized how little we know about how Willie runs things. He's got deals going in all directions. Not to mention The Bread Box money. By the way, anybody know where he moved the money to?" No one did.

When they arrived at Davis-Fischer, there were still a few reporters hanging around. "What's the latest on the governor? Is he really out of danger? Can we get an interview? Do they know any more about the guy who shot him? What was the motive? Who's gonna run the state while the governor's laid up?"

Joe Laundry was all for ignoring them, but PV stopped to give them what little information there was. The reporters scribbled away, but in truth there was nothing new to report.

Although the small hospital had fewer than 50 rooms, the staff had set up a makeshift VIP suite for Willie on the second floor. Doctors and nurses moved efficiently up and down the halls. When the head nurse, Elsa Honeycutt, saw the delegation, she directed them to Willie's room. "He's been expecting you. He asked us to show you in right away."

Willie's room was filled with flowers. He was hooked up to an IV drip and he was pale, but otherwise he looked pretty good considering what he had been through.

Laine went directly to Willie's side. He reached out and took her hand.

"How're you feeling, Villie?" Sol asked.

"I've been better, but I reckon I'll live," Willie said. "Least that's what the docs tell me."

"Lots of flowers," Pappy observed for want of something better to say.

"Yeah, looks like a damn funeral home," Willie answered. No one laughed. "Come on, lighten up. Looking at your faces makes me think I might really be in trouble." His voice was weak and talking was an obvious effort.

Obediently everyone smiled. "You certainly had us going for a while there last night," PV said. "Mother was *not* happy to have missed all the excitement."

Willie smiled.

"I reckon you've got everybody in the state praying for you, Boss…. half of 'em hoping you'll get better and the other half hoping you'll die," Chauncey said.

Every head in the room snapped in his direction. PV started to reprimand him, but Willie laughed, which lead to a coughing fit.

"Damnation, Chauncey, don't make me laugh. Hurts like hell." He took several deep breaths. "Lord, I'd love to see their faces…Bet Fry and his cronies cried in their Wheaties this morning when they heard I was still kicking." More coughing, which brought Nurse Honeycutt on the run.

"Here, here, no more of that," she said coming to Willie's aid. "I think you had better leave…"

Willie patted her hand. "Come on now, Nurse Honey, let them stay. I promise to make Chauncey stop telling me jokes. How's that?"

In spite of herself, she smiled. Willie could be very persuasive when he put his mind to it. "All right, but just ten minutes. That's it. No more." Nurse Honeycutt was a pretty woman and her manner and voice were warm, motherly. But, like any good mother, it was clear when she set limits she expected them to be observed.

Reminds me of my wife, Nette. Too bad you never had a chance to meet her.

"Yes Ma'am," Willie said with a wink. Then he turned to The Boys, "Do you know who shot me? Police find out why he did it?"

They hesitated. "The bodyguards didn't exactly conduct a lengthy *interrogation*, if you know what I mean…" said PV.

"Bagged him on the spot," Joe said.

"He vas carrying no ID. Probably never know who or why. Just some *meshuggener*, a crazy man with an ax to grind," said Sol.

Willie closed his eyes and The Boys exchanged glances. Willie had always been in charge. Seeing him like this was a new experience and they didn't quite know how to handle it.

"Thought you might want to see the first editions," Pappy said and laid the newspapers out on the bed. In addition to the *Atlanta Constitution*, he brought the *Macon Telegraph*, the *Savannah Morning News*, the *Columbus Ledger-Enquirer*, plus the New Orleans *Times Picayune*, the Chicago *Tribune*, the Houston *Chronicle* and *The New York Times*. "They're all here, Boss."

Willie couldn't resist the siren call of publicity. He opened his eyes and pulled himself up so he could see better. As he picked up each paper, a big smile crossed his face. "Well, damn, if I didn't make the front page all over. If I'd known getting shot would get this much coverage, I'd have arranged it myself long ago." Willie started to cough again and Laine handed him a glass of water. Nurse Honeycutt came into the room and stood protectively at the bedside of her patient. Out of Willie's line of vision, she pointed to her watch.

Willie looked up at Laine. "Sorry I ruined your evening, Miss Becker."

"As long as you promise never to do it again, I forgive you." She tried to keep her voice light and confident.

The Boys continued to talk, telling Willie what was going on and how the crowds of supporters were still waiting outside the hospital.

"I know you're enjoying all this attention, Governor, but you need your rest." To emphasize her point, Nurse Honeycutt gently shooed everyone out the door and down the hall out of sight of the governor's room.

Chauncey waited until she went to attend to another patient and then walked back to talk to Willie. His eyes were closed, so Chauncey lowered his voice so as not to startle him. "Chief, you awake?"

Without opening his eyes, Willie smiled slightly. "Heard you open the door. Yes, I'm awake."

"Well, I hate to bring it up at a time like this, but when you moved The Bread Box from the hotel, where'd you put it? We wanta make sure the wrong people don't get their hands on it"

Chauncey wondered if Willie had heard him. "The other reason I'm asking, Boss, is that we'd like to do a little investigating before the trail gets cold and we might need some... persuasion money."

Willie didn't seem to hear him.

"Chief?" Chauncey prompted.

"What? Oh yeah, the money. It's safe, don't worry. Nobody's gonna find it..." His voice trailed off.

"Can you just tell me...?

"Don't worry...I'll go over all that stuff tomorrow... tomorrow."

CHAPTER THIRTY-SEVEN

LATER THAT AFTERNOON, LAINE QUIETLY let herself back into Willie's room and took her place beside his bed. He slept most of the time but occasionally he would wake up and talk for a few minutes, then he'd drift off to sleep again. Dr. Williams came by to check on his patient several times and was talking to Laine when Dr. Sinclair came in. The doctors excused themselves and conferred for several minutes out of earshot in the hallway.

About 5:00 p.m., The Boys came back. They were all standing around the room when Willie put his hand to his chest. "God, my heart's racing. Thing's flying," he said to Laine, his eyes wide and frightened.

"Get Nurse Honeycutt," she said.

The nurse entered the room almost immediately, followed by a nurse's aide. Honeycutt took a quick look at Willie. "Get Dr. Williams quick." The aide ran down the hall trying to find the doctor. With practiced efficiency, Nurse Honeycutt hurried to Willie's bedside and took his blood pressure. No one breathed. The look on the nurse's face told them something was seriously wrong.

In a moment, Dr. Williams appeared. "His pulse is climbing and his blood pressure's dropping, Doctor."

"Might be internal bleeding," Williams said. "Get me a catheter." The young nurse disappeared out the door again. "Out, all of you out!" Banished to the hall, Laine and The Boys strained to hear what the doctor was saying.

When Dr. Williams inserted the catheter, it showed blood in Willie's urine, which confirmed his theory. "My guess is the bullet nicked the renal duct in the kidney. I'll have to go back in. Nurse, start running blood tests. We need to be prepared for transfusions. Start with that group hanging outside the door."

Glad for the chance to do something constructive, The Boys and Laine followed another nurse to an examining room where she efficiently checked blood types and drew blood from each of them. "Do we all match?" Chauncey asked.

"The governor's lucky. He's AB positive, he's a universal recipient. It means he can receive blood from any donor and from what the doctors are saying, he's going to need it."

"What?!"

"Oh, I mean…I overheard…I'm sure I was mistaken. Please just forget I said that, I'm so sorry…I…" She hurried out of the room.

Rumors flew around the hospital and in no time the press got wind of a major story in the making. Each one wanted a scoop for their newspaper, wanted to be the first to file their story. So in the absence of hard facts, they went with what they had. Bits of gossip, the worried expressions on the faces of Laine and The Boys. The *Constitution* put out another Extra. "Governor Back in Surgery. Outcome Uncertain." The Associated Press wire service picked up the story, but this time Willie wasn't aware of their interest and attention.

Laine found a phone booth in one of the waiting rooms and called her family in Ford Crossing again. She hated to be the bearer of bad tidings, but she didn't want them to hear the news on the radio first.

"The last we heard, he was doin' alright, Laine. What happened?"

"I don't know, Dad. He was sleeping on and off and then he said his heart was racing so I called the doctor. Seems like he's been bleeding inside and they're operating again to see if they can fix whatever's gone wrong…. They're working on him now and they've been in there a long time…Can I talk to Mama a minute?"

Louise took the phone. "Lainie, I know all about...I mean I know how much you...love Willie, and we do too. We're praying for him and the rest of the church folks—black and white—are praying, too. Is there anything else we can do?"

"No Ma'am, I don't think so. Oh Mama, we all thought he was doing fine. And now...what'll we do if he...." Laine's voice trailed off.

"You just keep praying, Child, that's all any of us can do now. It's in the hands of the Lord and we gotta have faith that he knows best about these things."

Laine hung up, but she didn't feel comforted. Leaving things in the hands of the Lord made her feel helpless. As far as she could tell, the Lord had no idea how important Willie Shorter was. He had no idea how many people depended on him. He had no idea how many things Willie still had to do. She didn't think God had any idea how much she loved Willie or how empty her life would be without him.

Dr. Williams, Dr. Sinclair and a hastily assembled team of doctors worked on Willie for more than four hours. In the end, they admitted Willie was beyond their ability to help him. Try as they might, they could not undo the damage that had already been done. Even with massive transfusions, the governor had lost too much blood.

Exhausted and covered in sweat, Dr. Williams came out to announce to Laine, The Boys, the state and the nation that at six minutes past 9:00 in the evening, Governor Jonathan William Shorter had been officially pronounced dead. It was just over 24 hours since he had been shot and two months past his 36th birthday.

As soon as they heard the news, the reporters rushed off in all directions like a startled covey of quail. Their patience had been rewarded with the biggest story of the year. They descended on every pay phone in the hospital and when nothing else was available they barged into offices and used any phone they could find.

Once they were gone, Laine and The Boys stood stunned and silent. No one moved. It was as if any movement, any action at all would somehow make the awful words they had just heard real. Finally, they found their coats and hats and started to leave. "Laine, can we take you home?" PV asked.

"I don't want to leave Willie."

"There's nothing you can do for him now," he said gently.

"I know, but I just want to stay a little while longer."

Slowly The Boys turned and walked out into the night.

When Laine was alone, memories began flying through her head so fast they made her dizzy. She sat down quickly, holding on to the arms of a chair. The nurse's aide who had been in Willie's room noticed her.

"Are you all right? You look pale. Just sit still, I'll get you a glass of water." Laine closed her eyes and willed the room to stop spinning. When the nurse returned, she took the water, drank it, and handed the glass back with no awareness of what she was doing. "My name's Rose. Do you want me to call someone?" Laine didn't respond. "Miss? Miss?" She touched Laine.

"What?"

"Do you want me to call someone?"

At first Laine didn't seem to understand the question then she shook her head. "My brother's at Georgia Tech, but I don't know how to… No, there's no one… I'll be all right." The nurse started to walk away, "Excuse me, Nurse, do you know where they've taken the governor?"

The young nurse hesitated then said in a whisper, "I can let you see him for just a minute, but that's all or I'll get in serious trouble."

Laine followed her down a flight of stairs and into a small bare room, number 103. Willie's body lay on an examining table. The nurse turned back the sheet. Laine stifled a cry. Willie looked so young and peaceful, almost boyish. She stepped to the table and touched his cheek. Cold. "I love you," she whispered.

"Miss, you have to go now."

With tears in her eyes, Laine nodded her thanks. Somehow she managed to get back upstairs, find a chair in a dark corner and sit down. She felt like an eggshell, so fragile that if anything or anyone touched her she would crumble. She had no idea how long she sat there but finally the young nurse appeared again.

"I hope you don't mind, but I called a cab for you. You really ought to go home." Laine allowed herself to be led outside where she got into the cab and gave the driver her home address.

CHAPTER THIRTY-EIGHT

ONCE IN HER APARTMENT, LAINE sat on the couch in the dark with her hands in her lap, her ankles crossed, her eyes unfocused. The bright flashes of memory started again, flickering by like images on a piece of film running off a spool. Disconnected, disjointed, distorted.

Willie's blue eyes through the screen door. Willie covered with lint inside the mill. His hands on her body. The Claxton check lying on the kitchen table. Dancing in the dirt. People's eager faces. Willie's eyes glazed over from too many numbers. Headlines, "Willie Wins." "Governor Shot." Governor Dead." Peeling wallpaper. A huge fan turning in lazy circles. Willie waving from a car. Opening a clinic. Serving school lunches. The magnolia tree at the ballpark. A roller coaster. The smell of rotten eggs. Bar-b-que. Willie in white tie and tails. Willie's blood.

It couldn't be over. It had to be a mistake, a bad dream. Willie couldn't be dead… But he was.

***

While Laine sat in the dark at home, back at the hospital the nurse's aide who had called a taxi for her ministered to the final needs of Willie Shorter.

Several years before, Rose Lorenzo had left a mill in Roswell, Georgia, and entered nursing school in Atlanta. Like Laine she was another smart, ambitious, hard-working mill-town girl. By putting in extra hours studying, she managed to stay at the top of her class. Her fellow nurses liked her, but they also considered her a bit too serious to be much fun. Most of the time she had her head in a book.

On the night Laine had been attending a glittering party looking like a princess in her black Chanel dress, Rose, in her starched white uniform, had reported for duty on the late shift at Davis-Fischer. As a nurse's aide, she performed routine duties. However, no matter how small they were, she made sure she did everything just right.

Her normal shift began at 11:00 p.m. and ended at 7:00 in the morning. Student nurses usually got the late duty but Rose didn't mind. She didn't have any family or a boyfriend in Atlanta and things were almost always quiet so she could count on undisturbed time to get some extra studying done. But not last night.

The entire hospital had been in an uproar. She'd heard the commotion in the emergency room about 1:30 a.m. "The governor's been shot!" At first she thought one of the interns was playing a joke, but the stricken looks on the faces around her quickly told her that wasn't the case. Why, she wondered, would anyone want to hurt that nice-looking, energetic young man who had done so much for the state? Rose heard about the new clinics in the rural areas, and it was her dream to get a job in one so she could work close to her family in Roswell.

When word came down that the bullet had been successfully removed and the governor was resting comfortably, Rose was proud of the work the doctors in "her" hospital had done.

But that was yesterday. Today everyone reported for duty early. The hospital was in an uproar again because the governor had been taken back into surgery. As his time in the operating room lengthened, doctors and nurses glanced at clocks and watches and shook their heads. The procedure was taking much too long.

When it was all over; the word that he was dead spread like an epidemic through the hospital corridors. Rose was in the waiting room when Dr. Williams made the announcement to the group of men and the young woman who were with the governor when he was brought in. Strange that he had no family with him. She knew she shouldn't have taken the young woman to see the governor's body, but she looked so sad, so alone. Rose hoped she got home all right.

Now the governor was dead and Rose had a job to do. In almost all tragedies, there are bit players who work mostly behind the scenes, fulfilling vital functions no one sees or appreciates.

Rose straightened her shoulders and with her usual efficiency walked briskly down the hall toward room 103. This wasn't her first experience with death. She knew the procedure and, once again, she followed all the rules. She had notified the morgue to expect the body, but while the governor was still at Davis-Fischer, he was her responsibility. It was her job to bathe him and dress him in a clean gown. She saw this as the last act of nursing care and she performed her duties with great respect for the patients who died.

Rose was a devout Catholic from a big Italian family. Since the governor was admitted to the hospital, she had stopped by the chapel whenever she had a minute to light a candle and say a special prayer for him. Rose believed in prayer.

Now as she walked down the hall, she thought she saw the call light over the door to Room 103 flash. Her heart stopped. That couldn't be. She had already been in the room and she knew the man who lay there was dead. Then she saw the light flash again. No doubt about it.

Could the doctors have made a mistake? They said the governor had slipped into a coma and been taken back into surgery. They said he died on the table. Could they have been wrong? Could her prayers have been answered? Could he somehow still be alive? "Dear God, let it be so," Rose said aloud. She made the Sign of the Cross and ran down the hall to open the door.

She slowly approached the table and looked down. The man lying there looked so serene. Younger than she remembered from his pictures in the papers. Against all hope, she looked closer; he was not breathing. She took the governor's wrist, he was cold. He had no pulse. Finally she forced herself to look closely at his face. He wore the peaceful mask of the dead. But she had seen the call light, she was sure of it.

This couldn't be happening. Suddenly she was afraid. She looked around to see if someone else was in the room. Then she glanced at the floor, and her heart sank. There, lying at her feet was the call button. When it fell off the side of the bed, the impact activated the flashing light. Quickly she picked it up, turned it off and tied it securely to the bed rail. She gently patted the governor's arm. "It's all right now, I'm here. Don't worry, I'll take care of you."

Rose felt unusually sad as she performed her duties. She had never met Willie Shorter, but she attended a rally once and heard him on the radio several times. Rose was used to dealing with the families of the deceased. Unlike her big extended family, this man didn't have anyone. She saw no wife, no mother or father, no brothers or sisters, no one. Yet his room had been full of people and the hallways full of reporters.

So on the night of February 12, nurse's aide, former mill-town girl, Rose Lorenzo carried out her prescribed tasks with tenderness and great care. She did this not because she was dealing with the Governor of the Great State of Georgia, but because she felt sorry for this young man who died alone.

CHAPTER THIRTY-NINE

LAINE MANAGED TO PULL HERSELF together enough to call home and talk to her parents. Through tears, Louise said, "Honey, I'll pass the word along to JW the next time he calls if he hadn't already heard about it on the radio. Try to get some rest if you can, we're all grieving right along with you."

Laine knew her mama meant well, but she didn't understand. Nobody did. She hung up the phone and sat in a stupor, unable to focus on even simple tasks. At some point she had put the old chenille bathrobe back on. She couldn't bring herself to eat, she didn't turn the lights on, and she slept in fits and starts sitting up on the couch. She didn't turn on the radio or go out for a paper. She already knew more than she wanted to about the shooting.

To everyone else, however, the assassination of the governor of Georgia was big news. It made the front page of every small town paper in the south and every major newspaper in the United States, as well as several in Europe. Willie would have been proud. Papers throughout Georgia ran stories detailing Willie's extraordinary rise to fame and power, the run-ins with the Fry machine, the land scandal, his accomplishments, and his ambitious plans for the future.

Sympathetic editors downplayed his dictatorial tendencies, his paranoia, and his relationship with Laine. Less sympathetic ones described him as a dangerous demagogue. The stories recounted all the shaky deals, the power plays, and his long-term affair with his "secretary." Once again, rumors of The Bread Box surfaced and were reported as both hard facts and urban legend.

The yellow journalism sheets focused on Laine and Willie. Their pages were filled with pictures of the two of them dancing at campaign functions, walking through the capitol with their heads together, and finally of her with his head in her lap, her hands holding the bloody napkins to his chest. The stories that gave The Boys pause were the ones demanding to know where the "missing millions" were hidden.

Grasping at every straw, Sly Fry immediately called for a new primary since he contended there was no clear cut chain of command to determine who should succeed the governor. As usual, he was mistaken. The Georgia State Constitution clearly stated that upon the death or incapacitation of the governor, "the President of the Senate shall exercise the executive powers of the government."

Wayne Gibbs had been appointed to the job——more or less legally——by Willie because he knew Wayne could be counted on to toe the Shorter line. The idea that he might actually have to run the state without Willie's guidance had never occurred to Wayne. He was a good man but he was terrified and the first to admit he was completely out of his depth. However, he made a valiant effort to hold things together and The Boys stepped in to make sure things were done in an orderly fashion.

The first order of business involved arranging for Willie's body to lie in state in the capitol rotunda. Simultaneously, people started coming out of the woodwork claiming to have this or that project going with the state. The Boys knew only too well that Willie tended to make deals on a handshake, no papers, no trails, no proof.

In her capacity as Keeper of the Numbers, Laine might have been able to shed some light on the subject. But since Willie and Laine had kept her involvement such a well-guarded secret, not even The Boys were aware of how much she knew about the inner workings of Willie's administration. They did know Willie wouldn't have put anything in writing or kept any records. They needed answers, but no one considered asking Laine for her help.

Without Willie she was forgotten. The House and Senate had their hands full trying to sort out matters that needed immediate attention. The Boys, however, were preoccupied with the location of the missing Bread Box and all the tithe money.

Finally it occurred to them they were overlooking their best source of information. "You know Laine might know where it is," Pappy said. "After all it was in her office the last time I saw it."

"True," Chauncey said, "but after that incident at the ball park, I know Willie moved it."

"Anybody know how much money we're talking about?" PV asked. The guesses ranged from $750,000 to a million. They all knew the money existed, they all knew the box containing the money existed. But nobody knew where Willie had put it!

Then they realized Laine had mysteriously disappeared. She hadn't been in her office and no one had seen her for days.

The Boys weren't the only ones wondering about Laine. Miss Amanda had hoped Laine might call, but so far she had heard nothing. Not wanting to worry Laine's parents in Ford Crossing, Miss Amanda took the practical approach and had her chauffeur drive her to Laine's apartment. She knocked and was appalled by the disheveled creature who finally opened the door. "My God!"

Laine's was still wearing the old bathrobe, her face was pale, her eyes red and swollen, her hair unwashed and uncombed. Miss Amanda's heart went out to her, but she had no intention of letting the situation continue unchecked.

"Laine, you must get yourself under control immediately. Go take a bath, wash your hair and put on some clean, suitable clothing."

Laine offered no resistance. She did as she was told. When she came back, she had wrapped a towel around her wet hair. She wore clean slacks and a matching sweater. Miss Amanda was in the kitchen scrambling eggs and squeezing orange juice.

"Sit down and eat."

Again Laine wordlessly followed orders. Surprisingly she discovered she was actually hungry and the orange juice tasted wonderful. Slowly some color came back into her face and her eyes cleared.

Over coffee, Miss Amanda filled her in on as much as she knew about what had gone on in her absence. PV had, of course, confided to Mother Ledbetter who had in turn confided in Miss Amanda. "No one quite seems to know what's happening, My Dear, least of all the man who is supposed to be running the state. I suspect you could be of some help in all this."

"They don't need me. The minute Willie was gone, I became invisible. Besides, I'm just a *secretary*, how could I possible help?" she asked coldly.

"Laine, that is beneath you. Now, get your things together, I'm taking you down to your office. Some matters must be attended to and you cannot stop living just because you want to."

So Laine went back to the capitol. The Boys had missed her and were glad to see her back. They tried to settle back into a normal routine.

She and PV had their usual lunch together. "Do you have any idea what happened to The Bread Box?" he asked as casually as he could.

"No. When Willie took it out of my office, he said he would put it in a safe place, but I have no idea what he did with it. I do have the ledger, if that would help."

PV nearly choked on his tea, "Oh yes, My Dear, I believe it would."

When they got back to the capitol, PV called the rest of The Boys into Laine's office. They made an effort not to appear too eager, but they were anxious to see the tangible proof of what they had only heard about in idle conversation.

Laine took the ledger out of her files and laid it on the desk. PV hesitated, then picked up the book and carefully turned to the last entry. When he saw the figure, he clutched the book to his heart and rolled his eyes toward heaven. He was breathing like an overworked steam engine. "Just look!" he said and held

the book out so they could see. The Bread Box funds totaled
$1,239,453.12

"In cash?" Pappy's voice cracked.

"As far as I know," Laine said. "Willie used to get the big bills
broken down when he needed it."

A stunned silence followed that revelation. Over a million
dollars in cash out there…somewhere. Propriety said they couldn't
begin a serious search—at least not until after the funeral.

"My God, the funeral!" Chauncey said. "I can't believe in
all the excitement about keeping the capitol rotunda open for
mourners, we completely overlooked the funeral. Nobody's done
anything about the actual burial."

"I'll take care of it," Laine volunteered and they gladly agreed.
When they left her office, she called Miss Amanda and explained
the situation. "I want to make sure Willie is buried in a place
he'd like and nobody's done anything about that. I'll pay for the
plot, but I'm afraid I'll just shame his name if anybody knows
what I'm doing. I saw this really nice place under a big oak tree at
Oakland Cemetery. If I give you the money, can you buy it and
then donate it or something?"

"That might be quite expensive, My Dear, are you…"

"Yes Ma'am, I'm sure. I want to do this."

"Then I will handle the necessary arrangements immediately
and the donation can come from Dev and me." She hesitated,
"Laine, before you hang up, I want to ask you a personal question.
Did you ever get Willie to make financial provision for you?"

Tears formed in Laine's eyes, but she blinked them away.
"Well, you know he bought me a house. It's big enough for my
whole family…if they want to come here…and I guess eventually
I'll start looking for a job…"

Miss Amanda sighed. "I see. My offer to pay for your college
education is still available if you are interested."

"Miss Amanda…"

"Perhaps it's too soon to be making plans, but just be aware that you can always come to me for advice or just to talk if that would prove useful."

"Thank you," Laine said.

No sooner had she hung up the phone, than Pappy called. "I need to see you in my office. We've got a problem."

CHAPTER FORTY

WHEN SHE WALKED IN, THE Boys were already there. "I just got a call from one of my newspaper buddies and Sly Fry is at it again. He says he's found proof that The Bread Box is stored in the safe at the Henry Grady Hotel. He's gonna have the police down there tomorrow morning to open it up and prove that Willie was stealing from state workers all along. My God, he's determined to disgrace Willie's memory before his body's put to rest."

"That's totally *ridiculous*," said PV. "The money's not there, it never was. We may not know where The Bread Box is, but we certainly know where it *isn't.*"

"Obviously Fry thinks he's on to something," Pappy said.

"So what's he going to open if there's no Bread Box there? Fry may be dumb as a post, but he's not going to embarrass himself in public. Anybody have any idea what he's up to?"

Chauncey cleared his throat. "If you remember, Willie *did* keep some money in the hotel safe. Just to make sure he hadn't put The Bread Box funds in there without telling anybody, I checked it yesterday. There's about $10,000 there. Maybe somebody at the hotel leaked that information to the press."

"Oh my God!" said PV.

"Take it easy, PV. We just need to think this thing through," Chauncey said.

"You know," Laine said slowly, "if Willie were here, he'd make this work to his advantage. Pappy, aren't you the one who always says the best defense is a good offense? What we need to do is beat Fry to the punch."

"And how do you propose we do that?" PV asked.

"Well…ah…let's notify the papers that… ah… that Willie said… if anything ever happened to him… the money in the safe was to be used… for something."

"I got it! I got it!" Chauncey exclaimed. "Oh, it's beautiful. We'll say the money came from Willie's salary, and he said if anything ever happened to him, it was to be used for his funeral. That way the state would not have to pay one red cent to bury Willie Shorter. What could be better than that? Now we have to plan a funeral…"

PV caught the spirit, "A train! A funeral *train*, like they did after Abraham Lincoln was shot. It can go through county seats in the rural areas. We'll give Willie back to the people who loved him most."

And so it came to pass, the next morning, with representatives from all the major newspapers in attendance, The Boys made a great show of opening the safe at the Henry Grady Hotel and showing the world the contents along with a letter from Willie outlining how the money was to be spent…if the occasion ever arose.

The Boys took charge and made plans to use the $10,000 to give Willie Shorter the biggest, most elaborate funeral any Southern politician had ever had. Once again, Willie had beaten Sly Fry at his own game.

Once the plans for the funeral train were made public, time was of the essence. Chauncey made arrangements with H. M. Patterson Funeral Home on Spring Street to provide a special coffin sealed with a glass top so everyone could see Willie lying in state.

PV called in a favor from one of Mother Ledbetter's friends at Southern Railroad to provide a special car with oversized windows so the glass coffin would be visible to those who lined the tracks to catch a glimpse of their hero. Laine planned a route that passed through all 121 rural counties, the ones whose county unit votes got Willie elected.

Draped in dark garlands, the train had five cars to accommodate The Boys, their families, Laine and her family, Sonny Cunningham and the Whippersnappers, as well as a who's-who of Georgia politicians and a select group of national figures. Space on the train was by invitation only. Sly Fry was not invited.

As the train pulled out of Terminal Station in Atlanta, a cold rain began to fall. Although it followed the path of the train through its journey, the rain didn't deter thousands of people, black and white, who came to say goodbye to Willie Shorter. Rather than a sea of funeral black, all along the route people waved bright colors, a fitting way to say good-bye to the man who had brought them such bright hope.

Upon returning to Atlanta, a hearse transported the casket to the Second Baptist Church on the corner of Washington and Mitchell, one block from the capitol. By the time the funeral service began, the church was full. People packed into the pews and stood shoulder to shoulder in the aisles. More people clustered under the open windows hoping to hear part of the service.

Laine sat quietly with her family on the second row. The Whippersnappers played and a colored choir from the Help for Hard Times Baptist Church in Ford Crossing sang *Amazing Grace*. The church was filled with flowers – expensive arrangements and small bouquets in Mason jars that lined the sills of all the stained-glass windows.

Dignitaries of all sorts spoke of Willie's accomplishments, his dedication to the state and his love for the common man. Death momentarily silenced even the harshest critics. The service was moving, but Laine and The Boys really outdid themselves with their arrangements for the procession to Oakland Cemetery *after* the service.

They hired every black Cadillac touring car, Buick Roadster, Packard and even a Maxwell or two, to transport anyone who wanted to go to Oakland for the graveside service. The big cars normally held seven people comfortably, but as many as ten or 12 crammed into most of them. People who couldn't get inside rode on the running boards or sat on the fenders holding on to the hood ornaments.

The Boys and their families rode behind the hearse in the cars provided by Patterson's Funeral Home. The next car in line was Willie's old Ford, conspicuous in the company of all those fine cars. With JW at the wheel, the Becker family rode to Oakland Cemetery in the car that first brought Willie to Ford Crossing over six years before.

Governor Jonathan William Shorter came to his final rest in a shady plot on a hill from which the dome of the Georgia state capitol was clearly visible. Officially the plot was donated by Mr. and Mrs. Endeavor M. Stratham, long-time friends and supporters of the governor.

Then it was over.

Almost.

As the mourners left Oakland Cemetery, they heard the Whippersnappers playing *When the Saints Go Marching In* and smelled the distinctive smoky bourbon-enriched aroma of Shorter bar-b-que. When they walked out the main gate, they saw tables lined up left and right along the high stone walls. Each table was piled high with bar-b-que sandwiches, Brunswick stew, and gallons and gallons of sweet ice tea. Willie was feeding the multitudes. Folks laughed and cried and ate their fill.

Next day the *New York Times* proclaimed, "Shorter Throws One Last Party."

For The Boys, the let down after the funeral was almost worse than the announcement of Willie's death. Now it was truly over. Reluctantly they went back to work. With Willie gone, it was far from business as usual, but it was something. Once more, Laine got lost in the shuffle.

For the past six years, Willie had been her life. He filled every hour of her days. A thousand times now she thought of something she wanted to tell him or some question only he could answer. The hole left by his passing was so enormous she had no idea how to cope with it.

Contrary to what she had always imagined, the nights weren't the worst part. She'd never been much of a drinker, so she found it only took a shot or two of bourbon to knock her out each night.

The hardest part was when she woke up in the morning. The first few seconds were fine. Willie Shorter was still alive and the world was full of the possibilities he promised for the future. Then reality hit her with the force of a sledgehammer. Willie was dead. He was never coming back. It was over.

For her, the future didn't exist. Each morning she faced one more day of endless hours to get through with nothing to do. She hardly knew the Acting Governor, Wayne Gibbs, and even if she had, he did not need her assistance.

Even so, she forced herself to get dressed and go to work, but no one at the capitol noticed her. After a week, she packed a few things and called JW to tell him she was going home.

Back in Ford Crossing she did what she had vowed never to do again. She went into the mill. She remembered complaining all those years ago that the machines were so loud she couldn't hear herself think. Now she blessed the noise because it was the only thing that blocked out her thoughts.

She expected one of the supervisors to see her standing around the first day and send her home. However, they didn't seem to be concerned with what happened on the floor anymore. They spent most of their time closed up in the second floor offices.

The workforce at the mill had been cut in half. The twins had been laid off just before Christmas. The few workers who were left kept to themselves. No one talked. They kept their heads down and hoped to escape notice. *Funny, I'm invisible wherever I go. Without Willie, I don't exist.*

Then several days later, at about 3:30 a.m., she woke with a start. She sat up in bed and realized the rest of the family was awake, too. She stumbled into the kitchen, shielding her eyes against the light. Louise, Jeb, the twins and Bo were already there.

"You're up, too. What is it? What's wrong?" And then she knew. The mill was silent. The heartbeat of the town had stopped.

The family pulled coats over their nightclothes and walked out on the front porch. In the moonlight, they saw their neighbors come out of their houses, walk into the street and head toward Claxton Mill. The mill noise had been replaced with a low rumble of voices and the sound of shuffling feet. Laine took her mother's hand and the family joined the group of ghostly looking figures.

CHAPTER FORTY-ONE

WHEN THEY GOT TO THE mill, they saw the gates were closed. A huge chain and several padlocks made entry impossible. All the interior lights were off. The few floodlights that were on gave the whole scene an eerie, haunted look. Then someone discovered a notice tacked to a board chained to the fence.

Claxton Mill Permanently Closed

Workers Will Vacate All Housing Within 30 Days

People looked at each other in stunned silence. There had been rumors for some time, but nothing official. The supervisors had said nothing, given no real warning.

Finally someone in the back of the crowd yelled out, "What about pay day? We've got wages coming at the end of this week." Like the lid blowing off a boiling pot, everyone started talking at once. Many of the workers were second generation with Claxton. They had never done anything else, never lived anywhere else. What were they going to do now with no jobs and no place to live?

Laine and her family separated themselves from the crowd and started home. It was inconceivable that within a month there would be no mill town, just empty houses and an empty, useless mill. Ford Crossing would cease to exist.

The Beckers took stock of their meager possessions. They owned their furniture, their clothes, a few pots, pans and dishes, but nothing else.

"Don't worry," Laine said. "I've got the house Willie bought for me in Atlanta. The tenants moved out last month and it's sitting there empty. There's plenty of room for all of us."

"I'm not going," Callie announced.

"What?!" Louise said.

"Me and Luther are getting married. He's got a job working in a print shop over in Waycross. It was gonna be a surprise. Pastor Bennett is gonna marry us right after church this Sunday. Bessie's gonna be my bridesmaid. Don't worry, we're gonna be OK." The family all hugged Callie and tried their best to sound genuinely happy for her.

Louise walked around the kitchen, running her hands over surfaces, opening and closing cabinet doors. "I can't believe it's all over. I feel kinda guilty knowing we have a place to go and some money laid up to get us through the hard times when folks we've known all our lives will walk away from here with nothing."

They were all silent for a moment. Then Jeb lit a cigarette. "You know, if JW hadn't got hurt and Willie Shorter hadn't come into our lives, we'd be out in the cold, too."

"They say the Lord works in mysterious ways and I guess this is a good example," Louise said. Then she turned to Callie, "Sweetie we didn't mean to overlook your announcement. Luther's a fine young man and we really are happy for you both. We'll call JW today and make sure he comes down for the wedding. I think you oughta tell folks at prayer meeting Wednesday night so they have something to look forward to. Everybody's gonna need some cheerin' up."

Jeb put his arm around Callie's shoulder, "We'll take some of the Claxton money to help you and Luther get started…the rest'll tide us over for a while, until we can find work up there in Atlanta."

Laine looked around the table. Work? What could they do? All they knew was the mill. Her dad might find something in Atlanta, but her mother and Bessie…. Short of cleaning other people's houses, they didn't know how to do anything else. Miss

Amanda might help, but Laine couldn't bear the thought of her mother and sister working as maids in one of those big Ansley Park mansions.

After the simple wedding ceremony on Sunday morning, the Beckers waved goodbye to the newly-weds who drove away in Luther's old pickup piled high with secondhand furniture. After the joy came the sadness. The congregation said teary good byes to friends and neighbors. Some folks planned to live with children who had moved away, some with other relatives. A few were staying on until the bitter end, promising to occupy their homes until the law evicted them. Already Ford Crossing had begun to look like a ghost town.

For the first time since Willie's death, Laine had a purpose. She called Pappy and told him about the mill closing. He sympathized and asked what he could do to help. "We have to vacate the house and I wondered…"

"Say no more. I'll send a DOT truck and crew to pick up everything your family wants to take with them. Are they moving here to Atlanta?"

"Yes, the house in Peachtree Hills is big enough for all of us. I wonder if Willie had a premonition…?"

"Don't torture yourself, Lass. What's done is done. Tell your family not to worry about the move. I'll take care of everything."

On moving day, JW drove home to help pack. When all the boxes and furniture were loaded on the truck, Jeb closed the door to the house. Laine, Bessie, and Bo got in the back seat of the Ford. No one knew where Louise was. Jeb went to look for her. He found her sitting on the back steps crying.

"Come on, Hon, it's time to go." He sat down and put his arm around her.

"Jeb, this mill town is all I know. It's all I've ever known. The kids think this is a great adventure, but for me…what am I gonna do up there in Atlanta where I don't know anybody?"

Jeb patted her back. "You sit right here, just a minute. I forgot to pack something."

Louise dried her eyes with the hem of her dress and smoothed her hair back into place. Then she saw Jeb carrying an old wash tub filled with...zinnias.

As bad as she felt, she had to laugh. "Jeb..."

"I dug up the plants. Reckon we can't leave 'em here to die. I guess you'll have to find a place for 'em in Atlanta."

Together they carried the heavy tub to the DOT truck and the driver helped load it in the back with the furniture. Louise got in the car next to JW and Jeb sat next to her. The truck headed toward Atlanta. Slowly JW drove past the mill one last time.

None of the Beckers had seen the house in Peachtree Hills until they pulled into the driveway. The DOT truck was already there and the crew was waiting to unload it.

"The house is so big," Louise said. "And all this land around it, is that yours, too?"

"It's all ours, Mama. Plenty of room for a garden." Louise instructed the crew to unload the zinnias and put the tub in the shade. Then she went off to explore the rest of the yard and the rest of the family started helping the crew unload the truck.

Louise's blue velvet couch and the rest of the living room furniture, a kitchen table and chairs, two double beds and a couple of dressers had been crowded in the little mill house. Now they floated around in the empty space of the big airy rooms.

Laine insisted her mother and father take the big corner bedroom upstairs. JW would continue to live in the dorm until he graduated in June. Since Callie was in Waycross with her new husband, both Bo and Bessie got a room of their own.

Laine had already moved her clothes and things from the Spring Street apartment into the little bedroom in the back. After many years, the Beckers once again lived under one roof.

Monday of the following week, Jeb took Bo to enroll him in school. Several hours later Jeb came home grinning from ear to ear. "You are now looking at the head of the maintenance department at Bo's school," he said. "They were having a problem with a leaky water heater in the cafeteria and I fixed it up good as new. The principal came by just as I was cleaning up and said if I wanted a job, it was mine."

At supper that night, Bessie proudly announced she had taken the streetcar downtown and signed up for business school. Laine was amazed at how quickly her family was adapting to big city life.

About a week later, just after daybreak, Laine heard a noise outside and went to investigate. There was her mother, with a hoe and a shovel breaking ground for a garden. Laine nearly cried when she realized that in her entire life, Louise had never had a whole day to do nothing but what *she wanted to do*.

After getting her family settled in, Laine went back to work. Since she was the one who always opened Willie's mail, her office was filled with mail bags full of condolence letters. In the absence of a family, the letters were simply addressed to "The Governor." They came from ordinary people, from black and white, from young and old, from rich and poor. In different ways they all said the same thing, "I thought of Willie Shorter as my friend; he will be missed."

More out of habit than design, Laine set up a filing system and discovered that although most of the letters were from Georgia, there were also cards and letters from Louisiana, Texas, Mississippi, Alabama, Tennessee, North and South Carolina and even as far away as New York and Michigan. One letter said, "We heard him on the radio and if he had run for president, he would have had our vote." Laine smiled. Willie would have enjoyed that.

In Willie's absence, Wayne Gibbs had surprised everyone by taking charge and holding things together. He spoke before both the Senate and the House and reiterated Willie's impassioned speech when he first took office asking both houses to work together for the good of the State. He reminded the legislators of all the progress that had been made and asked them to move forward with the Shorter plans that were already under way. The legislature needed time to regroup and working with the new governor seemed to be the safest thing to do, at least until the dust settled.

Without Willie making deals and pulling strings behind the scenes, the business of government settled down to pre-Shorter days. What would have taken Willie six weeks, now took six months or more. The Boys found the slower pace a lot easier on their nerves, but not nearly so much fun.

The Boys dropped by Laine's office from time to time but once she sorted through the piles of letters, Laine felt like the fifth wheel on the wagon. "Nobody's going to mind if you continue to show up and draw your pay," Chauncey said. "Hell, that's what half the people in this building do anyway."

"I couldn't do that."

"At least stay on long enough to sort out the stuff boxed up from Willie's office. Maybe you can find a clue as to where he put The Bread Box. At any rate, we don't want anybody else going through his files, no telling what else they might find."

Reluctantly, she agreed to stay.

CHAPTER FORTY-TWO

MORE THAN ANYONE ELSE, LAINE knew the importance of sorting through Willie's papers. He had an amazing facility for keeping information stored in his head, but he also had a bad habit of making notes and leaving them lying around everywhere. Separately they wouldn't mean much, but if someone took the time to put them together, the intent behind the research wouldn't be hard to figure out. In the end, she came up with a sorting system: burn immediately, discuss with The Boys, leave in the official files.

She also packed up his law books, the *Complete Humorous Sketches and Tales of Mark Twain*, Shakespeare's tragedies, a number of American history books, and a fairly extensive collection of Dashiell Hammett's books.

The location of The Bread Box, however, still remained a mystery. A million dollars would take up considerable space. It couldn't just be stuck in a drawer or go unnoticed in a filing cabinet. And, contrary to the evidence, it couldn't just disappear. So Laine organized a thorough search and she and The Boys went through every location they could think of where Willie might have stashed it.

They started with the old suite of offices at the Henry Grady. No luck. They searched Willie's single room upstairs. Nothing. Privately Laine searched their suite at the end of the hall, not there either. They tried the governor's mansion even though Willie had never lived there. A dead end.

They widened the search to his old office in Morganton and even to Miss Dorothy's boardinghouse and the Over-the-Hill

Boys Club and Museum. Again they came up empty. Laine asked
JW to check under the seats and in the trunk of Willie's old Ford.
He found nothing. On her own, Laine made a special trip back to
Ford Crossing to search their old house. The money was nowhere
to be found. Reluctantly, they gave up the search.

It was finally over. There was nothing more for her to do. To
postpone the inevitable, she decided to call Miss Amanda. They
talked briefly and Miss Amanda asked what Laine's plans were.
"Well, my dad's working, JW, Bessie and Bo are all in school,
Mama's having the time of her life staying home and working in
her garden, so I guess it's time for me to look for a job."

"How would you like to work for me? I need a personal
secretary, someone I can trust. We can convert a room in the East
Wing as an office. Would that interest you?"

"Miss Amanda, you don't have to do that for me…"

"I'm not doing it for you; I'm doing it for myself. I don't want
just anyone knowing my family business and I certainly would
not want anyone else working under my roof. Besides, I might
warn you that I will be a very strict boss and I expect nothing less
than total loyalty and discretion."

Laine knew about loyalty and discretion, so she gladly accepted
the job and any other demands Miss Amanda wanted to tack on.
When Laine hung up the phone, she looked around her office
at the capitol and sighed. One life over, another one beginning.

Knowing she had a job waiting for her made clearing out
her office somewhat easier. She destroyed all the files she had
created during Willie's first term in office: the voting patterns
and statistics, the mail logs, the donation lists, the requests for
money, the personal files, everything. The only things she kept
were Willie's old books and a shopping bag that contained the
private financial papers and ledgers she had created for Willie's
eyes only. She had a final lunch with The Boys at the Winecoff
dining room then took a taxi up town to the house in Peachtree
Hills.

When she checked the mailbox, she found a letter forwarded from her old Spring Street address. It was from the law firm of King, Spalding & Underwood, and directed her to be present at the reading of the last will and testament of one Jonathan William Shorter on Monday of the following week.

Laine knew her mother secretly hoped Willie had left her something in his will, but Laine knew despite all the rumors, Willie didn't own much to leave to anyone. On the appointed Monday, she dressed in her most conservative suit and appeared as directed in the law firm's office downtown on Peachtree Street. The Boys greeted her warmly. As she sat and listened to the men talk about what was going on at the capitol, she realized how far away she was from what had been the center of her life for so long.

Eventually an elegantly dressed secretary came to usher them into a large boardroom with a polished mahogany table, dark maroon leather chairs and a view looking over the interconnecting train tracks that were at the heart of Atlanta's—and the firm's—success. At each place was a folder bearing the firm's logo, a crystal glass filled with ice and a bottle of Coca-Cola, a visible nod to King and Spalding's sizable block of Coca-Cola stock.

As Laine had suspected, Willie's personal property was meager. There was some back pay, which had been collected and was divided among her and The Boys. They were each handed an envelope with their share of the money. Laine had to fight back the funny idea that Willie had probably taken the usual tithe out of these "pay envelopes" to add to The Bread Box…wherever it might be.

In addition to the cash, Willie owned a small plot of land in North Georgia, which he left to Pappy. "Excellent hunting" the lawyer commented. Another ten acres in South Georgia he left to Joe Laundry. "Good farm land." Several rather expensive gifts he had received as governor, he left to Chauncey. His private journals and letters, he left to Sol Goldman with the hope that through his connections in the Department of Education he might be instrumental in creating a special collection at Georgia Tech.

"To PV Ledbetter, I leave my eternal thanks, because there is absolutely nothing I own that you need or could possibly want." Even now, Willie could make them smile.

"To Laine Becker I leave all my personal effects, knowing she will find some way to put them to good use." Then the lawyer turned to a table behind him and picked up a battered old shoebox tied with a piece of rawhide. "This item is also bequeathed to you," he said and handed the box to Laine. She immediately recognized it as the box Willie used to keep under the seat of the flatbed truck when they first started campaigning.

The formalities ended, the group broke up quickly. Laine tucked the box under her arm. A line of official state vehicles stood waiting to take The Boys back to the capitol. "Can we offer you a lift?" Chauncey asked.

Laine smiled. "No thank you. The trolley will take me almost to my door." She waved to each one as they departed, and then walked to the corner and took the streetcar home.

Laine told her mother about the proceedings. She knew Louise was disappointed, but Laine had never expected anything in the first place. They opened the envelope containing her portion of Willie's back pay and found six crisp new $20 bills.

That night after dinner all the family except JW, who was busy at school, gathered around to look inside the box. It contained a few letters, which Jeb had written to Willie. "I never knew you and Willie wrote to each other," Laine said looking at her dad in surprise.

"Just once or twice. Guess he didn't have anybody else he thought would straighten him out when he needed it." Without opening them, she handed the letters to Jeb.

The box contained a dozen or so snapshots taken over the years. One picture was of a brassy young woman and a bright-eyed toddler. Willie and his mother, they guessed. Another tattered picture showed Willie and Uncle Aubrey selling Bibles and Peruna from the back of a wagon. A couple showed Willie and Laine kicking up dust dancing at a political rally in some small town.

A large envelope held copies of early flyers and drafts of news releases along with a newspaper clipping about Willie's victory over Claxton Mills. In the bottom lay a woman's ring with a small ruby in it. It didn't fit Laine, so she gave it to Bessie who slipped it on and flashed her fingers for everyone to see.

Laine also found a silver locket with a place for two pictures. It was empty. "You oughta wear that Lainie," Louise said, "It'll be pretty if we polish it up some and I'll find some little pictures of you and Willie that'll just fit."

Bo got a silver dollar and a pocket knife Laine found near the bottom of the box. Tucked under some old papers was a long narrow box, with a melted rubber band around it. The box contained a fancy white lace fan. "Wonder what that's doing in here?" Jeb said.

The small tag attached said, "For your grandmother." In spite of herself, Laine laughed.

"What does it mean?" Louise asked.

"I'm not sure, but I'll bet somebody gave it to Willie after they heard him talk about his grandmother, the one we all know he didn't have. It's too pretty to leave in the box. Here, Mama, I think Willie would like for you to have this."

Louise took the fan, expertly flipped it open and batted her eyes at Jeb over the top of it. The family all laughed.

Later that night as Laine sat in bed, she went through the box again, looking at the pictures, remembering. Down in one corner she found a small envelope she had overlooked before. Inside was a flat metal key with a number on it and a small scrap of paper. She unfolded it and saw a note written in Willie's barely readable scrawl. "Take this key down to the Greyhound Bus Station. My personal effects are in the suitcases in the locker. Willie." There was nothing else.

CHAPTER FORTY-THREE

EVERY TIME LAINE THOUGHT IT was over, Willie Shorter slid back into her life, looking over her shoulder. Willie would have smiled at the headlines in the *Constitution*, "Sly Fry Convicted in Government Fraud." Fry had always wanted to have a permanent place in Atlanta and now, thanks to the United States Government, he would be a long-term resident at the Federal Penitentiary south of the city.

She still had the key Willie left to his bus station locker. Laine just couldn't bring herself to tie up that one last loose end; to sever her last tie to Willie. Instead she threw herself into her new job, working for Miss Amanda. She never knew being rich—*responsibly* rich—as Miss Amanda said, was so much work. Just keeping Miss Amanda's social calendar organized proved to be a full time job. There were board meetings to attend, charity events to plan, scholarships to administer, and a steady stream of letters asking for assistance that had to be read, evaluated, and answered. Miss Amanda also turned over the bookkeeping for each charity she supported to Laine.

Laine justified a further delay in going to the bus station by telling herself that she didn't want to do anything to detract from JW's graduation. However, after graduation on the first of June, she ran out of excuses.

She asked JW to drive her downtown. At first they couldn't find the locker that matched the number on the key. Then an attendant told them the over-sized lockers were down a short hall. When she inserted the key and opened the locker door, Willie's familiar smell, Burma Shave and Old Spice, brought tears to her eyes. She turned away as JW pulled two old suitcases out of the locker.

"What's he got in these things, bricks?" JW said as he hauled the suitcases through the lobby. With some difficulty he got them into the back seat and when they got home, he dragged them into Laine's bedroom.

"After all this trouble, aren't you going to open them?"

"Not yet, I just can't…"

JW dropped the subject and walked out shaking his head and mumbling something about never understanding women.

Laine sat on the bed and looked at the battered old luggage for a long time. It looked familiar but it took her a while to realize where she had seen the suitcases before. They had been stacked in the corner of their unfinished bedroom at the hotel and Willie had used them as a table.

On an impulse, Laine removed the night stand beside her bed and replaced it with the suitcases. Then she put her lamp on top of them.

Louise asked about the suitcases, but when Laine said she didn't want to open them yet, her mother let it go…for a while. However, after she had dusted them for two weeks she said, "Laine, you need to open those suitcases. If they have some of Willie's old clothes or books, we can give them to the Salvation Army where they will do some good."

"Yeah, you're right. I'll take care of it tonight after supper."

That evening after the supper dishes were washed and put away, Laine went to her room and Jeb and Louise settled in on the back screen porch to read the evening paper. Shortly Jeb looked up to see Laine standing in the doorway, her face white as a sheet. Without speaking she motioned for them to follow her down the hall. Very carefully she opened her bedroom door.

"Look!" She had opened the suitcases and dumped the contents on the bed. $1,239,453.12. The Bread Box money.

"Lord God Almighty, Laine, what is all that?" her mother demanded.

"The Bread Box."

Her father looked confused, "But they already found that money at the hotel. The newspaper said so."

"As usual, the papers didn't know what they were talking about. The Bread Box was always kept in a safe in my office. Then when Willie got so paranoid, he moved it without telling anybody where it was. Chauncey tried to ask him about it in the hospital and Willie said he'd explain everything tomorrow but tomorrow…. The Boys and I have been looking all over for this."

"And now that you've found it, what exactly do you plan to do with it?" Jeb wanted to know.

"Willie left a note." Laine pushed some money out of the way and sat on the edge of the bed. Jeb and Louise followed suit. Laine took the note out of her pocket, smoothed it out and began to read.

Dear Laine,

If you are reading this, then you know I don't need what's here anymore. I had great plans, Laine, and I always intended to have you with me every step of the way. I never could have done any of it without you. I know you didn't want to be a governor's wife but I hope you wouldn't have turned down the chance to be First Lady.

"First Lady!?!" Louise asked. Laine held up her hand and continued to read.

I planned to use this money to finance my national campaign, but since you have it, things obviously didn't quite work out that way. Just in case there was trouble, I left some money in the safe at the Henry Grady before I hid the rest. I knew you or one of The Boys would figure out what to do about that.

I knew once the news of The Bread Box was made public, the legend would die. There are no records of this money except the ledgers you kept. Nobody's going to come looking for it. Take what you need for yourself and your folks. They are the family I wish I had had. I leave it to you to decide how to use the rest of the money. You'll do fine and like Uncle Aubrey once told me, you might also do some good.

It was a hell of a ride, Lainie, and no matter how it turns out, just know that I would not have changed a thing. Although I didn't say it nearly enough, from the first moment I saw you through the screen in Ford Crossing, I have loved you with all my heart.

Have a good life and think of me once in a while.

Willie (Governor Jonathan William Shorter)

EPILOGUE

LAINE CONTINUED TO WORK FOR Miss Amanda for several years. During that time the Stratham's youngest son, Mark, returned from Europe to join a prestigious Atlanta architecture firm. With a little encouragement from Miss Amanda, the young people met, fell in love and eventually were married in Saint Philip's Episcopal Church. A lavish reception followed at the newly opened Biltmore Hotel.

Since the Stratham family was extremely wealthy, no one batted an eye when the young couple became major donors to the arts, education, and a host of other worthwhile charities in Atlanta. Their donations did a lot of good for the arts.

On the tenth anniversary of Willie's death, Laine and Mark gave funds to build the Willie Shorter Library in downtown Atlanta. Laine made a short speech about Willie's love of books and his tireless efforts that resulted in free textbooks for every child in Georgia. She also donated the books she had boxed up from Willie's office at the capitol and made sure they were given a place of honor in the main lobby of the library. Mark's father, Dev, passed away shortly after the library opened and Miss Amanda followed him at the age of 98.

In 1962 the Atlanta Art Association chartered a Boeing 707 to take a large delegation of art lovers on a month-long tour to view the art treasures of Europe. Laine and Mark were among the first couples to sign up.

When the group took off, Mayor Ivan Allan was at the airport to see them off and to officially wish them good luck and Godspeed. For a mill-town girl from Ford Crossing it was the trip of a lifetime.

Laine wrote home frequently to tell her parents, who were then in their 80s, what a wonderful time she and Mark were having viewing masterpieces by Rembrandt, Raphael, and da Vinci. Relying on the knowledge she had gained from Miss Amanda, Laine acquired several pieces of significant artwork, antiques, and artifacts that she planned to donate to Georgia museums.

On June 2, the group returned from Rome to Paris and headed for Orly Airport on the south side of the city along the River Seine. They boarded the plane in high spirits bound for Idlewilde Airport in New York City.

No sooner had the plane began lift-off, than the pilot knew something was wrong. As the plane reached maximum take-off speed of 175 miles per hour, the nose lifted off the runway, but the body did not. The pilot had already used up well over half of the runway. He knew he had to slow the plane down before it was too late. He locked the brakes and the rubber on the tires immediately evaporated leaving the bare metal rims which gouged deep ruts in the tarmac. Unable to stand the stress, the rims collapsed too.

Still traveling at approximately 150 miles an hour, the plane veered off the runway, causing its left undercarriage to fall off and the number two engine to break into flames. The plane hurled out of control into the pillars supporting the landing lights then disintegrated as it gained speed sliding down a hill toward the River Seine directly into the side of an abandoned stone cottage. The final impact caused the fuselage, which contained the passengers and crew, to burst into flame. The entire catastrophe took less than 60 seconds. Of the 232 passengers and crew, 230 died. Only two stewardesses strapped into the tail section survived.

Once again, tragedy struck the state of Georgia and Atlanta mourned their loss. Sadly this time there was no body, no funeral, no burial, nothing but ashes. However, out of the ashes of the Orly plane crash, the people of Atlanta built the Memorial Arts Center which serves the city's art community to this day.

ABOUT THE AUTHOR

Grace Hawthorne is a freelance writer who has written everything from ad copy for septic tanks to the libretto for an opera and lyrics for *Sesame Street*.

She is the author of *It's Cool in the Furnace*, the longest selling children's musical in the history of sacred music—40 years and counting.

Shorter's Way is her first novel.

CPSIA information can be obtained at www.ICGtesting.com
Printed in the USA
LVOW06s0549120813

347426LV00006B/9/P